Trail's End

George W. Ogden

CHAPTER I

THE UNCONQUERED LAND

Bones.

Bones of dead buffalo, bones of dead horses, bones of dead men. The tribute exacted by the Kansas prairie: bones. A waste of bones, a sepulcher that did not hide its bones, but spread them, exulting in its treasures, to bleach and crumble under the stern sun upon its sterile wastes. Bones of deserted houses, skeletons of men's hopes sketched in the dimming furrows which the grasses were reclaiming for their own.

A land of desolation and defeat it seemed to the traveler, indeed, as he followed the old trail along which the commerce of the illimitable West once was borne. Although that highway had belonged to another generation, and years had passed since an ox train toiled over it on its creeping journey toward distant Santa Fé, the ruts of old wheels were deep in the soil, healed over by the sod again, it is true, but seamed like scars on a veteran's cheek. One could not go astray on that broad highway, for the eye could follow the many parallel trails, where new ones had been broken when the old ones wore deep and rutted.

Present-day traffic had broken a new trail between the old ones; it wound a dusty gray line through the early summer green of the prairie grass, endless, it seemed, to the eyes of the leg-weary traveler who bent his footsteps along it that sunny morning. This passenger, afoot on a road where it was almost an offense to travel by such lowly means, was a man of thirty or thereabout, tall and rather angular, who took the road in long strides much faster than the freighters' trains had traveled it in the days of his father. He carried a black, dingy leather bag swinging from his long arm, a very lean and unpromising repository, upon which the dust of the road lay spread.

Despite the numerous wheel tracks in the road, all of them apparently fresh, there was little traffic abroad. Not a wagon had passed him since morning, not a lift had been given him for a single mile. Now, mounting a ridge toward which he had been pressing forward the past hour, which had appeared a hill of consequence in the distance, but now flattened out to nothing more than a small local divide, he put down his bag, flung his dusty black hat beside it, and stood wiping his face with a large turkey-red handkerchief which he unknotted from about his neck.

His face was of that rugged type common among the pioneers of the West, lean and harsh-featured, yet nobly austere, the guarantee of a soul above corruption and small trickery, of a nature that endures patiently, of an anger slow to move. There were bright hues as of glistening metal in his close-cut light hair as he stood bareheaded in the sun.

Sheep sorrel was blooming by the wheel tracks of the road, purple and yellow; daisy-like flowers, with pale yellow petals and great wondering hearts like frightened eyes, grew low among the short grass; countless strange blooms spread on the prairie green, cheering for their brief day the stern face of a land that had broken the hearts of men in its unkindness and driven them away from its fair promises. The traveler sighed, unable to understand it quite.

All day he had been passing little sod houses whose walls were crumbling, whose roofs had fallen in, whose doors beckoned in the wind a sad invitation to come in and behold the desolation that lay within. Even here, close by the road, ran the grass-grown furrows of an abandoned field, the settler's dwelling-place unmarked by sod or stone. What tragedy was written in those wavering lines; what heartbreak of going away from some dear hope and broken dream! Here a teamster was cutting across the prairie to strike the road a little below the point where the traveler stood. Extra side boards were on his wagon-box, as they used to put them on in corn-gathering time back in the traveler's boyhood home in Indiana. The wagon was heaped high with white, dry bones.

Bones. Nothing left to haul out of that land but bones. The young man took up his valise and hat and struck off down the road to intercept the freighter of this prairie product, hoping for an invitation to ride, better pleased by the prospect of resting living bones on dead dry ones than racking them in that strain to reach the town on the railroad, his journey's end, on foot before nightfall.

The driver's hat was white, like his bones; it drooped in weather-beaten limpness about his ears, hiding his face, but he appeared to have an hospitable heart in spite of the cheerlessness of his pursuit. Coming to the road a little before the traveler reached the point of conjunction, he drew the team to a stand, waiting his approach.

"Have a ride?" the freighter invited, edging over on the backless spring seat as he spoke, making room.

The bone-wagon driver was a hollow-framed man, who looked as if he had starved with the country but endured past all bounds of hardship and discouragement. He looked hungry--hungry for food, hungry for change, hungry for the words of men. His long gray mustache hung far below his stubble-covered chin; there was a pallor of a lingering sickness in his skin, which the hot sun could not sere out of it. He sat dispiritedly on his broken seat, sagging forward with forearms across his thighs.

"Footin' it over to Ascalon?" he asked, as the traveler mounted beside him.

"Yes sir, I'm headin' that way."

"Come fur?"

"Well, yes," thoughtfully, as if he considered what might be counted far in that land of unobstructed horizons, "I have come a considerable little stretch."

"I thought maybe you was one of them new settlers in here, goin' over to Ascalon to ketch the train," the bone man ventured, putting his inquiry for further particulars as politely as he knew how.

"I'm not a settler yet, but I expect to try it here."

"You don't tell me?"

"Yes sir; that's my intention."

"Where you from?"

"Iowa."

The bone man looked his passenger over with interest, from his feet in their serviceable shoes, to his head under his round-crowned, wide-brimmed black hat.

"A good many of 'em used to come in here from Ioway and Newbrasky in the early days," he said. "You never walked plumb from there, did you?"

"I thought of stopping at Buffalo Creek, back fifteen or twenty miles, but I didn't like the country around there. They told me it was better at Ascalon, so I just struck out to walk across the loop of the railroad and take a close look at the land as I went along."

"You must be something of a walker," the bone man marveled.

"I used to follow a walking cultivator across an eighty-acre cornfield," the traveler replied.

"Yes, that'll stretch a feller's legs," the bone man admitted, reminiscently. "Nothing like follerin' a plow to give a man legs and wind. But they don't mostly walk around in this country; they kind of suspicion a man when they see him hoofin' it."

"There doesn't seem to be many of them to either walk or ride," the traveler commented, sweeping a look around the empty land.

"It used to be full of homesteaders all through this country--I seen 'em come and I seen 'em go."

"I've seen traces of them all along the railroad for the last hundred miles or more. It must have been a mighty exodus, a sad thing to see."

TRAIL'S END

"Accordin' to the way you look at it, I reckon," the bone man reflected. "They're comin' to this country ag'in, flocks of 'em. This makes the third time they've tried to break this part of Kansas to ride, and I don't know, on my soul, whether they'll ever do it or not. Maybe I'll have more bones to pick up in a year or two."

"It seems to be one big boneyard; I saw cars of bones on every sidetrack as I came through."

"Yes, I tell folks that come here and try to farm that bones was the best crop this country ever raised, and it'll be about the only one. I come in here with the railroad, I used to drive a team pickin' up the buffaloes the contractors' meat hunter killed."

"You know the history of its ups and downs, then," the young man said, with every evidence of deep interest.

"I guess I do, as well as any man. Bones was the first freight the railroad hauled out of here, and bones'll be the last. I follered the railroad camps after they built out of the buffalo country and didn't need me any more, pickin' up the bones. Then the settlers begun to come in, drawed on by the stuff them railroad colonization agents used to put in the papers back East. The country broke their backs and drove 'em out after four or five years. Then I follered around after them and picked up the bones.

"Yes, there used to be some familiar lookin' bones among 'em once in a while in them times. I used to bury that kind. A few of them settlers stuck, the ones that had money to put in cattle and let 'em increase on the range. They've done well--you'll see their ranches all along the Arkansaw when you travel down that way. This is a cattle country, son; that's what the Almighty made it for. It never can be anything else."

"And there was another wave of immigration, you say, after that?" the passenger asked, after sitting a while in silence turning over what the old pioneer had said.

"Yes, wave is about right. They come in by freight trainload, cars of horses and cattle, and machinery for farmin', from back there in Ohio and Indiany and Ellinoi--all over that country where things a man plants in the ground grows up and comes to something. They went into this pe-rairie and started a bustin' it up like the ones ahead of 'em did. Shucks! you can turn a ribbon of this blame sod a hundred miles long and never break it. What can a farmer do with land that holds together that way? Nothin'. But them fellers planted corn in them strips of sod, raised a few nubbins, some of 'em, some didn't raise even fodder. It run along that way a few years, hot winds cookin' their crops when they did git the ground softened up so stuff would begin to make roots and grow, cattle and horses dyin' off in the winter and burnin' up in the fires them fool fellers didn't know how to stop when they got started in this grass. They thinned out year after year, and I drove around over the country and picked up their bones.

"That crowd of settlers is about all gone now, only one here and there along some crick. Bones is gittin' scarce, too. I used to make more when I got four dollars a ton for 'em than I do now when they pay me ten. Grind 'em up to put on them farms back in the East, they tell me. Takin' the bones of famine from one place to put on fat in another. Funny, ain't it?"

The traveler said it was strange, indeed, but that it was the way of nature for the upstanding to flourish on the remains of the fallen. The bone man nodded, and allowed that it was so, world without end, according to his own observations in the scale of living things from grass blade to mankind.

"How are they coming in now--by the trainload?" the traveler asked, reverting to the influx of settlers.

"These seem to be a different class of men," the bone man replied, his perplexity plain in his face. "I don't make 'em out as easy as I did the ones ahead of 'em. These fellers generally come alone, scoutin' around to see the lay of the country--I run into 'em right along drivin' livery rigs, see 'em around for a couple or three weeks sometimes. Then they go away, and the first thing I know they're back with their immigrant car full of stuff, haulin' out to some place somebody went broke on back in the early days. They seem to be a calculatin' kind, but no man ain't deep enough to slip up on the blind side of this country and grab it by the mane like them fellers seems to think they're doin'. It'll throw 'em, and it'll throw 'em hard."

"It looks to me like it would be a good country for wheat," the traveler said.

"Wheat!"

The bone man pulled up on his horses, checking them as if he would stop and let this dangerous fellow off. He looked at the traveler with incredulous stare, into which a shading of pity came, drawing his naturally long face longer. "I'd just as well stop and let you start back right now, mister." He tightened up a little more on the lines.

There was merriment in the stranger's gray eyes, a smile on his homely face that softened its harsh lines.

"Has nobody ever tried it?" he inquired.

"There's been plenty of fools here, but none that wild that I ever heard of," the bone man said. "You're a hundred miles and more past the deadline for wheat--you'd just as well try to raise bananers here. Wheat! it'd freeze out in the winter and blow out by the roots in the spring if any of it got through."

The traveler swept a long look around the country, illusive, it seemed, according to its past treatment of men, in its restful beauty and secure feeling of peace. He was silent so long that the bone man looked at him again keenly, measuring him up and down as he would some monstrosity seen for the first time.

"Maybe you're right," the young man said at last.

The bone man grunted, with an inflection of superiority, and drove on, meditating the mental perversions of his kind.

"Over in Ascalon," he said, breaking silence by and by, "there's a feller by the name of Thayer--Judge Thayer, they call him, but he ain't never been a judge of nothin' since I've knowed him--lawyer and land agent for the railroad. He brings a lot of people in here and sells 'em railroad land. He says wheat'll grow in this country, tells them settlers that to fetch 'em here. You two ought to git together--you'd sure make a pair to draw to."

"Wouldn't we?" said the stranger, in hearty humor.

"What business did you foller back there in Ioway?" inquired the bone man, not much respect in him now for the man he had lifted out of the road.

"I was a professional optimist," the traveler replied, grave enough for all save his eyes.

The bone man thought it over a spell. "Well, I don't think you'll do much in Ascalon," he said. "People don't wear specs out here in this country much. Anybody that wants 'em goes to the feller that runs the jewelry store."

The stranger attempted no correction, but sat whistling a merry tune as he looked over the country. The bone man drove in silence until they rose a swell that brought the town of Ascalon into view, a passenger train just pulling into the station.

"Octomist! Wheat!" said the bone man, with discount on the words that left them so poor and worthless they would not have passed in the meanest exchange in the world.

CHAPTER II

THE MEAT HUNTER

There was one tree in the city of Ascalon, the catalpa in front of Judge Thayer's office. This blazing noonday it threw a shadow as big as an umbrella, or big enough that the judge, standing close by the trunk and holding himself up soldierly, was all in the shade but the gentle swell of his abdomen, over which his unbuttoned vest gaped to invite the breeze.

Judge Thayer was far too big for the tree, as he was too big for Ascalon, but, scholar and gentleman that he was, he made the most of both of them and accepted what they had to offer with grateful heart. Now he stood, his bearded face streaming sweat, his alpaca coat across his arm, his straw hat in his hand, his bald head red from the parboiling of that intense summer day, watching a band of Texas drovers who had just arrived with three or four thousand cattle over the long trail from the south.

These lank, wide-horned creatures were crowding and lowing around the water troughs in the loading pens, the herdsmen shouting their monotonous, melancholy urgings as they crowded more famished beasts into the enclosures. Judge Thayer regarded the dusty scene with troubled face.

"And so pitch hot!" said he, shaking his head in the manner of a man who sees complications ahead of him. He stood fanning himself with his hat, his brows drawn in concentration. "Twenty wild devils from the Nueces, four months on the trail, and this little patch of Hades at the end!"

The judge entered his office with that uneasy reflection, leaving the door standing open behind him, ran up his window shades, for the sun had turned from the front of his building, took off his collar, and settled down to work. One could see him from the station platform, substantial, rather aristocratic, sitting at his desk, his gray beard trimmed to a nicety, one polished shoe visible in line with the door.

Judge Thayer's office was a bit removed from the activities of Ascalon, which were mainly profane activities, to be sure, and not fit company for a gentleman even in the daylight hours. It was a snubby little building with square front like a store, "Real Estate" painted its width above the door. On one window, in crude black lettering:

WILLIAM THAYER ATTORNEY

NOTARY

On the other:

MAYOR'S OFFICE

The office stood not above two hundred feet from the railroad station, at the end of Main Street, where the buildings blended out into the prairie, unfenced, unprofaned by spade or plow. Beyond Judge Thayer's office were a coal yard and a livery barn; behind him the lots which he had charted off for sale, their bounds marked by white stakes.

Ascalon, in those early days of its history, was not very large in either the territory covered or the inhabitants numbered, but it was a town of national notoriety in spite of its size. People who did not live there believed it to be an exceedingly wicked place, and the farther one traveled from Ascalon, in any direction whatever, the faster this ill fame increased. It was said, no farther off than Kansas City, that Ascalon was the wickedest place in the United States. So, one can image what character the town had in St. Louis, and guess at the extent of its notoriety in Pittsburg and Buffalo.

Porters on trains had a holy fear of Ascalon. They announced the train's approach to it with suppressed breath, with eyes rolling white in fear that some citizen of the proscribed town might overhear and defend the reputation of his abiding-place in the one swift and incontrovertible argument then in vogue in that part of the earth. Passengers of adventurous nature flocked to the station platform during the brief pause the train made at Ascalon, prickling with admiration of their own temerity, so they might return home and tell of having set foot in the wickedest town in the world.

And that was the fame of Ascalon, new and raw, for the greater part of it, as it lay beside the railroad on that hot afternoon when Judge Thayer stood in the shade of his little catalpa tree watching the Texans drive their cattle into the loading pens.

Before the railroad reached out across the Great Plains, Ascalon was there as a fort, under another name. The railroad brought new consequence, new activities, and made it the most important loading place for Texas cattle, driven over the long route on their slow way to market.

It was a cattle town, living and fattening on the herds which grazed the vast prairie lands surrounding it, and on the countless thousands which came northward to its portal over the Chisholm Trail. As will have been gathered from the scene already passed, agriculture had tried and failed in that land. Ascalon was believed to be, in truth, far beyond the limit of that gentle art, which was despised and contemned by the men who roamed their herds over the free grass lands, and the gamesters who flourished at their expense.

Not that all in Ascalon were vicious and beyond the statutory and moral laws. There was a submerged desire for respectability in the grain of even the worst of them which came to the front at times, as in defense of the town's reputation, and on election day, when they put in such a man as Judge Thayer for mayor. With a man like Judge Thayer at the head of affairs, all charges of the town's utter abandonment to the powers of evil seemed to fall and fade. But the judge, in reality, was only a pillar set up for dignity and show. They elected him mayor, and went on running the town to suit themselves, for the city marshal was also an elective officer, and in his hands the scroll of the law reposed.

Now, in these summer days, there was a vacancy in this most important office, three months, only, after election. The term had almost two years to run, the appointment of a man to the vacancy being in the mayor's hands. As a consequence there was being exerted a great deal of secret and open pressure on the mayor in favor of certain favorites. It was from a conference with several of the town's financial powers that the mayor had returned to his office when you first beheld him under his catalpa tree. The sweat on his face was due as much to internal perplexity as outward heat, for Judge Thayer was a man who wanted to please his friends, and everybody that counted in Ascalon was his friend, although they were not all friends among themselves.

No later than the night before the vacancy in the marshalship had fallen; it would not do to allow the town to go unbridled for even another night. A strong man must be appointed to the place, and no fewer than three candidates were being urged by as many factions, each of which wanted its peculiar interests especially favored and protected. So Judge Thayer was in a sweat with good reason. He wished in his honest soul that he could reach out and pick up a disinterested man somewhere, set him into the office without the strings of fear or favor on him, and tell him to keep everybody within the deadline, regardless of whose business prospered most.

But there were not men raining down every day around Ascalon competent to fill the office of city marshal. Out of the material offered there was not the making of one side of a man. Two of them were creatures of the opposing gambling factions, the other a weak-kneed fellow with the pale eyes of a coward, put forward by the conservative business men who deplored much shooting in the name of the law.

How they were to get on without much shooting, Judge Thayer did not understand. Not a bit of it. What he wanted was a man who would do more shooting than ever had been done before, a man who would clean the place of the too-ready gun-slingers who had gathered there, making the town's notoriety their capital, invading even the respectable districts in their nightly debaucheries to such insolent boldness that a man's wife or daughter dared not show her ear on the street after nightfall.

Judge Thayer put the town's troubles from him with a sigh and leaned to his work. He was preparing a defense for a cattle thief whom he knew to be guilty, but whose case he had undertaken on account of his wife and several small children living in a tent behind the principal gambling-house. Because it seemed a hopeless case from the jump, Judge Thayer had set his beard firmer in the direction of the fight. Hopeless cases were the kind that had come most frequently his way all the days of his life. He had been fronting for the under pup so long that his own chances had dwindled down to a distant point in his gray-headed years. But there was lots of satisfaction behind him to contemplate even though there might not be a great deal of prosperity ahead. That helped a man wonderfully when it came to casting up accounts. So he was bent to the cattle thief's case when a man appeared in his door.

This was a tall, bony man with the dust of the long trail on him; a sour-faced man of thin visage, with long and melancholy nose, a lowering frown in his unfriendly, small red eyes. A large red mustache drooped over his mouth, the brim of his sombrero was pressed back against the crown as if he had arrived devil-come-headlong against a heavy wind.

Judge Thayer took him for a cattleman seeking legal counsel, and invited him in. The visitor shifted the chafed gear that bore his weapon, as if to ease it around his gaunt waist, and entered, removing his hat. He stood a little while looking down at Judge Thayer, a disturbance in his weathered face that might have been read for a smile, a half-mocking, half-humorous expression that twitched his big mustache with a catlike sneer.

"You're the mayor of this man's town, are you, Judge?" he asked.

As the visitor spoke, Judge Thayer's face cleared of the perplexity that had clouded it. He got up, beaming welcome, offering his hand.

"Seth Craddock, as sure as little apples! I knew you, and I didn't know you, you old scoundrel! Where have you been all these years?"

Seth Craddock only expanded his facial twitching at this friendly assault until it became a definite grin. It was a grin that needed no apology, for all evidence was in its favor that it was so seldom seen by the eyes of men that it could be forgiven without a plea.

"I've been ridin' the long trail," said Seth.

"With that bunch that just arrived?"

"Yeh. Drove up from the Nueces. I'm quittin'."

"The last time I saw you, Seth, you were butchering two tons of buffalo a day for the railroaders. I often wondered where you went after you finished your meat contract."

"I scouted a while for the gover'ment, but we run out of Indians. Then I went to Texas and rode with the rangers a year or two."

"I guess you kept your gun-barrel hot down in that country, Seth?"

"Yeh. Once in a while it was lively. Dyin' out down there now, quiet as a school."

"So you turned back to Kansas lookin' for high life. Heard of this burg, I guess?"

"I kind of thought something might be happenin' off up here, Judge."

"And I was sitting here frying out my soul for the sight of a full-sized man when you stepped in the door! Sit down; let's you and me have a talk."

Seth drew a dusty chair from against the wall and arranged himself in the draft between the front and back doors of the little house. He leaned his storm-beaten sombrero against the leg of his chair near his heel, as carefully as if making preparations for quick action in a hostile country, shook his head when the judge offered a cigar, shifted his worn cartridge belt a bit with a movement that appeared to be as unconscious as unnecessary.

"What's restin' so heavy on your mind, Judge?" he inquired.

"Our city marshal stepped in the way of a fool feller's bullet last night, and all the valuable property in this town is lying open and unguarded today."

"Don't nobody want the job?"

"Many are called, or seem to feel themselves nominated, but none is appointed. The appointment is in my hands; the job's yours if you'll do an old friend a favor and take it. It pays a hundred dollars a month."

Seth's heavy black hair lay in disorder on his high, sharp forehead, sweated in little ropes, more than half concealing his immense ears. He smoothed it back now with slow hand, holding a thoughtful silence; shifted his feet, crossed his legs, looked out through the open door into the dusty street.

"How does the land lay?" he asked at length.

"You know the name of the town, everybody knows the name of the town. Well, Seth, it's worse than its name. It's a job; it's a double man's job. If it was any less, I wouldn't lay it down before you."

"Crooks run things, heh?"

"I'm only a knot on a log. The marshal we had wasn't worth the powder that killed him. Oh-h, he did kill off a few of 'em, but what we need here is a man that can see both sides of the street and behind him at the same time."

"How many folks have you got in this man's town by now, Judge?"

"Between six and seven hundred. And we could double it in three months if we could clean things up and make it safe."

"How would you do it, Judge? marry everybody?"

"I mean we'd bring settlers in here and put 'em on the land. The railroad company could shoot farmers in here by the hundreds every month if it wasn't for the hard name this town's got all over the country. A good many chance it and come as it is. We could make this town the supply point for a big territory, we could build up a business that'd make us as respectable as we're open and notorious now. For I tell you, Seth, this country around here is God Almighty's granary--it's the wheat belt of the world."

Seth made no reply. He slewed himself a little to sweep the country over beyond the railroad station with his sullen red eyes. The heat was wavering up from the treeless, shrubless expanse; the white sun was over it as hot as a furnace blast. From the cattle pens the dusty, hoarse cries of the cowboys sounded, "Ho, ho, ho!" in what seemed derision of the judge's fervent claims.

"A lot of us have staked our all on the outcome here in Ascalon, we fellows who were here before the town turned out to be the sink-hole of perdition that it is today. We built our homes here, and brought our families out, and we can't afford to abandon it to these crooks and gamblers and gun-slingers from the four corners of the earth. I let them put me in for mayor, but I haven't got any more power than a stray dog. This chance to put in a marshal is the first one I've had to land them a kick in the gizzards, and by Jeems River, Seth, I want to double 'em up!"

"It looks like your trick, Judge."

"Yes, if I had the marshal with me the two of us could run this town the way it ought to be run. And we'd keep the county seat here as sure as sundown."

"Considerin' a change?"

"The folks over in Glenmore are--the question will come to a vote this fall. The county seat belongs here, not away off there at Glenmore, seven miles from the railroad."

"What's your chance?"

"Not very heavy right now. We can out-vote them in town, but the country's with Glenmore, all on account of our notorious name. Folks hate to come in here to court, it's got so bad. But we could do a lot of cleaning up between now and November, Seth."

Seth considered it in silence, his red eyes on the dusty activities of his late comrades at the cattle pens. He shifted his dusty feet as if dancing to his slow thoughts, scraping his boot soles grittily on the floor.

"Yes, I reckon we could, Judge."

"Half the people in Glenmore want to come over to the railroad. They'd vote with us if they could be made to feel this was a town to bring their families to."

Seth seemed to take this information like a pill under his tongue and dissolve it in his reflective way. Judge Thayer left him to his ruminations, apparently knowing his habits. After a little Seth reached down for his hat in the manner of a man about to depart.

"All right, Judge; we'll clean up the town and part its hair down the middle," he said.

Judge Thayer did not give vent to his elation on Seth Craddock's acceptance of the office of city marshal, although his satisfaction gleamed from his eyes and radiated from his kindly face. He merely shook hands with his new officer in the way of men sealing a bargain, swore him in, and gave him the large shield which had been worn by the many predecessors of the meat hunter in that uncomfortable office, three of whom had gone out of the world with lead enough in them to keep them from tossing in their graves.

This ceremony ended, Seth put his hat firmly on his small, reptilian head, adding greatly to the ferociousness of his thirsty countenance by his way of pulling the sombrero down upon his ears.

"Want to walk around with me and introduce me and show me off?" he asked.

"It'll be the biggest satisfaction in ten years!" Judge Thayer declared.

CHAPTER III

FIRST BLOOD

Judge Thayer had completed the round of Ascalon's business section with the town's new peace officer, introducing him in due form. They stood now in front of the hotel, the plank awning of which extended over the sidewalk breaking the sun, Judge Thayer about to go his way.

"We've got to change this condition of things, Seth," he said, sweeping his hand around the quiet square, where nothing seemed awake but a few loafers along the shady fronts: "we've got to make it a day town instead of a night roost for the buzzards that wake up after sundown."

Seth did not answer. He stood turning his red eyes up and down the street, as if calculating distances and advantages for future emergencies. And as he looked there came driving into the somnolent square two men on a wagonload of bones.

"Old Joe Lynch; he's loadin' another car of bones," Judge Thayer said.

"He used to pick up meat for me," said Seth in his sententious way, neither surprised nor pleased on finding this associate of his adventurous days here in this place of his new beginning.

Joe Lynch drove across the farther side of the square, a block away from the two officials of Ascalon. There he stopped only long enough to allow his passenger to alight, and continued on to the railroad siding where his car stood.

Judge Thayer lingered under the hotel awning, where the breeze struck refreshingly, perhaps making a pretense of being cooled that was greater than his necessity, curious to see who it was Lynch had brought to town on his melancholy load. The passenger, carrying his flat bag, came on toward the hotel.

"He's a stranger to me," said the judge. His interest ending there, he went his way to take up again the preparation of his case in defense of the cattle thief whom he knew to be a thief, and nothing but a thief.

Seth Craddock, the new marshal, glanced sharply at the stranger as he approached the hotel. It was nothing more severe than Seth's ordinary scrutiny, but it appeared to the traveler to be at once hostile and inhospitable, the look of a man who sneered out of his heart and carried a challenge in his eyes. The stranger made the mental observation that this citizen was a sour-looking customer, who apparently resented the coming of one more to the mills of Ascalon's obscene gods.

There was a cluster of flies on the open page of the hotel register, where somebody had put down a sticky piece of chocolate candy and left it. This choice confection covered three or four lines immediately below the last arrival's name, its little trickling rivulets, which the flies were licking up, spreading like a spider's legs. There was nobody in the office to receive the traveler's application for quarters, but evidence of somebody in the remote parts of the house, whence came the sound of a voice more penetrating than musical, raised in song.

With her apurn pinned round her, He took her for a swan, But oh and a-las, it was poor Pol-ly Bawn.

So she sang, the words of the ancient ballad cutting through the partition like a saw. There was a nasal quality in them, as if the singer were moved to tears by the pathos of Poor Polly's end. The traveler laid a finger on the little bell that stood on the cigar case, sending his alarm through the house.

The song ceased, the blue door with DINING-ROOM in pink across its panels, shut against the flies, opened with sudden jerk, as if by a petulant hand. There appeared one who might have been Polly Bawn herself, taken by the white apron that shrouded her figure from shoulders to floor. She stood a moment in the door, seeing that it was a stranger, half closing that gay portal to step behind it and give her hair that swift little adjustment which, with women the world over, is the most essential part of the toilet. She appeared smiling then, somewhat abashed and coy, a fair short girl with a nice figure and pretty, sophisticated face, auburn curls dangling long at her ears, a precise row of bangs coming down to her eyebrows. She was a pink and white little lady, quick on foot, quicker of the blue eyes which measured the waiting guest from dusty feet to dusty hat in the glance that flashed over him in business-like brevity.

"Was you wishin' a room?" she inquired.

"If you can accommodate me."

"Register," she said, in voice of command, whirling the book about. At the same time she discovered the forgotten confection, which she removed to the top of the cigar case with an annoyed ejaculation under her breath that sounded rather strong. She applied her apron to the page, not helping it much, spreading the brown paste rather than removing it.

"You'll have to skip three or four lines, mister, unless you've got a 'delible pencil."

"No, I haven't. I'll write down here where it's dry."

And there the traveler wrote, the girl looking on sharply, spelling the letters with silently moving lips as the pen trailed them:

Calvin Morgan, Des Moines, Ia.

"In and out, or regular?" the girl asked, twisting the book around to verify the upside-down spelling of his name.

"I expect it will be only for a few days," Morgan replied, smiling a little at the pert sufficiency of the clerk.

"It's a dollar a day for board and room--in advance in this man's town."

"Why in this man's town, any more than any other man's town?" the guest inquired, amused.

"What would you think of a man that would run up a three weeks' bill and then walk out there and let somebody put a bullet through him?" she returned by way of answer.

"I think it would be a mean way to beat a board bill," he told her, seriously. "Do they do that right along here?"

"One smarty from Texas done it three or four months ago. Since then it's cash in advance."

Morgan thought it was a very wise regulation for a town where perils were said to be so thick, all in keeping with the notoriety of Ascalon. He made inquiry about something to eat. The girl's face set in disfavoring cast as she tossed her head haughtily.

"Dinner's over long ago," she said.

Morgan made amends for this unwitting breach of the rules, wondering what there was in the air of Ascalon that made people combative. Even this fresh-faced girl, not twenty, he was sure, was resentful, snappish without cause, inclined to quarrel if a word got crosswise in a man's mouth. As he turned these things in mind, casting about for some place to stow his bag, the girl smiled across at him, the mockery going out of her bright eyes. Perhaps it was because she felt that she had defended the ancient right of hostelers to rise in dignified front when a traveler spoke of a meal out of the regular hour, perhaps because there was a gentleness and sincerity in the tall, honest-looking man before her that reached her with an appeal lacking in those who commonly came and went before her counter.

"Put your grip over there," she nodded, "and I'll see what I can find. If you don't mind a snack--" she hesitated.

"Anything--a slab of cold meat and a cup of coffee."

"I'll call you," she said, starting for the blue door.

The girl had reached the dining-room door when there entered from the street a man, lurching when he walked as if the earth tipped under him like the deck of a ship. He was a young and slender man, dressed rather loudly in black sateen shirt and scarlet necktie, with broad blue, tassel-ornamented sleeve holders about his arms. He wore neither coat nor vest, but was belted with a pistol and booted and spurred, his calling of cowboy impressed in every line.

The girl paused, hand on the door, waiting to see what he wanted, and turned back when he rested his arms on the cigar case, clicking the glass with a coin. While she was making change for him, the cowboy stood with his newly bought cigar in his mouth, scanning the register. He seemed sober enough when standing still, save for the vacant, liquor-dead look of his eyes.

"Who wrote that?" he asked, pointing to Morgan's name.

"That gentleman," the girl replied, placing his change before him.

The cowboy picked up his money with numb fingers, fumbled to put it in his pocket, dropping it on the floor. He kicked at it with a curse and let it lie, scowling meantime at Morgan with angry eyes.

"Too good to write your name next to mine, are you?" he sneered. "Afraid it'd touch your fancy little handwritin', was you?"

"I didn't know it was your name, pardner," Morgan returned, conciliating him as he would an irresponsible child. "Why, I'd walk a mile to write my name next to yours any day. There was something on the book----"

"You spit on it! You spit on my name!" the foolish fellow charged, laying hand to his pistol. "A man that's too good to write his name next to mine's too good to stay in the same house with me. You'll hit the breeze out of here, pardner, or you'll swaller lead!"

The girl came swiftly from behind the counter, and ran lightly to the door. Morgan put up his hand to silence the young man, knowing well that he could catch his slow arm before he could drag his gun two inches from the holster.

"Keep your gun where it is, old feller," he suggested, rather than warned, in good-natured tone. "I didn't mean any insult, but I'll take my hat off and apologize to you if you want me to. There was a piece of candy on the book right----"

"I'll put a piece of hot iron in your guts!" the cowboy threatened. He leaned over the register, hand still on his pistol, and tore out the offending page, crumpling it into a ball. "You'll eat this, then you'll hit the road back where you come from!"

The girl was beckoning to somebody from the door. Morgan was more annoyed and shamed by his part in this foolish scene than he was disturbed by any feeling of danger. He stood watching the young man's shooting arm. There was not more than five feet between them; a step, a sharp clip on the jaw, and the young fool would be helpless. Morgan was setting himself to act, for the cowboy, whose face was warrant that he was a simple, harmless fellow when sober, was dragging on his gun, when one came hastening in past the girl.

This was a no less important person than the new city marshal, whom Morgan had seen without knowing his official standing, as he arrived at the hotel.

"This man's raisin' a fuss here--he's tore the register--look what he's done--tore the register!" the indignant girl charged.

"You're arrested," said the marshal. "Come on."

The cowboy stood mouthing his cigar, a weak look of scorn and derision in his flushed face. His right hand was still on his pistol, the wadded page of the register in the other.

"You'd better take his gun," Morgan suggested to the marshal, "he's so drunk he might hurt himself with it."

Seth Craddock fixed Morgan a moment with his sullen red eyes, in which the sneer of his heart seemed to speak. But his lips added nothing to the insult of that disdainful look. He jerked his head toward the door in command to his prisoner to march.

"Come out! I'll fight both of you!" the cowboy challenged, making for the door. He was squarely in it, one foot lifted in his drunken balancing to step down, when Seth Craddock jerked out his pistol between the lifting and the falling of that unsteady foot, and shot the retreating man in the back. The cowboy pitched forward into the street, where he lay stretched and motionless, one spurred foot still in the door.

Morgan sprang forward with an exclamation of shocked protest at this unjustified slaughter, while the girl, her blue eyes wide in horror, shrunk against the counter, hands pressed to her cheeks, a cry of outraged pity ringing from her lips.

"Resist an officer, will you?" said the city marshal, as he strode forward and looked down on the first victim in Ascalon of the woeful harvest his pistol was to reap. So saying, as if publishing his justification, he sheathed his weapon and walked out, as little moved as if he had shot the bottom out of a tomato can in practice among friends.

A woman came hastening from the back of the house with dough on her hands, a worn-faced woman, whose eyes were harried and afraid as if they had looked on violence until horror had set its seal upon them. She exclaimed and questioned, panting, frantic, holding her dough-clogged fingers wide as she bent to look at the slain man in her door.

"It was the new marshal Judge Thayer was in here with just after dinner," the girl explained, the pink gone out of her pretty face, the reflection of her mother's horror in her eyes.

"My God!" said the woman, clutching her breast, looking with a wilder terror into Morgan's face.

"Oh, I wish they'd take him away! I wish they'd take him away!" the girl moaned, cringing against the counter, covering her face with her hands.

Outside a crowd collected around the fallen man, for common as death by violence was in the streets of Ascalon, the awe of its swift descent, the hushing mystery of its silence, fell as coldly over the hearts of men there as in the walks of peace. Presently the busy undertaker came with his black wagon to gather up this broken shape of what had been a man but a few minutes past.

The marshal did not trouble himself in the case further. Up the street Morgan saw him sauntering along, unmoved and unconcerned, from all outward show, as if this might have been just one incidental task in a busy day. Resentment rose in Morgan as he watched the undertaker and his helper load the body into the wagon with unfeeling roughness; as he saw the marshal go into a saloon with a crowd of noisy fellows from the stock pens who appeared to be applauding his deed.

This appeared to Morgan simply murder in the name of the law. That bragging, simple, whisky-numbed cowboy could not have hurt a cat. All desire for dinner was gone out of Morgan's stomach, all thought of preparing it from the girl's mind. She stood in the door with her mother, watching the black wagon away with this latest victim to be crushed in Ascalon's infernal mill, twisting her fingers in her apron, her face as white as the flour on her mother's hands. The undertaker's man came hurrying back with a bucket of water and broom. The women turned away out of the door then, while he briskly went to work washing up the dark little puddle that spread on the boards of the sidewalk.

"Dora, where's your pa?" the elder woman asked, stopping suddenly as she crossed the room, her face drawn in a quick stroke of fear, her hands lifted to ease the smothering in her breast again.

"I don't know, Ma. He ain't been around since dinner."

The woman went to the door again, to lean and peer up and down the street with that great anxiety and trouble in her face that made it old, and distorted the faint trace of lingering prettiness out of it as if it had been covered with ashes.

"He's comin'," she said presently, in voice of immeasurable relief. She turned away from the door without allowing her glance to fall directly on the wet spot left by the undertaker's man.

Mother and daughter talked together in low words, only a few of which now and then reached Morgan as he stood near the counter where the mutilated register lay, turning this melancholy event in his thoughts. He recovered the torn crumpled page from the floor, smoothed and replaced it in the book. A man came in, the woman turning with a quick glad lighting of the face to meet him.

"O Tommy! I was worried to death!" she said.

Tom Conboy, proprietor of the Elkhorn, as the hotel was called, grunted in discount of this anxiety as he turned his shifty eyes to the stranger, flicking them on and off like a fly. He saw the coins dropped by the cowboy, picked them up, put them in his pocket, face red from what evidently was unaccustomed effort as he straightened his back.

"You seem to be gettin' mighty flush with money around this joint," he said, severe censure in his tone.

"He dropped it--the man the marshal shot dropped it--it was his," the girl explained. "I wouldn't touch it!" she shuddered, "not for anything in the world!"

"Huh!" said Conboy, easily, entirely undisturbed by the dead man's money in his pocket.

"My God! I wish he hadn't done it here!" the woman moaned.

"I didn't think he'd shoot him or I wouldn't 'a' called him," the girl pleaded, pity for the deed in her shocked voice. "He didn't need to do it--he didn't have to do it, at all!"

"Sh-h-h! No niggers in Ireland, now--no-o-o niggers in Ireland!"

Conboy shook his head at her as he spoke, pronouncing this rather amazing and altogether irrelevant declaration with the utmost gravity, an admonitory, cautioning inflection in his naturally grave and resonant voice. The girl said no more on the needless sacrifice of the young man's life.

"I was goin' to get this gentleman some dinner," she said.

"You'd better go on and do it, then," her father directed, gently enough for a man of his stamp, rather surprisingly gentle, indeed, Morgan thought.

Tom Conboy was a short-statured man, slight; his carefully trimmed gray beard lending a look of serious wisdom to his face which the shiftiness of his insincere eyes at once seemed to controvert. He wore neither coat nor vest, but a white shirt with broad starched bosom, a large gold button in its collarless neckband. A diamond stud flashed in the middle of his bosom; red elastic bands an inch broad, with silver buckles, held up the slack of the sleeves which otherwise would have enveloped his hands.

"Are you goin' to stay in the office a while now, Tommy, and look after things while Dora and I do the work?" the woman asked.

"I've got to get the jury together for the inquest," Conboy returned, with the briskness of a man of importance.

"Will I be wanted to give my testimony at the inquest, do you suppose?" Morgan inquired. "I was here when it happened; I saw the whole thing."

He spoke in the hope that he might be given the opportunity of relieving the indignation, so strong in him that it was almost oppressive, before the coroner's jury. Tom Conboy shook his head.

"No, the marshal's testimony is all we'll need," Conboy replied. "Resistin' arrest and tryin' to escape after arrest. That's all there was to it. These fellers'll have to learn better than that with this new man. I know him of old--he's a man that always brings in the meat."

"But he didn't try to escape," Morgan protested. "He was so drunk he didn't know whether he was coming or going."

Conboy looked at him disfavoringly, as if to warn him to be discreet in matters of such remote concern to him as this.

"Tut, tut! no niggers in Ireland," said he, shaking his head with an expression between a caution and a threat.

CHAPTER IV

THE OPTIMIST EXPLAINS

Not more than two hours after the tragedy at the Elkhorn hotel, of which he was the indirect cause, Calvin Morgan appeared at Judge Thayer's little office. The judge had finished his preparation for the cattle thief's case, and now sat ruminating it over his cob pipe. He nodded encouragingly as Morgan hesitated at the door.

"Come in, Mr. Morgan," he invited, as cordially as if introductions had passed between them already and relations had been established on a footing pleasant and profitable to both.

Morgan smiled a little at this ready identification, remembering the torn page of the hotel register, which all the reading inhabitants of the town who were awake must have examined before this. He accepted the chair that Judge Thayer pushed toward him, nodding to the bone-wagon man who came sauntering past the door at that moment, the long lash of his bullhide whip trailing in the dust behind him.

"You've come to settle with us, I hear?" said the judge.

"I'm looking around with that thought, sir."

"I don't know how you'll do at the start in the optical way, Mr. Morgan--I'm afraid not much. I'd advise watch repairing and jewelry in addition. This town is going to be made a railroad division point before long, I could get you appointed watch inspector for the company. Now, I've got a nice little storeroom----"

"I'm afraid you've got me in the wrong deck," Morgan interrupted, unwilling to allow the judge to go on building his extravagant fancy. "I could no more fix a watch than I could repair a locomotive, and spectacles are as far out of my line as specters."

Judge Thayer's face reddened above his thick beard at this easy and fluent denial of all that he had constructed from a hasty and indefinite bit of information.

"I beg your pardon, Mr. Morgan. It was Joe Lynch, the fellow that drives the bone wagon, who got me wrong. He told me you were an oculist."

"I think that was his rendition of optimist, perhaps," Morgan said, laughing with the judge's hearty appreciation of the twist. "I told him, in response to a curious inquiry, that I was an optimist. I've tried hard--very hard, sometimes--to live up to it. My profession is one that makes a heavy drain on all the cheerfulness that nature or art ever stocked a man with, Judge Thayer."

"It sounds like you might be a lawyer," the judge speculated, "or maybe a doctor?"

"No, I'm simply an agriculturist, late professor of agronomy in the Iowa State Agricultural College. It takes optimism, believe me, sir, to try to get twenty bushels of wheat out of land where only twelve grew before, or two ears of corn where only two-thirds of one has been the standard."

"You're right," Judge Thayer agreed heartily; "it takes more faith, hope, and courage to be a farmer than any other calling on earth. I often consider the risks a farmer must take year by year in comparison with other lines of business, staking his all, very frequently, on what he puts into the furrows, turning his face to God when he has sown his seed, in faith that rains will fall and frosts will be stayed. It is heroic, sometimes it is sublimely heroic. And you are going to try your fortunes here on the soil?"

"I've had my eye on this country a good while in spite of the dismal tales of hardship and failure that have come eastward out of it. I've looked to it as the place for me to put some of my theories to the test. I believe alfalfa, or lucerne, as it is called back East, will thrive here, and I'm going to risk your derision and go a little farther. I believe this can be made the greatest wheat country in America."

Judge Thayer brought his hand down with a smack of the palm that made his papers fly, his face radiating the pleasure that words alone could not express.

"I've been telling them that for seven years, Morgan!" he said.

"Hasn't it ever been tried out?"

"Tried out? They don't stay long enough to try out anything, Morgan. They're here today and gone tomorrow, cursing Kansas as they go, slandering it, branding it as the Tophet of the earth. We've never had the right kind of people here, they didn't have the courage, the faith, and the vision. If a man hasn't got the grit and ability to stick through his losses at any game in this life, Morgan, he'll never win. And he'll never be anything but a little loser, put him down where you will."

"I've met hundreds of them dragging their bones out of Kansas the past four or five years," Morgan nodded. "From what I can gather by talking with them, the trouble lies in their poverty when they come here. As you say, they're not staked to play this stiff game. A man ought to provision himself for a campaign against this country like he would for an Arctic expedition. If he can't do it, he'd better stay away."

"I guess there's more to that than I ever stopped to consider myself," Judge Thayer admitted. "It is a hard country to break, but there are men somewhere who can subdue it and reap its rewards."

"I tried to induce the railroad company to back me in an experimental farm out here, but the officials couldn't see it," Morgan said. "I'm going to tackle it now on my lonesome. The best proof of a man's confidence in his own theories is to put them into practice himself, anyway."

"These cattlemen around here will laugh at you and try to discourage you, Morgan. I'm the standing joke of this country because I still stick to my theory of wheat."

"The farmers in Iowa laughed their teeth loose when we book farmers at the college told them they could add a million bushels a year to the corn crop of the state by putting a few more grains on the ends of the cobs. Well, they did it, just the same, in time."

"I heard about that," nodded the judge, quite warmed up to this long-backed stranger.

"Failure is written all over the face of this country," Morgan continued; "I took a long tramp across it this morning. But I believe I've got the formula that will tame it."

"I believe you, I believe you can do it," Judge Thayer indorsed him, with enthusiasm. "I believe you've brought the light of a new epoch into this country, I believe you're carrying the key that's going to unlock these prairies and liberate the gold under the grass roots."

"It may be nothing but a dream," said Morgan softly, his eyes fixed on the blue distances through the open door. "Maybe it will break me and scatter my bones on the prairie for that old scavenger of men to haul away."

Judge Thayer shook his head in denial of this possibility, making note of this rugged dreamer's strong face, strong arms, large, capable hands.

"We're not away out West, as most people seem to think," he said, "only a little past the middle of the state. My observation through several years here has been that it rains about as much and as often in this part of the country as it does in the eastern part of the state, enough to make two crops in three, anyway, and that's as good as you can count on without irrigation anywhere."

Morgan agreed with a nod. Judge Thayer went on, "The trouble is, this prairie sheds water like the roof of a house, shoots it off so quick into the draws and creeks it never has a chance to soak in. Plow it, I tell 'em, and keep on plowin' it, in season and out; fix it so it can soak up the rain and hold it. Is that right?"

"You've got the key to it yourself," Morgan told him, not a little surprised to hear this uncredited missionary preaching the very doctrine that men of Morgan's profession had found so hard to make converts to in the prairie country.

"But it will be two or three years, at least, before you can begin your experiment with wheat," Judge Thayer regretted. "By that time I'm afraid the settlers that are taking up land around here now will be broken and discouraged, gone to spread the curse against Kansas in the same old bitterness of heart."

"I hope to find a piece of land that somebody has abandoned or wants to sell, that has been farmed a year or two," Morgan confided. "If I can get hold of such a place I'll be able to put in a piece of wheat this fall--even a few acres will start me going. I could enlarge my fields with my experience."

Judge Thayer said he believed he had the very place Morgan was looking for, listed for sale. But there were so many of them listed for sale, the owners gone, their equities long since eaten up by unpaid taxes, that it took the judge a good while to find the particulars in this special case.

"Man by the name of Gerhart, mile and a half west of town--that would bring him pretty near the river--offers his quarter for three hundred dollars. He's been there about four years, wife died this spring. I think he's got about eighty acres broken out. Some of that land ought to be in pretty good shape for wheat by now."

As the day was declining to evening, and Judge Thayer's supper hour was near, they agreed on postponing until morning the drive out to look at the dissatisfied settler's land. Morgan was leaving when the judge called him back from the door.

"I was just wondering whether you'd ever had any editorial experience?" he said.

"No, I've never been an editor," Morgan returned, speculating alertly on what might be forthcoming.

"We--our editor--our editor," said the judge, fumbling with it as if he found the matter a difficult one to fit to the proper words, "fell into an unfortunate error of judgment a short time ago, with--um-m-m--somewhat melancholy--melancholy--" the judge paused, as if feeling of this word to see that it fitted properly, head bent thoughtfully--"results. Unlucky piece of business for this community, coming right in the thick of the contest for the county seat. There's a fight on here, Mr. Morgan, as you may have heard, between Ascalon, the present county seat, and Glenmore, a God-abandoned little flyspeck on the map seven miles south of here."

"I hadn't heard of it. And what happened to the editor?"

"Oh, one of our hot-headed boys shot him," said the judge, out of patience with such trivial and hasty yielding to passion. "Since then I've been getting out the paper myself--I hold a mortgage on the property, I'll be obliged to foreclose to protect myself--with the help of the printer. It's not much of a paper, Morgan, for I haven't got the time to devote to it with the July term of court coming on, but I have to get it out every week or lose the county printing contract. There's a hungry dog over at Glenmore looking on to snatch the bone on the least possible excuse, and he's got two of the county commissioners with him."

"No, I'm not an editor," Morgan repeated, speculatively, as if he saw possibilities of distinction in that road.

"Without the press, we are a community disarmed in the midst of our enemies," said the judge. "Glenmore will overwhelm us and rob us of our rights, without a champion whose voice is as the voice of a thousand men."

"I'd never be equal to that," Morgan said, shaking his head in all seriousness. "Is the editor out of it for good? Is he dead?"

"They have a devilish peculiarity of seldom wounding a man here in Ascalon, Mr. Morgan. I've wished more than once they were not so cursed proficient. The poor fellow fell dead, sir, at the first shot, while he was reaching for his gun."

"I've seen something of their proficiency here," Morgan said, with plain contempt.

Judge Thayer looked at him sharply. "You refer to that affair at the hotel this afternoon?"

"It was a brutal and uncalled-for sacrifice of human life! it was murder in the name of the law."

"I think you are somewhat hasty and unjust in your criticism, Mr. Morgan," the judge mildly protested. "I know the marshal to be a cool-headed man, a man who can see perils that you and I might overlook until too late for our own preservation. The fellow must have made some break for his gun that you didn't see."

"I hope it was that way," Morgan said, willing to give the marshal every shadow of justification possible.

"I've known Seth Craddock a long time; he was huntin' buffalo for the railroad contractors when I first came to this country. Why, I appointed Seth to the office not more than an hour before that mix-up at the hotel."

"He's beginning early," Morgan said.

"The man that's going to clean this town up must begin early and work late," Judge Thayer declared. "An officer that would allow a man to run a bluff on him wouldn't last two hours."

"I suppose not," Morgan admitted.

"As I told Seth when I swore him in, what we want in Ascalon is a marshal that will use his gun oftener, and to better purpose, than the men that have gone before him. This town must be purified, the offal of humanity that makes a stench until it offends the heavens and spreads our obscene notoriety to the ends of the earth, must be swept out before we can induce sober and substantial men to bring their families into this country."

"It looks reasonable enough," Morgan agreed.

"Hell's kettle is on the fire in this town, Mr. Morgan; the devil's own stew is bubbling in it. If I could induce you to defer your farming experiment a few months, as much as I approve it, anxious as I am to see you demonstrate your theories and mine, I believe we could accomplish the regeneration of this town. With a man of Craddock's caliber on the street, and you in the Headlight office speaking with the voice of a thousand men, we could reverse public opinion and draw friends to our side. Without some such support, I view the future with gloom and misgiving. Glenmore is bound to displace us as the capital of this county; Ascalon will decline to a whistling station by the side of the track."

"I'm afraid I wouldn't care to hitch up with Mr. Craddock in the regeneration of Ascalon," Morgan said. "We'd pull so hard in opposite directions we'd break the harness."

Judge Thayer expressed his regret while he slipped on his black alpaca coat, asking Morgan to wait until he locked his door, when he would walk with him as far as the hotel corner. On the way they met a young man who came bowling along with a great air of importance and self-assurance, a fresh cigar tilted up in his mouth to such an angle that it threatened the brim of his large white hat.

Judge Thayer introduced this man as Dell Hutton, county treasurer. Hutton wrung Morgan's hand with ardent grip, as if he welcomed him into the brotherhood of the elect in Ascalon, speaking out of the corner of his mouth around his cigar. He was a thin-mouthed man of twenty-five, or perhaps a year or two older, with a shrunken weazenness about his face that made him look like a very old man done over, and but poorly renovated. His eyes were pale, with shadows in them as of inquiry and distrust; his stature was short, his frame slight.

Hutton seemed to be deeply, even passionately, interested in the venture Morgan had come to make in that country. He offered his services in any exigency where they might be applied, shaking hands again with hard grip, accompanied by a wrinkling of his thin mouth about his cigar as he clamped his jaws in the fervor of his earnestness. But he appeared to be under a great pressure to go his way, his eyes controverting the sincerity of his words the while.

"He's rather a young man to be filling such a responsible position," Morgan ventured as they resumed their way.

"Dell wasn't elected to the office," Judge Thayer explained. "He's filling out his father's term."

"Did he--die?" Morgan inquired, marveling over the mortality among the notables of the town.

"He was a victim of this feud in the rivalry for the county seat," Judge Thayer explained, with sadness. "It was due to Hutton, more than any other force, that we didn't lose the county seat at the last election--he kept the cattlemen lined up, was a power among them, followed that business a long time himself. Yes. He was the first man that ever drove a herd of cattle from Texas to load for market when this railroad was put through. Some of those skulkers from Glenmore shot him down at his door two months after he took office."

"I thought the boy looked like he'd been trained on the range," Morgan said, thoughtfully.

"Yes, Dell was raised in the saddle, drove several trips from Texas up here. Dell"--softly, a little sorrowfully, Morgan thought--"was the other principal in that affair with our late editor."

"Oh, I see. He was exonerated?"

"Clear case of self-defense, proved that Smith--the editor was Smith--reached for his gun first."

Morgan did not comment, but he thought that this seemed a thing easily proved in Ascalon. He parted from the judge at the bank corner, which was across the way from the hotel.

The shadow of the hotel fell far into the public square, and in front of the building, their chairs placed in what would have been the gutter of the street if the thoroughfare had been paved, their feet braced with probably more comfort than grace against the low sidewalk, a row of men was stationed, like crows on a fence. There must have been twenty or more of them, in various stages of undress from vest down to suspenders, from bright cravats flaunting over woolen shirts and white shirts, and striped shirts and speckled shirts, to unconfined necks laid bare to the breeze.

Whether these were guests waiting supper, or merely loafers waiting anything that might happen next, Morgan had not been long enough in town to determine. He noticed the curious and, he thought, unfriendly eyes which they turned on him as he approached. And as Morgan set foot on the sidewalk porch of the hotel, Seth Craddock, the new city marshal, rose out of the third chair on the end of the row nearest him, hand lifted in commanding signal to halt.

"You've just got time to git your gripsack," Craddock said, coming forward as he spoke, but stopping a little to one side as if to allow Morgan passage to the door.

"Time's no object to me," Morgan returned, good-humored and undisturbed, thinking this must be one of the jokes at the expense of strangers for which Ascalon was famous.

Some of the loafers were standing by their chairs in attitude of indecision, others sat leaning forward to see and hear. Traffic both ways on the sidewalk came to a sudden halt at the spectacle of two men in a situation recognized at a glance in quick-triggered Ascalon as significant, those who came up behind Morgan clearing the way by edging from the sidewalk into the square.

"The train'll be here in twelve minutes," Craddock announced, watch in his palm.

"On time, is she?" Morgan said indifferently, starting for the door.

Again Seth Craddock lifted his hand. Those who had remained seated along the gutter perch up to this moment now got to their feet with such haste that chairs were upset. Craddock put his hand casually to his pistol, as a man rests his hand on his hip.

"You're leavin' on it," he said.

"I guess you've got the wrong man," Morgan suggested, noting everything with comprehensive eye, not a little concerned by the marshal's threatening attitude. If this were going to turn out a joke, Morgan wished it might begin very soon to show some of its risible features on the surface, in order that he might know which way to jump to make the best figure possible.

"No, I ain't got no wrong man!" Craddock returned, making mockery of the words, uttering them jeeringly out of the corner of his mouth. He blasted Morgan with the glare of his malevolent red eyes, redder now than before his weapon had moistened the street of Ascalon with blood. "You're the feller that's been shootin' off your mouth about murder in the name of the law, and you bein' able to take his gun away from that feller. Well, kid, I'm afraid it's goin' to be a little too rough for you in this town. You're leavin'--you won't have time to git your gripsack now, you can write for it!"

Morgan felt the blood flaming into his face with the hot swell of anger. A moment he stood eye to eye with Craddock, fighting down the defiance that rose for utterance to his lips. Then he started again toward the hotel door.

Craddock whipped out his pistol with arm so swift that the eye multiplied it like a spoke in a quick-spinning wheel. He stood holding the weapon so, his wrist rather limber, the muzzle of the pistol pointing in the general direction of Morgan's feet.

"Maybe you can take a gun away from me, little feller?" Craddock challenged in high mockery, one nostril of his long nose twitching, lifting his mustache on that side in a snarl.

"Don't point that gun at me, Craddock!" Morgan warned, his voice unshaken and cool, although the surge of his heart made his seasoned body vibrate to the finger tips.

"Scratch gravel for the depot!" Craddock commanded, lowering the muzzle of his gun as if he intended to hasten the going by a shot between the offender's feet.

The men were separated by not more than two yards, and Morgan made no movement to widen the breach immediately following the marshal's command to go. On the contrary, before any that saw him standing there in apparent indecision, and least of all among them Seth Craddock, could measure his intention, Morgan stepped aside quicker than the watchers calculated any living man could move, reached out his long arm a flash quicker than he had shifted on his feet, and laid hold of the city marshal's hairy wrist, wrenching it in a twist so bone-breaking that nerves and muscles failed their office. Nobody saw exactly how he accomplished it, but the next moment Morgan stepped back from the city marshal, that officer's revolver in his hand.

"Mr. Craddock," he said, in calm, advisory way, "I expect to stay around this part of the country some little time, and I'll be obliged to come to Ascalon once in a while. If you think you're going to feel uncomfortable every time you see me, I guess the best thing for you to do is leave. I'm not saying you must leave, I don't set myself up to tell a man when to come and go without I've got that right over him. I just suggest it for your comfort and peace of mind. If you stay here you'll have to get used to seeing me around."

Craddock stood for a breath glaring at the man who had humiliated him in his new dignity, clutching his half-paralyzed wrist. He said nothing, but there was the proclamation of a death feud in his eyes.

"Give him a gun, somebody!" said a fool in the crowd that pressed to the edge of the sidewalk at the marshal's back.

Tom Conboy, standing in his door ten feet away, interposed quickly, waving the crowd back.

"Tut, tut! No niggers in Ireland, now!" he said.

"He can have this one," said Morgan, still in the same measured, calm voice. He offered the pistol back to its owner, who snatched it with ungracious hand, shoved it into his battered scabbard, turned to the crowd at his back with an oath.

"Scatter out of here!" he ordered, covering his degradation as he might in this tyrannical exercise of authority.

Morgan looked into the curious faces of the people who blocked the sidewalk ahead of him, withdrawn a discreet distance, not yet venturing to come on. Except for the red handkerchief that he had worn about his neck, he was dressed as when he arrived in Ascalon in Joe Lynch's wagon, coatless, the dust of the road on his shoes. In place of the bright handkerchief he now wore a slender black necktie, the ends of it tucked into his gray woolen shirt.

He felt taller, rawer, more angular than nature had built him as he stood there looking at the people who had gathered like leaves against a rock in a brook. He was ashamed of his part in the public show, sorry that anybody had been by to witness it. In his embarrassment he pushed his hat back from his forehead, looking around him again as if he would break through the ranks and hide himself from such confusing publicity.

The crowd was beginning to disperse at Seth Craddock's urging, although those who had come to a stand on the sidewalk seemed timid about passing Morgan. They still held back as if to give him room, or in uncertainty whether it was all over yet. Perhaps they expected Craddock to turn on Morgan again when he had cleared a proper space for his activities.

As for Morgan, he had dismissed the city marshal from his thoughts, for something else had risen in his vision more worthy the attention of a man. This was the face of a girl on the edge of the crowd in front of him, a tall, strong, pliant creature who leaned a little as if she looked for her reflection in a stream. She was garbed in a brown duck riding skirt, white waist with a bright wisp of cravat blowing at her breast like the red of bittersweet against snow. Her dusty sombrero threw a shadow over her eyes, but Morgan could see that they were dark and friendly eyes, as no shadow but night could obscure. The other faces became in that moment but the incidental background for one; his heart lifted and leaped as the heart moves and yearns with tender quickening at the sound of some old melody that makes it glad.

Morgan stepped back, thinking only of her, seeing only her, making a way for her, only, to pass. That others might follow was not in his mind. He stepped out of the way for her.

She came on toward him now, one finished, one refined, among that press of crudity, one unlooked for in that place of wild lusts and dark passions unrestrained. She carried a packet of newspapers and letters under her bent arm, telling of her mission on the street; the thong of her riding quirt was about her wrist. Her soft dark hair was low on her neck, a flush as of the pleasure that speaks in bounding blood when friend meets friend glowed in her face. Morgan removed his hat as she passed him. She looked into his face and smiled.

The little crowd broke and followed, but Morgan, oblivious to the movement around him, stood on the sidewalk edge looking after her, his hat in his hand.

CHAPTER V

ASCALON AWAKE

Ascalon was laid out according to the Spanish tradition for arranging towns that dominated the builders of the West and Southwest in the days when Santa Fé extended its trade influence over a vast territory. Although Ascalon was only a stage station in the latter days of traffic over the Santa Fé Trail, its builders, when it came occasion to expand, were men who had traded in that capital of the gray desert wastes at the trail's end, and nothing would serve them but a plaza, with the courthouse in the middle of it, the principal business establishments facing it the four sides around.

There were many who called it the plaza still, especially visitors from along the Rio Grande who came driving their long-horned, lean-flanked cattle northward over the Chisholm Trail. Santa Fé, at its worst, could not have been dustier than this town of Ascalon, and especially the plaza, or public square, in these summer days. Galloping horses set its dust flying in obscuring clouds; the restless wind that blew from sunrise till sunset day in and day out from the southwest, whipped it in sudden gusts of temper, and drove it through open doors, spreading it like a sun-defying hoarfrost on the low roofs. All considered, Ascalon was as dry, uncomfortable, unpromising of romance, as any place that man ever built or nature ever harassed with wearing wind and warping sun.

The courthouse in the middle of the public square was built of bricks, of that porous, fiery sort which seem so peculiarly designed to the monstrous vagaries of rural architecture. Here in Ascalon they fitted well with the arid appearance of things, as a fiery face goes best with white eyebrows, anywhere.

The courthouse was a two-storied structure, with the cupola as indispensable to the old-time Kansas courthouse as a steeple to a church. The jail was in the basement of it, thus sparing culprits a certain punishment by concealing the building's raw, red, and crude lines from the eye. Not that anybody in jail or out of it ever thought of this advantage, or appreciated it, indeed, for Ascalon was proud of the courthouse, and fired with a desire and determination to keep it there in the plaza forever and a day.

There were precedents before them, and plenty of them in that part of the country, where county seats had been changed, courthouses of red bricks and gray stones put on skids and moved away, leaving desolation that neither maledictions could assuage nor oratory could repair. For prosperity went with the courthouse in those days, and dignity, and consequence among the peoples of the earth.

Hitching racks, like crude apparatus for athletic exercises, were built around the courthouse, with good driving distance between them and the plank sidewalks. Here the riders from distant ranges tied their jaded mounts, here such as made use of wagons in that land of horseback-going men hitched their teams when they drove in for supplies.

There was not a shrub in the courthouse square, not the dead and stricken trunk of a tree standing monument of any attempt to mitigate the curse of sun. There was not a blade of grass, not a struggling, wind-blown flower. Only here and there chickweed grew, spreading its green tracery over the white soil in such sequestered spots as the hoofs of beast and the feet of men did not stamp and chafe and wear; and in the angles of the courthouse walls, the Russian thistle, barbed with its thousand thorns. Men did not consider beauty in Ascalon, this Tophet at trail's end, save it might be the beauty of human flesh, and then it must be rouged and powdered, and enforced with every cosmetic mixture to win attention in an atmosphere where life was lived in a ferment of ugly strife.

There was in Ascalon in those bloody days a standing coroner's jury, of which Tom Conboy was the foreman, composed of certain gamblers and town politicians whose interests were with the vicious element. To these men the wide notoriety of the town was capital. Therefore, it was seldom, indeed, that anybody was slain in Ascalon without justification, according to the findings of this coroner's jury. In this way the gamblers and divekeepers, and such respectable citizens as chose to exercise their hands in this exhilarating pastime, were regularly absolved.

The result of this amicable agreement between the county officials and the people of the town was that Ascalon became, more than ever, a refuge for the outlawed and proscribed of other communities. Every train brought them, and dumped them down on the station platform to find their way like wolves to their kind into the activities of the town.

Gamblers and gun-slingers, tricksters and sharpers, attended by the carrion flock of women who always hover after these wreckers and wastrels, came to Ascalon by scores. It began to appear a question, in time, of what they were to subsist upon, even though they turned to the ravening of one another.

But the broad notoriety of Ascalon attended to this, bringing with the outlawed and debased a fresh and eager train of victims. The sons of families came from afar, sated with the diversions and debaucheries of eastern cities, looking for strange thrills and adventures to heat their surfeited blood. Unsophisticated young men came, following the lure of romance; farm boys from the midwestern states came, with a thought of pioneering and making a new empire of the plow, as their fathers had smoothed the land in the states already called old.

All of these came with money in their pockets, and nearly all of them, one day first or last, became contributors to the support of Ascalon's prostituted population. New victims came to replace the plucked, new crowds of cowherders rode in from the long trails to the south, relays of them galloped night after night from the far ranches stretching along the sandy Arkansas. There was no want of grain to sow in the gaping furrows struck out by the hands of sin in the raw, treeless, unpainted city of Ascalon.

And into all this fever of coming and going, this heartbreak of shame and loss, of quickly drawn weapon, of flash, despairing cry, and death--this sowing of recklessness and harvesting of despair--into all this had come Calvin Morgan, a man with a clean heart, a clean purpose in his soul.

Ascalon once had been illuminated at night about the public square by kerosene lamps set on posts, after the manner of gas lights in a city, but the expense of supplying glass day after day to repair the damage done by roysterers during the night had become so heavy that the town had abandoned lights long before Morgan's advent there. Only the posts stood now, scarred by bullets, gnawed by horses which had stood hitched to them forgotten by their owners who reveled their wages in Ascalon's beguiling fires. At the time of Morgan's coming, starlight and moonlight, and such beams as fell through the windows of houses upon the uneven sidewalk around the square, provided all the illumination that brightened the streets of Ascalon by night.

On the evening of his mildly adventurous first day in the town, Morgan sat in front of the Elkhorn hotel, his chair in the gutter, according to the custom, his feet braced comfortably against the outer edge of the sidewalk, flanked by other guests and citizens who filled the remaining seats. Little was said to him of his encounter with the new city marshal, and that little Morgan made less, and brought to short ending by his refusal to be led into the matter at all. And as he sat there, chatting in desultory way, the fretting wind died to a breath, the line of men in the chairs grew indistinct in the gloom of early night, and Ascalon rose up like a sleeping wolf, shaking off the drowse of the day, and sat on its haunches to howl.

This awakening began with the sound of fiddles and pianos in the big dance hall whose roof covered all the vices which thrive best in the dark. Later a trombone and cornet joined the original musical din, lifting their brassy notes on the vexed night air. Bands of horsemen came galloping in, yelping the short, coyote cries of the cattle lands. Sometimes one of them let off his pistol as he wheeled his horse up to the hitching rack, the relief of a simple mind that had no other expression for its momentary exuberance.

Sidewalks became thronged with people tramping the little round of the town's diversions, but of different stamp from those who had sparsely trickled through its sunlight on legitimate business that afternoon. Cowboys hobbled by in their peggy, high-heeled gait, as clumsy afoot as penguins; men in white shirts without coats, their skin too tender to withstand the sun, walked with superior aloofness among the sheep which had come to their shearing pens, preoccupied in manner, yet alert, watching, watching, on every hand.

Now and then women passed, but they, also, were of the night, gaudily bedecked in tinsel and glittering finery that would have been fustian by day to the least discriminating eye. Respectability was not abroad in Ascalon by night. With the last gleam of day it left the stage to wantonness.

As the activity of the growing night increased, high-pitched voices of cowboys who called figures of the dances quavered above the confusion of sounds, a melancholy note in the long-drawn syllables that seemed a lament for the waste of youth, and a prophecy of desolation. When the music fell to momentary silence the clash of pool balls sounded, and the tramp of feet, and quavering wild feminine laughter rising sharply, trailing away to distance as if the revelers sailed by on the storm of their flaming passions, to land by and by on the shores of morning, draggled, dry-lipped, perhaps with a heartache for the far places left behind forever.

Morgan was not moved by a curiosity great enough to impel him to make the round. All this he had seen before, time over, in the frontier towns of Nebraska, with less noise and open display, certainly, for here in Ascalon viciousness had a nation-wide notoriety to maintain, and must intensify all that it touched. He was wondering how the townspeople who had honest business in life managed to sleep through that rioting, with the added chance of some fool cowboy sending a bullet through their thin walls as he galloped away to his distant camp, when Tom Conboy came through the sidewalk stream to sit beside him in a gutter chair.

The proprietor of the Elkhorn hotel appeared to be under a depression of spirits. He answered those who addressed him in short words, with manner withdrawn. Morgan noted that the diamond stud was gone out of the desert of Conboy's shirt bosom, and that he was belted with a pistol. Presently the man on Conboy's other hand, who had been trying with little result to draw him into a conversation, got up and made his way toward the bright front of the dance hall. Conboy touched Morgan's knee.

"Come into the office, kind of like it happened, a little while after me," he said, speaking in low voice behind his hand. He rose, stretching and yawning as if to give his movements a casual appearance, stood a little while on the edge of the sidewalk, went into the hotel. Morgan followed him in a few minutes, to find him apparently busy with his accounts behind the desk.

A little while the proprietor worked on his bookkeeping, Morgan lounging idly before the cigar case.

"Some fellers up the street lookin' for you," Conboy said, not turning his head.

"What fellows? What do they want?"

"That bunch of cowboys from the Chisholm Trail."

"I don't know them," said Morgan, not yet getting the drift of what Conboy evidently meant as a warning.

"They're friends of the city marshal; he belonged to the same outfit," Conboy explained, ostensibly setting down figures in his book.

"Thank you," said Morgan, starting for the door.

"Where you goin' to?" Conboy demanded, forgetting caution and possible complications in his haste to interpose.

"To find out what they want."

"There's no sense in a man runnin' his arm down a lion's throat to see if he's hungry," Conboy said, making a feint now of moving the cigar boxes around in the case.

"This town isn't so big that they'd miss a man if they went out to hunt him. Where are they?"

"I left them at Peden's, the big dance hall up the street. Ain't you got a gun?"

"No," Morgan returned thoughtfully, as if he had not even considered one before.

"The best thing you can do is to take a walk out into the country and forget your way back, kid. Them fellers are goin' to be jangled up just about right for anything in an hour or so more. I'd advise you to go--I'll send your grip to you wherever you say."

"You're very kind. How many of them are there?"

"Seven besides Craddock, the rest of them went to Kansas City with the cattle you saw leave in them three extras this evening. Craddock's celebratin' his new job, he's leadin' 'em around throwin' everything wide open to 'em without a cent to pay. 'Charge it to me' he said to Peden--I was there when they came in--'charge it to me, I'm payin' this bill.' You know what that means."

"I suppose it means that the collection will be deferred," Morgon said, grinning over the city marshal's easy cut to generosity.

"Indefinitely postponed," said Conboy, gloomily. "I'm goin' to put all my good cigars in the safe, and do it right now."

"Here's something you may put in the safe for me, too," said Morgan, handing over his pocketbook.

"Ain't you goin' to leave town?" Conboy asked, hand stayed hesitantly to take the purse.

"I've got an appointment with Judge Thayer to look at a piece of land in the morning," Morgan returned.

"Well, keep out enough to buy a gun, two of 'em if you're a double-handed man," Conboy counseled.

"I've got what I need," said Morgan, putting the purse in Conboy's hand.

"I'd say for you to take a walk out to Judge Thayer's and stay all night with him, but them fellers will be around here a couple of weeks, I expect--till the rest of the outfit comes back for their horses. Just one night away wouldn't do you any good."

"I couldn't think of it," said Morgan, coldly.

"You know your business, I guess," Conboy yielded, doubtfully, "but don't play your luck too far. You made a good grab when you took that feller's gun away from him, but you can't grab eight guns."

"You're right," Morgan agreed.

"If you're a reasonable man, you'll hit the grit out of this burg," Conboy urged.

"You said they were at Peden's?"

"First dance house you come to, the biggest one in town. You don't need to tip it off that I said anything. No niggers in Ireland, you know."

"Not a nigger," said Morgan.

As he stepped into the street, Morgan had no thought of going in any direction save that which would bring him in conjunction with the men who sought him. If he began to run at that stage of his experiences, he reasoned, he would better make a streak of it that would take him out of the country as fast as his feet would carry him. If those riders of the Chisholm Trail were going to be there a week or two, he could not dodge them, and it might be that by facing them unexpectedly and talking it over man to man before they got too far along in their spree, the grievance they held against him on Seth Craddock's account could be adjusted.

He had come to Ascalon in the belief that he could succeed and prosper in that land which had lured and beckoned, discouraged and broken and driven forth again ten thousand men. Already there was somebody in it who had looked for a moment into his soul and called it courageous, and passed on her way again, he knew not whither. But if Ascalon was so small that a man whom men sought could not hide in it, the country around it was not vast enough to swallow one whom his heart desired to find again.

He would find her; that he had determined hours ago. That should be his first and greatest purpose in this country now. No man, or band of men, that ever rode the Chisholm Trail could set his face away from it. He went on to meet them, his dream before him, the wild sound of Ascalon's obscene revelry in his ears.

CHAPTER VI

RIDERS OF THE CHISHOLM TRAIL

Peden's emporium of viciousness was a notable establishment in its day. By far the largest in Ascalon, it housed nearly every branch of entertainment at which men hazard their fortunes and degrade their morality. It was a vast shell of planks and shingles, with skeleton joists and rafters bare overhead, built hastily and crudely to serve its ephemeral day.

In the farther end there was a stage, upon which mephitic females displayed their physical lures, to come down and sell drinks at a commission in the house, and dance with the patrons, at intervals. Beyond the many small round tables which stood directly in front of the stage was a clear space for dancing, and on the border of this festival arena, in the front of the house, the gambling devices. A bar ran the length of the building on one side from door to orchestra railing. It was the pride of Ascalon that a hundred men could stand and regale themselves before this counter at one time.

Five bartenders stood behind this altar of alcohol when Morgan set foot in the place intent on putting himself in the way of the riders of the Chisholm Trail. These Texas cowboys were easily identified among the early activities of the place by the unusual amount of Mexican silver and leather ornamentation of their apparel. They were a road-worn and dusty crew, growing noisy and hilarious in their celebration of one of their number being elevated to the place of so conspicuous power as city marshal of that famous town. It appeared to have its humorous side from the loud laughter they were spending over it, and the caressing thumps which they laid on Seth Craddock's bony back.

They were lined up against the bar, Craddock in the midst of them, a regiment of bottles before them. Morgan drew near, ordered a drink, stood waiting the moment of his discovery and what might follow it. The Texans were trying everything in the stock, from gin to champagne, gay in the wide choice the marvelous influence of their comrade opened to them without money or the hint of price.

Morgan lounged at the bar, turning meditatively the little glass of amber liquor that was the passport to the estate of a proper man in Ascalon, as in many places neither so notorious nor perilous in those times. Each of the big metal kerosene lamps swung high on the joists threw a circular blotch of shadow on the floor, but the light from them fell brightly on the bar, increased in brilliancy by reflection from the long row of mirrors.

In this sparkle of glass and bar furniture Morgan stood, conspicuous by being apart, like a solitary who had ridden in for a jambouree of his own without companion or friend. He wore his broad-brimmed black hat with the high crown uncreased, and only for the lack of boots and pistol he might have passed for a man of the range. The bartender who served him looked at him with rather puzzled and frequent sidelong turning of the eyes as he stood brooding over the untasted liquor, as if he sought to place him in memory, or to classify him among the drift of men who came in varying moods to his mahogany altar to pay their devotions to its bottled gods.

Morgan's hat cast a shadow over half his face, making it as stern as a Covenanter's portrait. His eyes were on the bar, where his great hand turned and turned the glass, as if his mind were withdrawn a thousand leagues from the noisy scene about him. But for all that apparently wrapt and self-centered contemplation, Morgan knew the moment when Seth Craddock looked his direction and discovered him. At that moment he lifted his glass and drank.

Craddock turned to his companions, upon whom a quiet settled as they drew together in brief conference. Presently the city marshal sauntered out, leaving his comrades of the long trail to carry on their revelry alone. A gangling young man, swart-faced, fired by the contending crosses of alcoholic concoctions which he had swallowed, approached Morgan where he leaned against the bar. This fellow straddled as if he had a horse between his legs, and he was dusty and road-rough, but newly shaved and clipped, and perfumed with all the strong scents of the barber's stock.

"Good evenin', bud. How does your copperosticies seems to segastuate this evenin'?" he hailed, in a bantering, insolent, overriding way.

"I'm able to be up and around and take a little grub," Morgan returned, as good-humoredly as if there had been no insulting sneer in the cowboy's words.

"I hear you're leaving town this evenin'?"

"I guess that's a mistake of the printer," Morgan said with casual ease.

The other men in the party drew around Morgan, some of them challenging him with insolent glances, all of them holding their peace but the one who had spoken, who appeared to have been selected for that office.

"A friend of mine told me you was hittin' the grit out of here tonight," the young man insisted, putting that in his voice which seemed to admit no controversy. "This country ain't no place for a granger, bud; farmin's the unhealthiest business here a man ever took up, they tell me, he don't live no time at it. Sure, you're hittin' the road out of here tonight--my friend appointed us a committee to see you off."

"I'm sorry to disappoint you, boys, but your friend's got the wrong information on me and my movements, whoever he is. I'm goin' to hang around this town some little time, till my farming tools come, anyhow. Just pass that word along to your friend, will you, sport?"

"You ain't got erry gun stuck around in your pants, have you, bud?" the Texan inquired with persuasive gentleness.

"Not the ghost of a gun."

"Grangers burn their eyebrows off and shoot theirselves through the feet when they go totin' guns around," the fellow said, speaking in the wheedling, ingratiating way that one addresses an irresponsible child or a man in alcoholic paresis. The others appeared to find a subtle humor in their comrade's mode of handling a granger. Morgan grinned with them as if he found it funny himself.

One fellow stood a little apart from the rest of the band, studying Morgan with an expression of insolence such as might well warrant the belief that he held feud with all grangers and made their discomfiture, dislodgment, and extermination the chief business of his life. This was a man of unlikely proportions for a trade aback of a horse--short of legs, heavy of body, long in the reach of his arms. His face was round and full, fair for one who rode abroad in all seasons under sun and storm, his teeth small and far apart.

This man said nothing, took no part in the side comment that passed among his comrades, only grinned occasionally, his eyes unwaveringly on Morgan's face. Morgan was drawn to note him particularly among this mainly trifling and innocuous bunch, uneasily impressed by the cold curiosity of his round, tigerish eyes. He thought the fellow appeared to be calculating on how much blood a granger of that bulk contained, and how long it would take him to drink it.

"You ain't got a twenty-two hid around in your pocket nowhere?" the inquisitor pressed, with comically feigned surprise. Morgan denied the ownership of even a twenty-two. "I'll have to feel over you and see--I never saw a granger in my life that didn't tote a twenty-two," the Texan declared, stepping up to Morgan to put his declaration into effect.

Morgan had stood through this mocking inquisition in careless posture, elbows on the bar at his back, with as much good humor as if he were a member of the band taking his turn as the butt of the evening's merrymaking. Now, as the young Texan approached with the evident intention of searching him for a weapon, Morgan came suddenly out of his lounging posture into one of watchfulness and defense. He put up his hand in admonitory gesture to stay the impending degradation.

"Hands off, pardner!" he warned.

The cowboy stopped, turned to his comrades in simulated amazement.

"Did you hear the pore feller make that noise?" he asked, turning his head as if he listened, not quite convinced that his ears had not deceived him.

"He's sick, he orto have a dose of turkentime for the holler horn," said one.

"He's got the botts--drench him for the botts," another prescribed.

That suggestion appealed to their humor. It was endorsed with laughter as they pressed around Morgan to cut off his escape.

"I was told you men were looking for me," Morgan said, estimating them individually and collectively with calculative eyes, "so I stepped in here where you could find me if you had anything worth a man's time to say to me. I guess you've shot your wad, and you've got my answer. You can tell your friend I'm stopping at the Elkhorn hotel, if he don't know it already."

Morgan moved away from the bar as if to leave the place. They bunched in front of him to bar his passage, one laying hold of his arm.

"We're fixin' up a little drink for you," this detainer said, indicating the former spokesman, who was busy at the bar pouring something of the contents of the various bottles into one that bore a champagne label.

"I've had my drink, it isn't time for another," Morgan said, swinging his arm, sending the fellow who clung to it headlong through the ranks of his companions.

At this show of resistance the mask of humor that had covered their sinister intention was flung aside. The man with the wide-set teeth stepped into action there, the others giving place to him as to a recognized champion. He whirled into Morgan, planting a blow just above the bridge of his nose that sent him back against the bar with a jolt that made the bottles dance.

It was such a sudden and mighty blow that Morgan was dazed for a moment, almost blinded. He saw his assailant before him in wavering lines as he guarded instinctively rather than scientifically against the fierce follow-up by which the fellow seemed determined to make an inglorious end of it for the despised granger. Morgan cleared out of the mists of this sudden assault in a moment, for he was a man who had taken and given hard blows in more than one knock-down and drag-out in his day. He caught the swing that was meant for a knock-out on his left guard, and drove his able right fist into the fellow's face.

The pugilistic cowboy, rare fellow among his kind, went to the floor. But there was good stuff in him, worthy the confidence his comrades reposed. For a breath or two he lay on his back as he fell, twisted to his side with a springy movement of incredible swiftness, and sprang to his feet. Blood was running from his battered nose and already puffed lips.
The cheers of his comrades warmed him back to battle, and the onlookers who came pressing from all quarters, drew aside to give them room to fight.

They began to mix it at a furious pace, both of them sledging heavily, the advantage of reach and height sparing Morgan much of the heavy punishment his opponent lacked the cleverness to avoid. While the fellow doubtless was a champion among the men of his range, he had little chance against Morgan, imperfect as he was at that game. In a few minutes of incessant hammering, no breathing spell to break the fierce encounter, Morgan had chopped the cowboy's face severely. Five times Morgan knocked him down in less than half as many minutes, the elastic, enduring fellow coming back each time with admirable courage and vigor.

Morgan's hands were cut from this bare-knuckled mauling, but his opponent had not landed a damaging blow on his face since the first unexpected and unguarded one. He could see, from their crowding and attempts to interfere, that the spirit of fairness had gone out of the rest of the bunch. An end must be made speedily, or they would climb him like a pack of wildcats and crush him like a rabbit in a fall. With this menace plainly before him, Morgan put his best into the rush and wallop that he meant to finish the fight.

The cowboy's extraordinary resistance broke with the blow; he lay so long like a dead man where he fell that his comrades brought whisky to revive him. Presently he struggled to hands and knees, where he stood coughing blood, Morgan waiting by to see what would follow.

"Take them knucks away from him! he slugged me!" Morgan was amazed to hear the fellow charge.

"That's not so!" Morgan denied. "Here--search me," he offered, lifting his arms.

In the code governing personal encounter in those days of the frontier, which was not so very long ago, just one tick in the great clock of history, it was permissible to straddle one's enemy when one got him down, and churn his head against the ground; to gouge out his eyes; to bite off his ears; to kick him, carve him, mutilate him in various and unsportsman-like and unspeakable ways. But it was the high crime of the code to slug him with brass or steel knuckles, commonly called knucks. The man who carried this reenforcement for the natural fist in his pocket and used it in a fight was held the lowest of all contemptible and namelessly vile things. So, these Texas cowboys turned on Morgan at their comrade's accusation, deaf to any denial, flaming with vengeful resentment.

They probably would have made an end of Morgan then and there, but for the interference of Peden, proprietor of the place, who appeared on the scene of the turmoil at that moment, calm and unruffled, expensive white sombrero on the back of his head, fresh cigar in his mouth, black frock coat striking him almost to the knees.

Peden pushed in among the cowboys as they made a rush for Morgan, who stood his ground, back to the bar, regretting now the foolish impulse that had led him into this pack of wolves. Peden stepped in front of Morgan, authority in his very calmness, and restrained the inflamed Texans.

He asked them to consider the ladies. The ladies were in a terrible panic, he said, sweeping his hand toward the farther end of the room where a dozen or so of the creatures whom he dignified with the name were huddled under the restraint of the chief fiddler, who stood before them with fiddle in one hand, bow in the other, like sword and buckler.

There was more curiosity than fright in the women, as the most unsophisticated observer could have read in their kalsomined countenances. Peden's only object in keeping them back from a closer enjoyment of the battle was entirely commercial, humanity and delicacy being no part of his business plan. A live lady was worth a great deal more to his establishment than one with a stray bullet in her skin, waiting burial at his expense in the busy undertaker's morgue.

The cowboys yielded immediately to Peden's appeal in behalf of the ladies, although they very likely would have resented a more obscure citizen's interference with their plans. They fronted the bar again on Peden's invitation to pour another drink. Two of them lifted from the floor the man whom Morgan had fought, and supported him in a weak-kneed advance upon the bar. They cheered him in his half-blind and bleeding wretchedness with promise of what that marvelous elixir, whisky, would do for him once he began to feel the quickening of its potent flame.

Peden indicated by a lifting of the eyebrows, a slight movement of the head toward the door, that Morgan was to improve this moment by making a quiet and expeditious get-away. Morgan needed no urging, being quite willing to allow matters to rest where they stood. He started for the door, making a little detour to put a faro table, around which several men were standing, between himself and the men to whom Seth Craddock had delegated the business of his expulsion from the town. One of the men supporting their defeated champion saw Morgan as he rounded the table, and set up the alarm that the granger was breaking for the range.

Even then Morgan could have escaped by a running dash, for those high-heeled horseback men were not much on foot. But he could not pay that much for safety before the public of Ascalon, despicable as those of it gathered there might be. He made a pretense of watching the faro game while the Texans put down their glasses to rush after him and make him prisoner, threatening him with clubbed pistols above his head.

The lookout at the faro game, whose patrons were annoyed by this renewal of the brawl, jumped from his high seat and took a hand in the row. Friends of the marshal or friends of the devil, he said, made no difference to him. They'd have to go outside to finish their fuss. This man, a notorious slayer of his kind, quicker of hand than any man in Ascalon, it was said, urged them all toward the door.

The cowboys protested against this breach of hospitality, but Peden stood in his customary pose of calmness to enforce his bouncer's word, hand pushing back his long black coat where it fell over the holster at his belt.

Morgan was in no mind to go with them, for he began to have a disturbing alarm over what these men might do in their drunken vengeance, relieved as they thought themselves to be of all responsibility to law by the liberty their friend Craddock had given them. Without regard to the bouncer's orders or Peden's threatening pose, he began to lay about him with his fists, making a breach in the ranks of his captors that would have opened the way to the door in a moment, the outbreak was so unexpected and violent, if it had not been for a quieting tap the bouncer gave him with one of the lethal instruments which he carried for such exigencies.

Morgan was conscious of a sensation of expulsion, which seemed swift, soft, and soundless, with a dim sense of falling at the end. When his dispersed senses returned to their seat again, he found himself in the open night, stretched on the ground, hands bound behind his back.

CHAPTER VII

A GENTLE COWBOY JOKE

As Morgan's faculties cleared out of their turgid whirl, and the stars began to leave off their frivolous capers and stand still, he heard voices about him in the dark, and they were discussing the very interesting question of whether he should be hung like a horse thief or loaded upon a train and shipped away like sheep.

Morgan's bruised senses assembled and righted at the first conscious grasp of this argument, as a laboring, buffeted ship rights when its shifted cargo is flung back to place by the shock of a mighty surge. Nature was on guard again in a moment, straining and tense in its sentry over the habitation of a soul so nearly deserted but a minute before. Morgan listened, sweating in the desperation of his plight.

They had taken him away from the main part of town, as he was aware by the sound of its revelry in the near distance. Close at hand a railroad engine was frying and gasping; farther off another was snorting impatiently as it jerked the iron vertebrae of a long freight train. And these men whom he could not see around him in the darkness were discussing the expediency of hanging him while unconscious, against the morality of waiting for him to come to himself so he might have the felon's last appeal of prayer.

One maintained that it was against all precedent to hang an unconscious man and send him off to perdition without a chance to enter a plea for his soul, and he argued soberly, in the manner of a man who had a spirit of fairness in him, and a little gleam of reason and morality left. To Morgan's relief and hope this man went further as he put his view of the case, even so far as to question their right to hang the granger at all. They clamored against him and tried to scoff him down, moving with drunken, scuffing feet near the spot where Morgan lay, as if to put the sentence into immediate execution.

"Wait a minute now, boys," this unknown, unseen champion pleaded, "let's me and you talk this thing over some more. That kid put up a man's fight, even if he is a granger--you'll have to give him credit for that. I didn't find no knucks on him, and you didn't. He couldn't 'a' dropped 'em on the floor, and he couldn't 'a' swallered 'em. He didn't have no knucks, boys--that hard-hoofed granger just naturally tore into the Dutchman with his bare hands. I know he did, his hands is all cut and swelled up--here, wait till I strike a match and show you."

Morgan thought it wise to feign insensibility while this apparently sober man among the crew struck a match and rolled his body over to show the granger's battered hands. The others were not convinced by this evidence, nor softened in the least. He was a granger, anyhow, a fencer of the range, an interloper who had come into their ancient domain like others of his grasshopper tribe to fence up the grazing lands and drive them from the one calling that they knew. If for no other reason, he deserved hanging for that. Ask anybody; they'd say the same.

"That ain't no kind of talk," said the defender, reprovingly, "your daddies and mine was grangers before us, and our kids'll have to be grangers or nothin' after a while--if any of us ever has any. I was in for havin' a little fun with this feller; I was in on it with the rest of you to see the Dutchman hammer him flat, but the Dutchman wasn't a big enough feller for the job. Where's he at?"

"Layin' up there on the depot platform," somebody said.

"This feller flattened him out, done it like he had him on a anvil," the granger's advocate chuckled. "That there freight's goin' to pull out in a little while--let's look along till we find a empty car and chuck him in it. By morning he'll be in La Junta. He's had his lesson out of the cowman's book, he'll never come back to plow up this range."

Morgan thought that, perhaps by adding his own argument to this unknown friend's, he might move the rest of the bunch from their cruel determination to have his life. He moved, making a breathing like a man coming to his senses, and struggled to sit up.

There were exclamations of satisfaction that he had revived in time to relieve them of the responsibility of sending a man out of the world without a chance to pray. The man who had championed Morgan's cause helped him to sit up, asking him with a curious rough kindness if he wanted a drink. Morgan replied that he did. A bottle was put to his lips, bruised and swollen until they stood open by the rough usage his captors had given him while unconscious. He took a swallow of the whisky, shutting the rest out with tongue against teeth when the fellow insisted that he take a man's dose.

They drew close around Morgan where he sat, back against this kind fellow's knee. Morgan could see them plainly now, although it was too dark to trace their features. One of them dropped the noose of a rope over his head as the one who stood behind him took the flask from his lips. Morgan knew by the feel of it against his neck that it was a platted rawhide, such as the Mexicans term reata.

"Granger, if you got anything to say, say it," this one directed. Morgan recognized him as the one who had opened the trouble in Peden's hall.

Morgan had considerable to say, and he said it without whimper or tremor, his only appeal being to their fairness and sense of justice between man and man. He went back a little farther in his simple history than he had gone with Judge Thayer that afternoon, telling them how he once had been a cowboy like themselves on the Nebraska and Wyoming range, leading up briefly, so they might feel they knew him, to his arrival in Ascalon that day, and his manner of incurring Seth Craddock's enmity, for which they were considering such an unreasonable punishment.

Inflamed as they were by liquor, and all but insensible to reasonable argument, this simple story, enforced by the renewed plea of the one who befriended him, turned two or three others in Morgan's favor. They probably would have set him free if it had not been for the Dutchman, who joined them, apparently sober and bitterly vindictive, as they were considering that step.

The Dutchman was for vengeance on his own account, Seth Craddock out of the consideration entirely. The granger had slugged him, he maintained; no man that ever walked on the grass was able to lay him out with bare hands. If they didn't hang the granger he'd shoot him, then and there, even though he would have to throw ashes on his stinking blood to keep it from driving everybody out of town.

Wait a minute, the young man with the straddle suggested, speaking eagerly, as if he had been struck by an inspiration. The freight train was just pulling out; suppose they put the rope around the granger's body instead of his neck, leave his hands tied as they were, and hitch him to a car! In that way he'd hang himself. It would be plain suicide, as anybody with eyes could see.

The innocence and humor of this sportful proposal appealed to them at once. It also satisfied the Dutchman, who seconded it loudly, with excited enthusiasm. The protests of the granger's defender and friend were unavailing. They pushed him back, even threatening him with their guns when he would have interfered to stay the execution of this inspired sentence.

The train was getting under way; three of the gang laid hold of the reata and ran, dragging Morgan against his best efforts to brace his feet and hold them, the others pushing him toward the moving train. The long freight was bound westward. Morgan and his tormenters were beyond the railroad station, not far from Judge Thayer's little white office building, which Morgan could see through the gloom as he vainly turned his eyes about in the hope of some passing stranger to whom he could appeal.

Luckily for Morgan, railroad trains did not get under way as quickly in those days of hand brakes and small engines as now. Added to the weight of the long string of empty cattle cars which the engine was laboring to get going was a grade, with several short curves to make it harder where the road wound in and out among small sand hills. By the time Morgan's captors had attached the rope to the ladder of a car, the headway of the train had increased until they were obliged to trot to keep up with it. Not being fleet of foot in their hobbling footgear when sober, they were at a double disadvantage when drunk and weaving on their legs. They made no attempt to follow Morgan and revel in his sufferings and peril, but fell back, content to enjoy their pleasantry at ease.

Morgan lurched on over the uneven ground, still dizzy and weak from the bludgeoning he had undergone, unable to help his precarious balance by the use of his arms, doubly bound now by the rope about his middle which the Texans had drawn in running noose. It was Morgan's hope in the first few rods of this frightful journey that a brakeman might appear on top of the train, whose attention he might attract before the speed became so great he could no longer maintain it, or a lurch or a stumble in the ditch at the trackside might throw him under the wheels.

A quick glance forward and back dispelled this hope; there was not the gleam of a lantern in sight. But somebody was running after him, almost beside him, and there were yells and shots out of the dark behind. Now the runner was beside Morgan, hand on his shoulder as if to steady himself, and Morgan's heart swelled with thankful gratitude for the unknown friend who had thus risked the displeasure of his comrades to set him free.

The train was picking up speed rapidly, taxing Morgan's strength to hold pace with it trussed up as he was, the strain of the hauling rope feeling as if it would cut his arms to the bone. The man who labored to hold abreast of Morgan was slashing at the rope. Morgan felt the blade strike it, the tension yield for a second as if several strands had been cut. But not severed, not weakened enough to break it. It stiffened again immediately and the man, clinging desperately to Morgan's shoulder to hold his place in the quickening race, struck at it again and missed.

There came more shots and shouts. Morgan's heroic friend stumbled, lost his hold on the shoulder of the man he was trying to save, fell behind out of sight.

Morgan's poor hope for release from present torture and impending death now rested in the breaking of the rawhide rope where it had been weakened by that one desperate slash of the knife. He tried lunging back against the rope, but the speed of the train was too great; he could not brace a foot, he could not pause. There were gravel and small boulders in the ditch here. Morgan feared he would lose his footing and be dragged to his miserable end.

But onward through the dark he struggled and stumbled, at a pace that would have taxed an unhampered man to maintain, the strain of the cutting rope about his body and arms like a band of hot iron. Should a brakeman appear now on top of the car to which he was tied, Morgan knew he had little chance of making himself heard through the noise of the train, spent as he was already, gasping short breaths which he seemed unable to drive into his burning lungs.

How long could human strength and determination to cling to life endure this punishment! how long until he must fall and drag, unable to regain his feet, to be pounded at that cruel rope's end into a mangled, abhorrent thing!

On, the grind of wheels, the jolt of loose-jointed cars over the clanking track drowning even the noise of the engine laboring up that merciful grade; on, staggering and swaying, flung like a pebble on a cord, shoulder now against the car, feet now flying, half lifted from the ground, among the stones of the ditch, over the uneven earth, across gullies, over crossings where there paused no traveler in the black despair of that night to give him the help for which he perished.

On, the breath that he drew in gasping stridulation like liquid fire in his throat; on, the calm stars of the unemotional universe above his head; on, the wind of the wide prairie lands striking his face with their indefinable sweet scents which even clutching death did not deny his turbulent senses; on, pain in every nerve; on, joints straining and starting in their sockets; on, dragged, whipped, lashed from ditch to ties' end, flung from rocking car to crumbling bank, where jagged rocks cut his face and freed his blood to streak coldly upon his cheek.

There was no likelihood that the train would stop in many miles--even now it was gaining speed, the engine over the crest of the grade. Only for a post that he might snub that stubborn strand of leather upon! only for a bridge where his swinging weight might break it!

Faster--the train was going faster! The pain of his torture dulling as overcharged nerves refused to carry the growing load, Morgan still clung to his feet, pounding along in the dark. He was growing numb in body and mind, as one overwhelmed by a narcotic drug, yet he clung to the desperate necessity of keeping on his feet.

How far he had come, how long he might yet endure, he had no thought to measure. He lived only for the insistent, tenacious purpose of keeping on his feet, rather than of keeping on his feet to live. He must run and pant, under the lash of nature that would not let him drop down and die, as long as a spark of consciousness remained or flying limbs could equal the speed of the train, helped on by the drag of that rawhide strand that would not break.

No thought of death appalled him now as at first; its revolting terror at that rope's end had no place in his thought this crowded, surging moment. Only to live, to fight and live, to run, unfeeling feet striking like wood upon the wayside stones, and run, as a maimed, scorched creature before a fire, to fall into some cool place and live. And live! and live! In spite of all, to live!

And presently the ground fell away beneath his feet, a swish of branches was about him, the soft, cool touch of leaves against his face. A moment he was flung and tangled among willows--it was a strange revelation through a chink of consciousness in that turmoil of life and death that swept the identifying scent of willows into his nostrils--and then he dropped, striking softly where water ran, and closed his eyes, thinking it must be the end.

CHAPTER VIII

THE AVATISM OF A MAN

Morgan knew that the cogs of the slow machinery by which he had been hoisted from the saddle to the professorial chair had slipped. As he lay there on his back in the shallow ripple of the Arkansas River, the long centipede railroad bridge dark-lined across the broad stream, he turned it in his mind and knew that it was so.

He had gone back in that brief time of terrific torture to the plane from which he had risen by hard and determined effort to make of himself a man in the world of consequence and achievement; back to the savagery of the old days when he rode the range in summer glare and winter storm. For it was his life's one aim and intention now to rise from that cool bed in the river presently and go back to Ascalon, try by sound of voice those who had subjected him to this torture, separating by that test his heroic friend from the guilty. The others he intended to kill, man by man, down to the last unfeeling brute.

The water was not more than two or three inches deep where he lay, but a little way beyond he could hear it passing with greater volume among the spiles of the bridge. Fortune had spared him a fall into the deeper channel, where even a foot of water might have drowned him, strengthless and fettered as he was. Fate had reserved him for this hour of vengeance. He turned, wallowing in the shallow water to soak the rawhide rope, which was already growing soft, the pressure and pain of it considerably eased on his arms.

He drank, and buried his face in the tepid water, grateful for life, exulting in the fierce fire that rose in him, triumphing already in the swift atonement he would call on those wretches to make. Back again to the ethical standard of those old, hard-riding, hard-drinking, hard-swearing days on the range, the refinements of his education submerged, and not one regret for the slip.

Morgan did not realize in that moment of surrender to the primitive desires which clamored within him how badly he was wrenched and mauled. He tried the rawhide, swelling his bound arms in the hope that the slipknot would give a little, but was unable to bring pressure enough on the rope to ease it in the least.

Eager to begin his harvest of revenge before the men from the Nueces struck south again over the long trail, Morgan determined to start at once in search of somebody to free him from his bonds. He could not return to Ascalon in this shameful plight, his ignominy upon him, an object of derision. There must be somebody living along the river close at hand who would cut his bonds and give him a plaster to stick over the wound he could feel drawing and gaping in his cheek.

When it came to getting to his feet, Morgan learned that his desire had outgrown his strength. A sickness swept him as he struggled to his knees; blood burst from his nostrils, the taste of blood was on his tongue. Dizzy, sick to the core of his heart, sore with a thousand bruises, shot with a thousand pains which set up with every movement like the clamor of harassing wolves, he dragged himself on his knees to the edge of the water, where he lay on his face in the warm sand.

He waited there a long time for the gathering of strength enough to carry him on his quest of a friendly hand. Only the savage determination to strike his enemies down, head by head, kept him from perishing as he lay there sore and bruised, chilled to the marrow in his welling agony even that hot summer night.

Dawn was breaking when he at last found strength to mount the low bank through the encumbering brush and vines. His arms were senseless below the elbows, swollen almost to bursting of veins and skin by the gorged blood. There was no choice in directions, only to avoid the town. He faced up the river and trudged on, the cottonwood leaves beginning their everlasting symphony, that is like the murmur of rain, as the wakening wind moved them overhead.

Morgan stumbled over tin cans at the edge of the tall grass when the rising sun was shining across his unprotected eyes. He stood for a little while, wondering at first sight if this were only another mirage of the plagued imagination, such as had risen like ephemera while he lay on the sand bar at the river's edge. He stood with weak legs braced wide apart to fix his reeling senses on the sight--the amazing, comforting sight, of a field of growing corn. Only a little field, more properly a patch, but it was tall and green, in full tassel, the delicate sweet of its blossoms strong on the dew-damp morning.

Beyond the field he could see the roof of a sod house, and a little of the brown wall that rose not much higher than the corn. Grass had grown on the roof, for it was made of strips of sod, also, and turned sere and brown in the sun. A wire fence stood a prickly barrier between roaming cattle and this little field of succulent fodder. Morgan directed his course to skirt the field, and came at last to the cabin door.

In front of the house there was no fence, but a dooryard that seemed to embrace the rest of the earth. Around the door the ground was trampled and bare; in front of the house three horses stood, saddled and waiting, bridle reins on the ground. It looked like a cow camp to Morgan; it seemed as if he had come back home. A dog rose slowly from where it lay across the door, bristles rising, foot lifted as if the creature paused between flight and attack, setting up such an alarm that the horses bolted a little way and stood wondering.

A woman came to the door, lifted her hands in silent astonishment, leaning a little to see.

"Heavens above! look at that man!" she cried, her words sounding as from a great distance in Morgan's dulling ears.

Morgan saw her start toward him, running. He tried to step forward to meet her, but only his body moved in accord with his will. The earth seemed to rise and embrace him, letting him down softly, as the arms of a friend.

It was a new pain that brought Morgan to his senses, the pain of returning life to his half-dead arms. Somebody was standing beside him holding these members raised to let the blood drain out of them, chafing them, and there was a smell of camphor and strong spirits in the place.

"The rope wouldn't 'a' slipped down, if they was tryin' to hang him, anyhow," somebody said with conclusive finality.

"Looks like they lassoed him and drug him," another said, full of the awe that hushes the human voice when one stands beside the dead.

"Whoever done it ought to be skinned alive!" a woman declared, and Morgan thanked her in his heart for her sympathy, although there was a weight of such absolute weakness on his eyes that he could not open them to see her face.

There was a dim sound of something being stirred in a glass, and the nerve-waking scent of more ardent spirits.

"If this don't fetch him to," said the voice of the first speaker, the deep pectoral tone of a seasoned man, "you jump your horse and go for the doctor, Fred."

Morgan shook his head to throw that obstinate weight from his eyes, or thought he shook it, but it was only the shadow of a movement. Slight as it was it brought an exclamation of relief in another voice, a woman's voice, also, tuned in the music of youth.

"Oh! he moved!" she said. And she was the one who stood beside him, holding aloft and chafing his blood-gorged arm.

"Blamed if he didn't! Here--try a little of this, son."

Morgan was gathering headway out of the fog so rapidly now that he began to feel ashamed of this helpless situation in which so many kind hands were ministering to him as if he were a sick horse. He made a more determined effort to open his eyes, succeeding this time, although it seemed to call for as much strength to lift his lids as to shoulder a sack of wheat. He saw a large hand holding a spoon hovering near his mouth, and the outline of big shoulders in a red shirt. Morgan swallowed what was offered him, to feel it go tingling through his nerves with vivifying warmth, like a message of cheer over a telegraph wire. The large man who administered the dose was delighted. He spoke encouragingly, working the spoon faster, as a man blows eagerly when he sees a flame start weakly in a doubtful fire. The woman with the voice of youth, who stood on Morgan's left hand, gently put his arm down, as if modesty would no longer countenance this office of tenderness to a conscious man.

"Any feelin' in your hands?" the man inquired, bending a whiskered face down near Morgan's.

"Plenty of it, thank you," Morgan replied, his voice stubborn as a rusty hinge.

"You'll be all right then, there's no bones broken as far as I can locate 'em. You just stretch out and take it easy, you'll be all right."

TRAIL'S END

"I gave up--I gave up--too easy," Morgan said, slowly, like a very tired man.

"Lands alive! gave up!" said the matron of the household, who still held Morgan's arm up to drain off the congested blood. "Look at your face, look at your feet! Gave up--lands alive!"

"You're busted up purty bad, old feller," said a young man who seemed to appear suddenly at Morgan's feet, where he stood looking down with the most friendly and feeling expression imaginable in his wholesome brown face.

"That cut on your face ain't deep, it could be closed up and stuck with strips of plaster and only leave a shallow scar, but it ought to be done while it's fresh," the boss of the ranch said.

"I'd be greatly obliged to you," Morgan told him, by way of agreement to the dressing of his wound.

By the time the pioneer of the Arkansas had treated his mysteriously injured patient's hurts, Morgan had come to himself completely. He was relieved to know that his collapse at the threshold of that hospitable home was due to the suffering of his bound arms, rather than any internal rupture or concussion as he at first feared.

Already his thoughts were running forward, his blood was pounding in his arteries, in vengeful eagerness to take up the trail of the men who had subjected him to this inhuman ordeal. He could not hope to repay them cruelty for cruelty, for he was not a man who did much crippling when it came to handling a gun, but if he had to follow them to the Nueces, even to the Rio Grande, for his toll, then he would follow.

The business that had brought him into the Kansas plains could wait; there was but one big purpose in his life now. He was eager to be up, with the weight of a certain dependable pistol in his holster, the feel of a certain rifle in its scabbard on the saddle under his knee.

Sore and bruised as he was, sorer that he would be tomorrow, Morgan wanted to get up as soon as the long rough cut on his cheek had been comfortably patched with adhesive tape. He asked the rancher if he would oblige him with a horse to go to Ascalon, where his trunk containing his much-needed wardrobe was still in the baggage-room at the depot.

"You couldn't ride to Ascalon this morning, son," the rancher told him, severely kind.

"You'll do if you can make it in a week," the young man added his opinion cheerfully.

"Yes, and then some, the way it looks to me," the elder declared.

Morgan started as if to spring from the low couch where they had laid him when they carried him in, dusty and bloody, fearful and repulsive sight of maimed flesh and torn clothing that he was.

"I can't stay a week--I can't wait a day! They'll be gone, man!" he said.

"Maybe they will, son," the rancher agreed, gently pushing him back; "maybe. But they'll leave tracks."

"Yes, by God! they'll leave tracks!" Morgan muttered.

"Don't you think I'd better send my boy over to town for the doctor?" the rancher asked.

"Not unless you're uneasy about me."

"No, your head's all right and your bones are whole. You'll heal up, but it'll take some time."

Morgan said he felt that more had been done for him already than any number of doctors could have accomplished, for the service had been one of humanity, with no thought of reward. They would let the doctor stay in Ascalon, and Morgan would go to him if he felt the need coming on. The rancher disclaimed credit for a service such as one man owed another the world over, he said. But it was plain that he was touched by the outspoken gratitude of this wreckage of humanity that had come halting in bonds to his door.

"I'm a stranger to this country," Morgan explained, "I arrived in Ascalon yesterday--" pausing to ponder it, thinking it must have been longer than a day ago--"yesterday"--with conviction, "a little after noon. Morgan is my name. I came here to settle on land."

"You're the man that took the new marshal's gun away from him," the rancher said, nodding slowly. "My daughter knew you the minute she saw you--she was over there yesterday after the mail."

Morgan's heart jumped. He looked about the room for her, but she and her mother had withdrawn.

"I guess I made a mistake when I mixed up with him," Morgan said, as if he excused himself to the absent girl.

"The only mistake you made was when you handed him back his gun. You ought to 'a' handed it back to a corpse," the rancher said.

"We knew that feller he killed," the younger man explained, with a world of significance in his voice.

"He used to live up here in this country before he went to Abilene; he'd come back to blow his money in Ascalon, I guess," the rancher said. "He was one of them harmless bluffin' boys you could take by the ear and lead around like he had a ring in his nose."

"That's what I told them," Morgan commented, in thoughtful, distracted way.

"You sized him up right. He wouldn't 'a' pulled his gun, quick as he was to slap his hand on it and run a sandy. I guess it was just as well it happened to him then as some other time. Somebody was bound to kill him when he got away among strangers."

The rancher, who introduced himself as Stilwell, asked for the details of the killing, which Morgan gave, together with the trivial thing that led up to it. The big rancher sighed, shaking his head sadly.

"You ought to took his gun away from him and bent it around his fool head," he said.

"It would have been better for him, and for me, I guess," Morgan agreed.

"Yes, that marshal was purty sore on you for takin' his gun away from him right out in public, it looks like," the rancher suggested, a bid in his manner for the details of his misfortune which Morgan felt were his by right of hospitality.

"I ran into some of his friends later on. He'd turned the town over to them, a bunch of cowpunchers just up from the Nueces."

The rancher started at the word, exchanging a startled, meaning look with his son.

"That outfit that loaded over at Ascalon yesterday?" he inquired.

"Yes; seven or eight of them stayed behind to look after the horses--eight with the marshal, he's one of the outfit."

"Did them fellers rope you and drag you away out here?" Stilwell inquired, leaning over in the tensity of his feeling, his tanned face growing pale, as if the thought of such atrocity turned his blood cold.

"They hitched me to a freight train. The rope broke at the river."

The rancher turned to his son again, making a motion with open hand outflung as if displaying evidence in some controversy between them that clinched it on his side without another word. The younger man came a step nearer Morgan's couch, where he stood with grave face, hesitant, as if something came forward in his mind to speak. The elder strode to the door and looked out into the sun of early morning, and the cool shadows of the cottonwood trees at the riverside which reached almost to his walls.

"To a train! God A'mighty--to a train!" Morgan heard him say.

"How far is it from Ascalon to the river?" Morgan asked.

"Over two miles! And your hands tied--God A'mighty!"

"You take it easy, they'll not leave Ascalon till Sol Drumm, their boss, comes back from Kansas City," the young man said. "We're layin' for him ourselves, we've got a bill against him."

"And we've got about as much show to collect it as we have to dip a hatful of stars out of the river," Stilwell said, turning gloomily from the door.

"We'll see about that!" the younger one returned, in high and defiant stubbornness.

"We've already lost upwards of five hundred head of stock from that feller's trespass on our range," Stilwell explained. "That gang drove in here three weeks ago to rest and feed up for market, payin' no attention to anybody's range or anybody's warning to keep off. They had the men with them to go where they pleased. Them Texas cattle come up here loaded with fever ticks, and the bite of them little bugs means death to a northern herd. They sowed ticks all over my range. I'm still a losin' cattle, and Lord knows where it will stop."

"You've been working to get a quarantine law passed, I remember," Morgan said, feeling this outrage as if the cattle were his own.

"Yes, but Congress is asleep, and them fellers down in Texas never shut their eyes. I warned Drumm to keep off my range, asked him first like a gentleman, but he drove in one night between my pickets and mixed his poison cattle with mine out of pure cussidness. He claimed they got away, and him with fifteen or twenty men to ride herd! It's cost me ten thousand dollars, at the lowest figure, already, and more goin'. It looks like it would clean me out."

"You ought to have some recourse against him in law," Morgan said.

"Yes, I thought so, too. I went to the county attorney and wanted to bring an attachment on Drumm's herd, but he told me there wasn't any law he could act under, it was anybody's range as much as mine, Texas fever or no Texas fever. I could sue him, he said, but it was a slim chance. Well, I'm goin' to see another lawyer--I'll take it up with Judge Thayer, and see what he can do."

"Drumm'll pay it, down to the last dime!" the young man declared.

"We can't hold him up and take it away from him, Fred," the older man reproved. "That would be as big a crime as his."

"He'll pay it!" Fred repeated, with what Morgan thought to be admirable tenacity, even though his means to the desired end might be hard to justify.

They helped Morgan to another room, where they outfitted him with clothing to replace his own shredded garments. Stilwell insisted that he remain as his guest until his hurts were mended, although, he explained, he could not stay at home to keep him company. His wife and daughter would talk his arm off without help from the rest of the family. He would call them in and introduce them.

"My girl's got a new piano--lucky I sent for it before that Texas outfit struck this range--she can try it out on you," Stilwell said, a laugh still left in him for an amusing situation in spite of the ruin he faced.

Morgan could hear the girl and her mother talking in the kitchen, their voices quite distinct at times as they passed an open door that he could not see. Lame and aching, hands swollen and purple, he sat in a rocking-chair by the open window, not so broken by his experiences nor so depressed by his pains but he yet had the pleasure of anticipation in meeting this girl. He had determined only a few hours ago that the country was not big enough to hide her from him. Now Fate had jerked him with rough hand to the end of his quest before it was fairly begun.

As he thought this, Stilwell came back, convoying his ample red-faced wife, and almost as ample, and quite as red-faced, daughter. So, there must have been more than one young lady after mail in Ascalon yesterday afternoon, thought Morgan, as he got up ruefully, with much pain in his feet and ankles, rather shamed and taken back, and bowed the best way he could to this girl who was not his girl, after all his eager anticipation.

CHAPTER IX

NEWS FROM ASCALON

"Down here in the river bottom, where the water rises close to the top of the ground, you can raise a little corn and stuff, but take it back on the prairie a little way and you can't make your seed back, year in and year out. Plenty of them have come here from the East and tried it--I suppose you must 'a' seen the traces of them scattered around as you come through the country east of Ascalon."

Morgan admitted that he had seen such traces, melancholy records of failure that they were.

"It's all over this country the same way. It broke 'em as fast as they came, starved 'em and took the heart out of 'em and drove 'em away. You can't farm this country, Morgan; no man ever learnt anything out of books that will make him master of these plains with a plow."

So spoke Stilwell, the cattleman, sitting at night before his long, low, L-shaped sod house with his guest who had been dragged into his hospitality at the end of a rope. Eight days Morgan had been sequestered in that primitive home, which had many comforts in spite of the crudity of its exterior. His soreness had passed from the green and superficially painful stage to the deeper ache of bruised bones. He walked with a limp, stiff and stoved in his joints as a foundered horse. But his hands and arms had recovered their suppleness, and, like an overgrown fledgling at the edge of the nest, he was thinking of projecting a flight.

During the time Morgan had been in the Stilwell ranchhouse no news had come to him from Ascalon. Close as they lived to the town, the Stilwells had been too deeply taken up with their own problem of pending ruin due to the loss of their herd from Texas fever infection, to make a trip even to the post-office for their mail. Violet, the daughter, was on the range more than half the time, doing what she could to drive the sick cattle to the river where they might have a better chance to fight the dread malady.

Morgan's injuries had turned out to be deeper seated and more serious than he had at first supposed. For several days he was racked with a fever that threatened to floor him, due to the mental torture of that terrible night. It had passed, and with it much of his pain, and he would have gone to Ascalon for his reckoning with the men from the Nueces two days ago if Stilwell had not argued the folly of attempting an adjustment under the handicap of his injuries.

Wait a few days longer, the rancher sagely advised, eat and rest, and rub that good fiery horse liniment of his on the sore spots and swollen joints. Even if they were gone, which Stilwell knew would not be the case for Drumm would not have made it back from Kansas City yet, Morgan could follow them. And to do that he must be sound and strong.

Stilwell had put off even his own case against the Texas stockman, he had been so urged for time in getting his sick cattle down to the shade and water along the river. Now the job seemed over, for all he could do, and was taking his ease at home this night, intending to go early in the morning and put his case for damages against Drumm into Judge Thayer's hands.

Through Morgan's days of sickness and waiting for strength, he was attended tenderly by Mrs. Stilwell, and sometimes of an afternoon, when Violet came in from the hot, dry range, she would play for him on her new piano. She played a great deal better than he had any reason to expect of her, self-taught in her isolation on the banks of the shallow Arkansas.

Violet was a girl of large frame, large bones in her wrists, large fingers to her useful, kindly ministering hands. Her face was somewhat too long and thin to be called handsome, but it was refined by a wistfulness that told of inner striving for something beyond the horizon of her days there in her prairie-circled home. And now as the two men talked outside the door, the new moonlight white on the dust of the trampled yard, Violet was at her piano, playing a simple melody with a soft, expressive tenderness as sweet to him as any music Morgan ever had heard. For he understood that the instrument was the medium of expression for this prairie girl's soul, reaching out from its shelter of sod laid upon sod to what aspirations, following what longings, mounting to what ambitions, none in her daily contact ever knew.

Stilwell was downcast by the blow he had received in the loss of more than half his herd through the Texas scourge. It had taken years of hardship and striving, fighting drouth and winter storm, preying wolves and preying men, to build the herd up to the point where profits were about ready to be enjoyed.

Nothing but a frost would put an end to the scourge of Texas fever; in those days no other remedy had been discovered. Before nature could send this relief Stilwell feared the rest of his cattle would die, although he had driven them from the contaminated range. If that happened he would be wiped out, for he was too old, he said, to start at the bottom and build up another herd.

It was at this point that Morgan suggested Stilwell turn to the soil instead of range cattle as a future business, a thing that called down the cattleman's scorn and derision, and citation of the wreckage that country had made of men's hopes. He dismissed that subject very soon as one unworthy of even acrimonious debate or further denunciation, to dwell on his losses and the bleakness of the future as it presented itself through the bones of his dead cattle.

As they sat talking, the soft notes of Violet's melody soothing to the ears as a distant song, the young man Fred came riding in from Ascalon, the bearer of news. He began to talk before he struck the ground, breathlessly, like a man who had beheld unbelievable things.

"That gang from Texas has took the town--everybody's hidin' out," he reported.

"Took the town?" said Stilwell, incredulously.

"Stores all shut up, post-office locked and old man Flower settin' in the upstairs winder with his Winchester across his leg waitin' for them to bust in the door and steal the gover'ment money!"

"Listen to that!" said Stilwell, as the young man stood there hat off, mopping the sweat of excitement from his forehead. "Where's that man-eatin' marshal feller at?"

"He's killin' off everybody in town but his friends--he's killed eight men, a man a day, since he's been in office. He's got everybody lookin' for a hole."

"A man a day!" said Morgan, scarcely able to believe the news.

"Who was they?" Stilwell inquired, bringing his chair down from its easy slant against the sod wall, leaning forward to catch the particulars of this unequaled record of slaughter.

"I didn't hear," said Fred, panting faster than his hard-ridden horse.

"I hope none of the boys off of this range around here got into it with him," Stilwell said.

"They say he's closed up all the gamblin' joints and saloons but Peden's, and the bank's been shut four or five days, Judge Thayer and a bunch of fellers inside of it with rifles. Tom Conboy told me the judge had telegraphed to the governor asking him to send soldiers to restore law and order in the town."

"Law and order!" Stilwell scorned. "All the law and order they ever had in that hell-hole a man'd never miss."

"Where's the sheriff--what's he doing to restore order?" Morgan inquired.

"The sheriff ain't doin' nothing. I ain't been over there, but I know that much," Stilwell said.

"They say he's out after some rustlers," Fred replied.

"Yes, and he'll stay out till the trouble's over and come back without a hide or hair of a rustler. What else are they doin'?"

"Rairin' and shootin'," said Fred, winded by the enormity of this outlawry, even though bred in an atmosphere of violence.

"Are they hittin' anybody, or just shootin' for noise?" Stilwell asked.

"Well, I know they took a crack at me when I went out of Conboy's to git my horse."

Mrs. Stilwell and Violet, who had hastened out on Fred's excited arrival, exclaimed in concern at this, the mother going to her boy to feel him over as for wounds, standing by him a little while with arm around him.

"Did you shoot back?" Stilwell wanted to know.

"I hope I did," Fred replied.

Stilwell got up, and stood looking at the moon a little while as if calculating the time of night.

"They need a man or two over there to clean that gang up," he said. "Well, it ain't my business to do it, as long as they didn't hit you."

Mrs. Stilwell chided him sharply, perhaps having history behind her to justify her alarm at these symptoms.

"Let them fight it out among themselves, the wolves!" she said.

Morgan had drawn a little apart from the family group, walking to the corner of the house where he stood looking off toward Ascalon, still and tense as if he listened for the sounds of conflict. He was dressed in Stilwell's clothes, which were somewhat too roomy of body but nothing too large otherwise, for both of them had the stature of proper men. His feet were in slippers, his ankles bandaged and soaked with the penetrating liniment designed alike for the ailments of man and beast.

Violet studied him as he stood there between her and the moon, his face sterner for the ordeal of suffering that had tried his manhood in that two-mile run beside the train, where nothing but a sublime defiance of death had held him to his feet.

He had told her of his seven-years' struggle upward from the cowboy's saddle to a place of honor in the faculty of the institution where he had beaten out the hard, slow path to learning; she knew of his purpose in coming to the western Kansas plains. Until this moment she had believed it to be a misleading and destructive illusion that would break his heart and rive his soul, as it had the hearts and souls of thousands of brave men and women before him.

Now she had a new revelation, the moonlight on his face, bright in his fair hair, picturing him as rugged as a rock uplifted against the dim sky. She knew him then for a man such as she never had met in the narrow circle of her life before, a man strong to live in his purpose and strong to die in it if the need might be. He would conquer where others had failed; the strength of his soul was written in his earnest face.

"I think I'll go over to Ascalon," Morgan said presently, turning to them, speaking slowly. "Will you let me have a horse?"

"Go to Ascalon! Lands save us!" Mrs. Stilwell exclaimed.

"No, no--not tonight!" Violet protested, hurrying forward as if she would stay him by force.

"You wait till morning, son," Stilwell counseled calmly, so calmly, indeed, that his wife turned to him sharply. "Maybe I'll go with you in the morning."

"You've got no business there--let them kill each other off if they want to, but you keep out of it!" said his wife.

"If you'll let me have a horse--" Morgan began again, with the insistence of a man unmoved.

"You forgot about our cattle, Mother," Stilwell chided, ignoring Morgan's request. "I'm goin' to sue Sol Drumm, I'm goin' to have the papers ready to serve on him the minute he steps off of the train. If there's any way to make him pay for the damage he's done me I'm goin' to do it."

"There's more than one way," said Fred. "If the law can't----"

"Then we lose," his father finished for him, in the calm resignation of a just man.

Morgan's intention of going to Ascalon to square accounts with his persecutors as soon as he had the strength to warrant such a move was no secret in the Stilwell family. Fred had offered his services at the beginning, and the one cowboy now left out of the five but recently employed by Stilwell had laid his pistol on the table and told Morgan that he was the man who went with it, both of them at his service when the hour of reckoning should arrive. Now Stilwell himself was beginning to show the pistol itch in his palm.

Morgan was grateful for all this uprising on the part of his new friends in his behalf, to whom his suffering and the cruelty of his ordeal appealed strongly for sympathy, but he could not accept any assistance at their hands. There could be no satisfaction in justice applied by any hand but his own. If otherwise, he might as well go to the county attorney, lodge complaints, obtain warrants and send his enemies to jail.

No, it was a case for personal attention; it was a one-man job. What they were to suffer for their great wrong against him, he must inflict with his own weapon, like the savage Comanche whose camp fires were scarcely cold in that place.

So Morgan spoke again of going that night to Ascalon, only to be set upon by all of them and argued into submission. Eager as Fred was to go along and have a hand in the fray, he was against going that night. Violet came and laid her good wholesome, sympathetic hand on Morgan's arm and looked into his face with a plea in her eyes that was stronger than words. He couldn't bear his feet in the stirrups with his ankles all swollen and sore as they were, she said; wait a day or two--wait a week. What did it matter if they should leave in the meantime, and go back down the wild trail to Texas? So much the better; let them go.

Morgan smiled to hear her say it would be better if they should get away, for she was one of the forgiving of this world, in whose breast the fire of vengeance would find no fuel to nurse its hot spark and burst into raging flame. He yielded to their entreaties and reasoning, agreeing to defer his expedition against his enemies until morning, but not an hour longer.

When the others had gone to bed, Morgan went down to the river through the broad notch in the low bank where the Santa Fé Trail used to cross. This old road was brush-grown now, with only a dusty path winding along it where the cattle passed to drink. The hoof-cut soil was warm and soft to his bruised feet; the bitter scent of the willows was strong on the cooling night as he brushed among them. Out across the broad golden bars he went, seeking the shallow ripple to which the stream shrunk in the summer days between rains, sitting by it when he came to it at last, bathing his feet in the tepid water.

There he sat for the cure of the water on his bruised, fevered joints, raking the fire of his hatred together until it grew and leaped within him like a tempest. As the Indian warrior watches the night out with song of defiance and dance of death to inflame him to his grim purpose of the dawn, so this man fallen from the ways of gentleness into the abyss of savagery spurred himself to a grim and terrible frenzy by visiting his wrath in anticipation upon his enemies.

Unworthy as they were, obscure and trivial; riotous, ignorant, bestial in their lives, he would lower himself to their level for one blood-red hour to carry to them a punishment more terrible than the noose. As from the dead he would rise up to strike them with terror. In the morning, when the sun was striking long shadows of shrub and bunched bluestem over the prairie levels; in the morning, when the wind was as weak as a young fawn.

CHAPTER X

THE HOUR OF VENGEANCE

The proscribed of the earth were sleeping late in Ascalon that morning, as they slept late every morning, bright or cloudy, head-heavy with the late watch and debaucheries of the night. Few were on the street in pursuit of the small amount of legitimate business the town transacted during the burning hours when the moles of the night lay housed in gloom, when Morgan walked from the baggage-room of the railroad depot.

Few who saw Morgan on the day of his arrival in Ascalon would have recognized him now. He had been obliged to go to the bottom of his trunk for the outfit that he treasured out of sentiment for the old days rather than in any expectation of needing it again--the rig he had worn into the college town, a matter of six hundred miles from his range, to begin a new life. Now he had fallen from the eminence. He was going back to the old.

The gray wool shirt was wrinkled and stained by weather and wear, the roomy corduroy trousers were worn from saddle chafing, the big spurs were rusted of rowel and shank. But the boots were new--he had bought them before leaving the range, to wear in college, laying them aside with regret when he found them not just the thing in vogue--and they were still brave in glossy bronze of quilted tops, little marred by that last long ride out of his far-away past. His cream-colored hat was battered and old, for he had worn it five years in all weather, crushed from the pressure of packing, but he pinched the tall crown to a point as he used to wear it, and turned the broad brim back from his forehead according to the habit of his former days.

This had been his gala costume in other times, kept in the bunkhouse at the ranch for days of fiesta, nights of dancing, and wild dissipation when he rode with his fellows to the three-days' distant town. His old pistol was in his holster, and his empty cartridge belt about his middle, the rifle, in saddle holster, that he used to carry for wolves and rustlers, in his hand.

Morgan stood a moment, leaning the rifle against the depot end, to take the bright silk handkerchief from about his neck, as if he considered it as being too festive for the somber business before him. The station agent stood at the corner of the building, watching him curiously.

The horse that Morgan had borrowed from Stilwell lifted its head with a start as he approached where it stood at the side of the station platform, as if it questioned him on the reason for this transformation and the honesty of his purpose. Morgan did not mount the horse, although he walked with difficulty in the tight boots which had lain like the shed habits of his past so many years unstretched by a foot. He went leading the horse, rein over his arm, to the hitching rack in front of the hotel, under the plank canopy of which Stilwell and his son waited his coming.

Stilwell had made it plain to Morgan at the beginning, to save his feelings and his pride, that they were not attending him on the expedition against his enemies with any intention of helping him. Just to be there in case of outside interference, and to enjoy the spectacle of justice being done by a strong hand. Stilwell's account, personally, was not against these men, he said, although they had driven their herd upon his range and spread infection among his cattle. That would be taken up with Sol Drumm when he came back from Kansas City with the money from his cattle sale.

Morgan went to the hardware store, two doors from the hotel, from which he presently emerged with a coil of new rope, a row of new cartridges in his belt, and pockets heavy with a reserve supply. Tom Conboy was standing in his door, looking up and down the street in the manner of a man who felt his position insecure. Morgan saw that he was haggard and worn as from long vigils and anxieties, although he had about him still an air of assurance and self-sufficiency. Morgan passed him in the door and entered the office unrecognized, although Conboy searched him with a disfavoring and suspicious eye.

In the office there was evidence of conflict and turmoil. The showcase was broken, the large iron safe lay overturned on the floor. The blue door leading into the dining-room had been burst from its hinges, its panels cracked, and now stood in the office leaning against the partition like a champion against the ropes. Conboy turned from his watch at the street door with reluctance, to see what the visitor desired, and at the same moment Dora appeared in the doorless frame within.

"Mr. Morgan!" she cried, incredulity, surprise, pleasure, mingled in her voice.

She paused a moment, eyes round, hands lifted, her pretty mouth agape, but came on again almost at once, eagerness brushing all other emotions out of her face. "Wherever in the world have you been? What in the name of goodness is the matter with your face?" She turned Morgan a little to let the light fall on his wound.

Grim as Morgan's business was that morning, bitter as his savage heart, he had a nook in his soul for sympathetic Dora, and a smile that came so hard and vanished so quickly that it seemed it must have hurt him in the giving more than the breaking of a bone.

"Mister Morgan!" said Dora, hardly a breath between her last word and the next, "whatever have you been doin' to your face?"

"No niggers in Ireland, now--no-o-o niggers in Ireland!" Conboy warned her, coming forward with no less interest than his daughter's to peer into Morgan's bruised and marred face. "Well, well!"--with much surprise altogether genuine, "you're back again, Mr. Morgan?"

"Wherever have you been?" Dora persisted, no more interested in niggers in Ireland than elsewhere.

"I fell among thieves," Morgan told her, gravely. Then to Conboy: "Is that gang from Texas stopping here?"

"No, they lay up at Peden's on the floor where they happen to fall," Conboy replied. "If there ever was a curse turned loose on a town that gang--look at that showcase, look at that door, look at that safe. They took the town last night, a decent woman didn't dare to show her face outside the door and wasn't safe in the house. They tried to blow that safe with powder when I wouldn't open it and give them the money. But they didn't even jar it--your money's in there, Mr. Morgan, safe."

"Oh, it was awful!" said Dora. "Oh, you've got your gun! If some man----"

"Sh-h-h! No nig----"

"Where's the marshal?" Morgan asked.

"Took the train east last night. The operator told me he got a wire from Sol Drumm, boss of the outfit, to meet him in Abilene today. He swore them six ruffians in as deputies before he went and left them in charge of the town."

"Six? Where's the other one?"

Conboy looked at him with quick flashing of his shifty eyes. "Don't you know?" he asked, with significant shrewdness, smiling a little as if to show his friendly appreciation of the joke.

"What in the hell do you mean?" Morgan demanded.

"No niggers in Ireland, now," Conboy said soothingly, his face growing white. "One of them was killed down by the railroad track the night you left. They said you shot him and hopped a freight."

Morgan said no more, but turned toward the door to leave.

"The inquest hasn't been held over him yet, we've been kept so busy with the marshal's cases we didn't get around to him," Conboy explained. "Maybe you can throw some light on that case?"

"I can throw a lot of it," Morgan said, and walked out with that word to where he had left his horse.

There Morgan cut six lengths from his new rope, drawing the pieces through his belt in the manner of a man carrying string for sewing grain sacks. He took the rifle from the saddle, filled its magazine, and started toward Peden's place, which was on the next corner beyond the hotel, on the same side of the square. When he had gone a few rods, halting on his lame feet, alert as a hunter who expects the game to break from cover, Stilwell and Fred got up from their apparently disinterested lounging in front of the hotel and followed leisurely after him.

Many of the little business houses around the square were closed. There was a litter of glass on the plank sidewalk, where proprietors stood gloomily looking at broken windows, or were setting about replacing them with boards after the hurricane of deviltry that swept the town the night past. Those who were abroad in the sunlight of early morning making their purchases for the day, moved with trepidation, putting their feet down quietly, hastening on their way.

An old man who walked ahead of Morgan appeared to be the only unshaken and unconcerned person in this place of sleeping passions. He carried a thick hickory stick with immense crook, which he pegged down in time to his short steps, relying on it for support not at all, his lean old jaw chopping his cud as nimbly as a sheep's. But when Morgan's shadow, stretching far ahead, fell beside him, he started like a dozing horse, whirled about with stick upraised, and stood so in attitude of menace and defense until the stranger had passed on.

Conboy was alert in his door, watching to see what new nest of trouble Morgan was about to stir with that threatening rifle. Others seemed to feel the threat that stalked with this grim man. Life quickened in the somnolent town as to the sound of a fire bell as he passed; people stood watching after him; came to doors and windows to lean and look. A few moments after his passing the street behind him became almost magically alive, although it was a silent, expectant, fearful interest that communicated itself in whispers and low breath.

Who was this stranger with the mark of conflict on his face, this unusual weapon in the brawls and tragedies of Ascalon held ready in his hands? What grievance had he? what authority? Was he the bringer of peace in the name of the law that had been so long degraded and defied, or only another gambler in the lives of men? They waited, whispering, in silence as of a deserted city, to see and hear.

There was only one priest of alcohol attending the long altar where men sacrificed their manhood in Peden's deserted hall that morning. He was quite sufficient for all the demands of the hour, his only customers being the unprofitable gang of cattle herders whom Morgan sought. True to their training in early rising, no matter what the stress of the night past, no matter how broken by alarm and storm, they were all awake, like sailors called to their watch. They were improving while it might last the delegated authority of Seth Craddock, which opened the treasures of a thousand bottles at a word.

The gambling tables in the front of the house were covered with black cloths, which draped them almost to the floor, like palls of the dead. Down at the farther end of the long hall a man was sweeping up the débris of the night, his steps echoing in the silence of the place. For there was no hilarity in the sodden crew lined up at the bar for the first drink of the day. They were red-eyed, crumpled, dirty; frowsled of hair as they had risen from the floor.

Peden's hall was not designed for the traffic of daylight. There was gloom among its bare girders, shadows lay along its walls. Only through the open door came in a broad and healthy band of light, which spread as it reached and faltered as it groped, spending itself a little way beyond the place where the lone bartender served his profitless customers.

Morgan walked into the place down this path of light unnoticed by the men at the bar or the one who served them, for they were wrangling with him over some demand that he seemed reluctant to supply. At the end of the bar, not a rod separating them, Morgan stopped like a casual customer, waiting his moment.

The question between bartender and the gang quartered upon the town was one of champagne. It was no drink, said the bartender, to lay the foundation of a day's business with the bottle upon. Whisky was the article to put inside a man's skin at that hour of the morning, and then in small shots, not too often. They deferred to his experience, accepting whisky. As they lined up with breastbones against the bar to pour down the charge, Morgan threw his rifle down on them.

No chance to drop a hand to a gun standing shoulder to shoulder with gizzards pressed against the bar; no chance to swerve or duck and make a quick sling of it and a quicker shot, with the bore of that big rifle ready to cough sixteen chunks of lead in half as many seconds, any one of them hitting hard enough to drill through them, man by man, down to the last head in the line. So their arms went up and strained high above their heads, as if eager to show their desire to comply without reservation to the unspoken command. Morgan had not said a word.

The bartender, accepting the situation as generally inclusive, put his hands up along with his deadbeat patrons. And there they stood one straining moment, the man with the broom down in the gloom of the farther end of the building, unconscious of what was going on, whistling as he swept among the peanut hulls.

Morgan signaled with his head for the bartender to come over the barrier, which he did, with alacrity, and stood at the farther end of the line, hands up, a raw-fisted, hollow-faced Irishman with bristling short hair. Morgan jerked his head again, repeating the signal when the bartender looked in puzzled fright into his face to read the meaning. Then the fellow got it, and came forward, a vast relief spreading in his combative features.

Morgan indicated the rope ends dangling at his belt. Almost beaming, quite triumphant in his eagerness, the bartender grasped his meaning at a glance. He began tying the ruffians' hands behind their backs, and tying them well, with a zest in his work that increased as he traveled down the line.

"Champagne, is it?" said he, mocking them, a big foot in the small of the victim's back as he pulled so hard it made him squeal. "Nothing short of champoggany wather will suit the taste av ye this fine marin', and you with a thousand dollars' wort' of goods swilled into your paunches the past week! I'll give you a dose of champoggany wather you'll not soon forget, ye strivin' devils! This sheriff is the man that'll hang ye for your murthers and crimes, ye bastes!" And with each expletive a kick, but not administered in any case until he had turned his head with sly caution to see whether it would be permitted by this silent avenger who had come to Ascalon in the hour of its darkest need.

While Morgan's captives cursed him, knowing now who he was, and cursed the bartender whom they had overriden and mocked, insulted and abused in the security of their collective strength and notorious deeds, the shadow of two men fell across the threshold of Peden's door. There the shadows lay through the brief moments of this little drama's enactment, immovable, as though cast by men who watched.

The porter came forward from his sweeping to look on this degradation of the desperados, mocking them, returning them curse for curse, voluble in picturesque combinations of damning sentences as if he had practiced excommunication longer than the oldest pope who ever lived. In the

TRAIL'S END

excess of his scorn for their fallen might he smeared his filthy broom across their faces, paying back insult for insult, bold and secure under the protection of this stern eagle of a man who had dropped on Ascalon as from a cloud.

When the last man was bound, the last kick applied by the bartender's great, square-toed foot, Morgan motioned his sullen captives toward the door.

"Wait a minute--have something on the house," the bartender urged.

Morgan lifted his hand in gesture at once silencing and denying, and marched out after the heroes of the Chisholm Trail. Through it all he had not spoken.

They cursed Morgan as he drove them into the street, and surged against their bonds, the only silent one among them the Dutchman, and the only sober one. Now and then Morgan saw his face as the others bunched and shifted in their struggles to break loose, his mocking, sneering, pasty white face, his wide-set teeth small and white as a young pup's. His eyes were hateful as a rattlesnake's; lecherous eyes, debased.

Morgan herded them into the public square beyond the line of hitching racks which stood like a skeleton fence between courthouse and business buildings. People came pouring from every house to see, hurrying, crowding, talking in hushed voices, wondering in a hundred conjectures what this man was going to do. Gamblers and nighthawks, roused by the very feeling of something unusual, hastened out half dressed, to stand in slippers and collarless shirts, looking on in silent speculation.

Citizens, respectable and otherwise, who had suffered loss and humiliation, danger and terror at the hands of these men, exulted now in their downfall. Some said this man was a sheriff from Texas, who had tracked them to Ascalon and was now taking them to jail to await a train; some said he was a special government officer, others that the governor had sent him in place of troops, knowing him to be sufficient in himself. Boys ran along in open-mouthed admiration, pattering their bare feet in the thick dust, as Morgan drove his captives down the inside of the hitching racks; the outpouring of citizens, parasites, outcasts of the earth, swept after in a growing stream.

From all sides they came to witness this great adventure, unusual for Ascalon in that the guilty had been humbled and the arrogant brought low. Across the square they came running, on the courthouse steps they stood. In front of the hotel there was a crowd, which moved forward to meet Morgan as he came marching like an avenger behind his captives, who were now beginning to show alarm, sobered by their unexampled situation, sweating in the agony of their quaking hearts.

At the hitching rack where his horse stood, Morgan halted the six men.

He took the remainder of his new rope from the saddle, laced it through the bonds on the Texans' wrists, backed them up to the horizontal pole of the hitching rack, and tied them there in a line, facing inward upon the square. As he moved about his business with deliberate, yet swift and sure hand of vengeance well plotted in advance, Morgan kept his rifle leaning near, watching the crowd for any outbreak of friends who might rise in defense of these men, or any movement that might threaten interference with his plans.

When he had finished binding the six men, backs to the rack, Morgan beckoned a group of boys to him, spoke to them in undertone that even the nearest in the crowd did not hear. Off the youngsters ran, so full of the importance of their part in that great event that they would not stay to be questioned nor halt for the briefest word.

In a little while the lads came hurrying back, with empty goods boxes and barrels, fragments of packing cases, all sorts of dry wood to which they could lay their eager hands. This they piled where Morgan indicated, to stand by panting, eyes big in excitement and wondering admiration for this mighty man.

Mrs. Conboy, standing at the edge of the sidewalk before her door, not more than ten yards from the spot where Morgan was making these unaccountable preparations, leaned with a new horror in her fear-haunted eyes to see.

"My God! he's goin' to burn them!" she said. "Oh, my God!"

CHAPTER XI

THE PENALTY

Whatever the stranger's intention toward the rough riders of the Chisholm Trail who had terrorized good and bad alike in Ascalon for a week, whether to roast them alive as they stood in a row with backs to the hitching rack, or to inflict some other equally terrible punishment; or whether he was simply staking them there while he cooked his breakfast cowboy fashion, not willing to trust them out of sight while he regaled himself in a restaurant, nobody quite understood. Mrs. Conboy's exclamation appeared to voice the general belief of the crowd. Murmurs of disapproval began to rise.

One of the leading moralists of the town, proprietor of a knock-down-and-drag-out, was loudest in his protestations that such a happening in the public square of Ascalon, in the broad light of day, the assembled inhabitants looking on, would give the place a name from which it never would recover. This fellow, a gross man of swinging paunch, a goitre enlarging and disfiguring his naturally thick, ugly neck, had scrambled from his bed in haste at the thrilling of the general alarm of something unusual in the daylight annals of the town. His bare feet were thrust into slippers, his great white shirt was collarless, dainty narrow blue silk suspenders held up his hogshead-measure pantaloons. The redness of unfinished sleep was in his eyes.

"I tell you, men, this ain't a goin' to do--this ain't no town down south where they take niggers out and burn 'em," he said. "I ain't got no use for that gang, myself, but I've got the good of the town and my business to consider, like all the rest of you have."

There must have been in town that day forty or more cowboys from Texas and the Nation, as the Cherokee country south was called. These for the greater part were still sober, not having been paid off, still on duty caring for the horses left behind them when the cattle were loaded and shipped, or for the herds resting and grazing close by after the long drive. They began to gather curiously around the fat man who had the fair repute of Ascalon so close to his heart, listening to his efforts to set a current of resentment against the stranger stirring in the awed crowd. They began to turn toward Morgan now, with close talk among themselves, regarding him yet as something more than a common man, not keen to spring into somebody else's trouble and get their fingers scorched.

"What's he going to do with them?" one of these inquired.

"Burn 'em," the fat man replied, as readily as if he had it from Morgan's own mouth, and as strongly denunciatory as though the disgrace of it reached to his fair fame and good business already. "You boys ain't goin' to stand around here and see men from your own country burnt like niggers, are you? Well, you don't look like a bunch that'd do it--you don't look like it to me."

"What did they do to him?" one of the cowboys asked, not greatly fired by the fat man's sectional appeal.

Stilwell came loitering among them at that point, a man of their own calling, sympathies, and traditions, with the shoulder-lurching gait of a man who had spent most of his years in the saddle. He told them in a few feeling, picturesque words the extent of Morgan's grievance against the six, and left it with them to say whether he was to be interfered with in his exaction of a just and fitting payment.

"I don't know what he's goin' to do," Stilwell said, "but if he wants to roast 'em and eat 'em"--looking about him with stern eyes--"this is his day."

"If he needs any help there's plenty of it here," said a cowboy from the Nation, hooking his thumb with lazy but expressive movement under the cartridge belt around his slim waist.

The fat publican subsided, seeing his little ripple of protest flattened out by the spirit of fair play. He backed to the sidewalk, where he stood in conference with Tom Conboy, and there was heard a reference to niggers in Ireland, pronounced with wise twisting of the head.

Morgan selected, in the face of this little flurry of opposition and defense, a box from among the odds and ends brought him by the boys, sat on it facing his prisoners and broke bits of wood for a fire. People began pressing a little nearer to see what was to come, but when Morgan, with eye watchful to see even the shifting of a foot in the crowd, reached for his rifle and laid it across his lap, there was an immediate scramble to the sidewalk. This left twenty feet of dusty white road unoccupied, a margin on the page where this remarkable incident in Ascalon's record of tragedies was being written.

Midway of his line of captives, six feet in front of the nearest man, Morgan kindled a fire, adding wood as the blaze grew, apparently as oblivious of his surroundings as if in a camp a hundred miles from a house. When he had the fire established to his liking, he took from his saddle an iron implement, at the sight of which a murmur and a movement of new interest stirred the crowd.

This iron contrivance was a rod, little thicker than a man's finger, which terminated in a flat plate wrought with some kind of open-work device. This flat portion, which was about as broad as the span of a man's two hands and perhaps six or eight inches long, appeared to be a continuation of the handle, bent and hammered to form the crude pattern, and the wonderment and speculation, contriving and guessing, all passed out of the people when they beheld this thing. That was a cattle country; they knew it for a branding iron.

Morgan thrust the brand into the fire, piled wood around it, leaning over it a little in watchful intent. This relic of his past he also had retrieved from the bottom of his trunk along with boots and spurs, corduroys and hat, and it had been a long time, indeed, since he heated it to apply the Three Crow brand to the shoulder of a beast. That brand, his father's brand in the early days in the Sioux country where he was the pioneer cattleman, never had been heated to come in contact with such base skins as these, Morgan reflected, and it would not be so dishonored now if cattle were carrying it on any range.

When the Indians killed his father and drove off the last of the herd, the Three Crow became a discontinued brand in the Northwest. The son had kept this iron which his father had carried at his saddle horn as a souvenir of the times when life was not worth much between the Black Hills and the Platte. The brand was not recorded anywhere today; the brand books of the cattle-growers' associations did not contain it. But it was his mark; he intended to set it on these cattle, disfiguration of face for disfiguration, and turn them loose to return smelling of the hot iron among their kind.

Sodden with the dregs of last night's carousel, slow-headed, surly as the Texans were when Morgan encountered them, they were all alert and fully cognizant of their peril now. No rough jest passed from mouth to mouth; there was no sneer, no laugh of bravado, no defiance. Some of them had curses left in them as they sweated in the fear of Morgan's silent preparations and lunged on their ropes in the hope of breaking loose. All but the Dutchman appealed to the crowd to interfere, promising rewards, making pledges in the name of their absent patron, Seth Craddock, the dreaded slayer of men.

Now and again one of them shouted a name, generally Peden's name, or the name of some dealer or bouncer in his hall. Nobody answered, nobody raised hand or voice to interfere or protest. During their short reign of pillage and debauchery under the protection of the city marshal, the members of the gang had not made a friend who cared to risk his skin to save theirs.

To add to their disgrace and humiliation, their big pistols hung in the holsters on their thighs. People, especially the men of the range, remarked this full armament, marveling how the stranger had taken six men of such desperate notoriety all strapped with their guns, but they understood at once his purpose in allowing the weapons to hang under their impotent hands. It was a mockery of their bravado, a belittlement of their bluff and swagger in the brief day of their oppression.

Morgan withdrew the brand from the fire, knocking the clinging bits of wood from it against the ground.

The Dutchman was first in the line at Morgan's right hand as he turned from the fire with the branding iron red-hot in his hand. Near the Dutchman stood Morgan's borrowed horse, drowsing in the sun with head down, its weight on three legs, one ear set in its inherited caution to catch the least alarm. From the first moment of his encounter with these scoundrels Morgan had not lowered himself to address them a single word. Such commands as he had given them had been in dumb show, as to driven creatures. This rule of silence he held still as he approached the first object of his vengeance.

The Dutchman started back from the iron in sudden rousing from his brooding silence, fear and hate convulsing his snarling face, shrinking back against the timber of the hitching rack as far as he could withdraw, where he stood with shoulders hunched about his neck, savage as a chained wolf. He began to writhe and kick as Morgan laid hold of his neck to hold him steady for the cruel kiss of the iron.

The fellow squirmed and lunged, with head lowered, trying to get on the other side of the rack, his companions who were within reach joining in kicking at Morgan, adding their curses and cries to the Dutchman's silent fight to save his skin. They raised such a commotion of noise and dust that it spread to the crowd, which pressed up with a great clamor of derision, pity, laughter, and shrill cries.

The cowboys, feeling themselves privileged spectators by reason of craft affiliation, made a ring around the scene of punishment, shouting in enjoyment of the spectacle, for it was quite in harmony with the cruel jokes and wild pranks which made up the humorous diversions of their lives.

"You'll have to hog-tie that feller," said one, drawing nearer than the rest in his interest.

Morgan paused a moment, brand uplifted, as if he considered the friendly suggestion. The Dutchman was cringing before him, head drawn between his shoulders, face as near the ground as he could strain the ropes which bound him. Morgan kicked the fellow's feet from under him, leaving him hanging by his hands.

The spectators cheered this adroit movement, laughing at the spectacle of the Dutchman hanging face downward on his ropes, and Morgan, sweating in the heat of the fire and sun, exertion and passion, careless of everything, thoughtless of all but his unsatisfied vengeance, straddled the Dutchman's neck as if he were a calf. He brought the iron down within an inch or two of the Dutchman's face, calculating how much of the crude device of three flying crows he could get between mouth and ear, and as Morgan stood so with the hot iron poised, the Dutchman choking between his clamping knees, a hand clutched his arm, jerking the hovering brand away.

Morgan had not heard a step near him through the turmoil of his hate, nor seen any person approaching to interfere. Now he whirled, pistol slung out, facing about to account with the one who dared break in to stay his hand in the administration of a punishment that he considered all too inadequate and humane.

There was a girl standing by him, her restraining hand still on his arm, the sun glinting in the gloss of her dark hair, her dark eyes fixed on him in denial, in a softness of pity that Morgan knew was not for his victims alone. And so in that revel of base surrender to his primal passions she had come to him, she whom his heart sought among the faces of women; in that manner she had found him, and found him, as Morgan knew in his abased heart, at his worst.

There was not a word, not the whisper of a word, in the crowd around them. There was scarcely the moving of a breath.

"Give me that iron, Mr. Morgan!" she demanded in voice that trembled from the surge of her perturbed breast.

Morgan stood confronting her in the fierce pose of a man prepared to contend to the last extreme with any who had come to stay his hand in his hour of requital. The glowing iron, from which little wavers of heat rose in the sun, he grasped in one hand; in the other his pistol, elbow close to his side, threatening the quarter from which interference had come. Still he demurred at her demand, refusing the outstretched hand.

"Give it to me!" she said again, drawing nearer, but a little space between them now, so near he fancied her breath, panting from her open lips, on his cheek.

Silent, grim, still clouded by the vapors of his passion, Morgan stood denying her, not able to adjust himself in wrench so sudden to the calm plane of his normal life.

"Not for their sake--for your own!" she pleaded, her hand gentle on his arm.

The set muscles of his pistol arm relaxed, the muzzle of the weapon dropped slowly with the surge of dark passion in his breast.

"They deserve it, and worse, but not from you, Mr. Morgan. Leave them to the law--give me that iron."

Morgan yielded it into her hand, slowly slipped his pistol back into the holster, slowly raised his hand to his forehead, pushed back his hat, swept his hand across his eyes like one waking from an oppressive dream. He looked around at the silent people, hundreds of them, it seemed to him, for the first time fully conscious of the spectacular drama he had been playing before their astonished eyes.

The Dutchman had struggled to his knees, where he leaned with neck outstretched as if he waited the stroke of the headsman's sword, unable to regain his feet. The girl looked with serious eyes into Morgan's face, the hot branding iron in her hand.

"I think you'd better lock them up in jail, Mr. Morgan," she said.

Morgan did not reply. He stood with bent head, his emotions roiled like a turgid brook, a feeling over him of awakening daze, such as one experiences in a sweat of agony after dreaming of falling from some terrifying height. Morgan had just struck the bottom of the precipice in his wild, self-effacing dream. The shock of waking was numbing; there was no room for anything in his righted consciousness but a vast, down-bearing sense of shame. She had seen a side of his nature long submerged, long fought, long ago conquered as he believed; the vindictive, the savage part of him, the cruel and unforgiving.

Public interest in the line of captives along the hitching rack was waking in a new direction all around the sun-burned square. It was beginning to come home to every staid and sober man in the assembly that he had a close interest in the disposition of these men.

"I don't know about that jail business and the law, Miss Retty," said a severe dark man who pushed into the space where Morgan and the girl stood. "We've been dressin' and feedin' and standin' the loss through breakin' and stealin' these fellers have imposed on this town for a week and more now, and I'm one that don't think much of lockin' them up in jail to lay there and eat off of the county and maybe be turned loose after a while. You'd just as well try to carry water up here from the river in a gunny sack as convict a crook in this county any more."

This man found supporters at once. They came pushing forward, the resentment of insult and oppression darkening their faces, to shake threatening fists in the faces of the Dutchman and his companions.

"The best medicine for a gang like this is a cottonwood limb and a rope," the man who had spoken declared.

It began to look exceedingly dark for the unlucky desperadoes inside of the next minute. The suggestion of hanging them immediately became an avowed intention; preparations for carrying it into effect began on the spot. While some ran to the hardware store for rope, others discussed the means of employing it to carry out the public sentence.

Hanging never had been popular in Ascalon, mainly because of the barrenness of the country, which offered no convenient branches except on the cottonwoods along the river. Wagon tongues upended and propped by neckyokes had been known to serve in their time, and telegraph poles when the railroad built through. But gibbets of this sort had their shortcomings and vexations. There was nothing so comfortable for all concerned as a tree, and trees did not grow by nature or by art in Ascalon. So there was talk of an expedition to the river, where all the six might be accommodated on one tree.

The girl who had taken the branding iron from Morgan and cooled the heat of his resentment and vengeance quicker than the iron had cooled, stood looking about into the serious faces of the men who suddenly had determined to finish for Morgan the business he had begun. Her face was white, horror distended her eyes; she seemed to have no words for a plea against this rapidly growing plan.

One of the doomed men behind her began to whimper and beg, appealing to her in his mother's name to save him. He was a young man, whose weak face was lined by the excesses of his unrestrained days in Ascalon. His hat had fallen off, his foretop of brown hair straggled over his wild eyes.

"Come away from here," said Morgan, turning to her now, his voice rough and still shaken by his subsiding passion. He took the hot iron from her, thinking of the trough at the public well where he might cool it.

"Don't let them do it," she implored, putting out her hands to him in appeal.

"Now Miss Rhetta, you'd better run along," a man urged kindly.

Morgan stood beside her in the narrowing circle about the six men who had been condemned by public sentiment in less than sixty seconds and scarcely more words, the hot end of the branding iron in the dust at his feet. He was silent, yet apparently agitated by a strong emotion, as a man might be who had leaped a crevasse in fleeing a pressing peril, upon which he feared to look back.

She whom the man had called Rhetta picked up the young cowboy's hat and put it on his head.

"Hush!" she charged, in reply to his whimpering intercession for mercy. "Mr. Morgan isn't going to let them hang you."

Morgan started out of his thoughtful glooming as if a reviving wind had struck his face, all alert again in a moment, but silent and inscrutable as before. He leaned his brand against the hitching post, recovered his rifle where it lay in the dust beside the scattered sticks of his fire, making himself a little room as he moved about.

Those who had talked of hanging the six now suspended sentence while waiting the outcome of this new activity on the part of the avenger. A man who came from somewhere with a coil of rope on his arm stood at the edge of the newly widened circle with fallen countenance, like one who arrived too late at some great event in which he had expected to be the leading actor.

Morgan began stripping belts and pistols from his captives, throwing the gear at the foot of the post where his branding iron stood. When he had stripped the last one he paused a moment as if considering something, the weapon in his hand. The girl Rhetta had not added a word to her appeal in behalf of the unworthy rascals who stood sweating in terror before the threatening crowd. But she looked now into Morgan's face with hopeful understanding, the color coming back to her drained cheeks, a light of admiration in her eyes. As for Morgan, his own face appeared to have cleared of a cloud. There was a gleam of deep-kindling humor in his eyes.

"Gentlemen, there will not be any hanging in Ascalon this morning," he announced.

He threw the last pistol down with the others, nodded Stilwell to him, whispered a word or two. Stilwell went shouldering off through the crowd. Morgan sheathed his rifle in the battered scabbard that hung on his saddle. In a little while Stilwell came back with a saw.

Morgan took the tool and sawed through the pole to which his captives were made fast. Stilwell held up the severed end while Morgan cut the other, freeing from the bolted posts the four-inch section of pole to which the cowboys were tied, leaving it hanging from the ropes at their wrists, dangling a little below their hands.

The late lords of the plains were such a dejected and altogether sneaking looking crew, shorn of their power by the hands of one man, stripped of their roaring weapons, tied like cattle to a hurdle, that the vengeful spirit of Ascalon veered in a glance to humorous appreciation of the comedy that was beginning before their eyes.

The cowboys who had stood ready a few minutes past to help hang the outfit, fairly rolled with laughter at the sight of this miserable example of complete degradation, through which the meanness of their kind was so ludicrously apparent. The citizenry and floating population of the town joined in the merriment, and the lowering clouds of tragedy were swept away on a gale of laughter that echoed along the jagged business front.

But the girl Rhetta was not laughing. Perplexed, troubled, she laid her hand on Morgan's arm as he stood beside his horse about to mount.

"What are you going to do with them now, Mr. Morgan?" she inquired.

"They're going to start for Texas down the Chisholm Trail," he said, smiling down at her from the saddle.

And in that manner they set out from Ascalon, carrying the pole at their backs, Morgan driving them ahead of him, starting them in a trot which increased to a hobbling run as they bore away past the railroad station and struck the broad trampled highway to the south.

Afoot and horseback the town and the visitors in it came after them, shooting and shouting, getting far more enjoyment out of it than they would have got out of a hanging, as even the most contrary among them admitted. For this was a drama in which the boys and girls took part, and even the Baptist preacher, who had a church as big as a mouse trap, stood grinning in appreciation as they passed, and said something about it being a parallel of Samson, and the foxes with their tails tied together being driven away into the Philistines' corn.

The crowd followed to the rise half a mile south of town, where most of it halted, only the cowboys and mounted men accompanying Morgan to the river. There they turned back, also, leaving it to Morgan to carry out the rest of his program alone, it being the general opinion that he intended to herd the six beyond the cottonwoods on the farther shore and despatch them clean-handed, according to what was owing to him on their account.

Morgan urged his captives on, still keeping them on the trot, although it was becoming a staggering and wabbling progression, the weaker in the line held up by the more enduring. They were experiencing in a small and colorless measure, as faint by comparison, certainly, as the smell of smoke to the feel of fire on the naked skin, what they had given Morgan in the hour of their cruel mastery.

At last one of them could stumble on no farther. He fell, dragging down two others who were not able to sustain his weight. There Morgan left them, a mile or more beyond the river, knowing they would not have far to travel before they came across somebody who would set them free.

The Dutchman, stronger and fresher than any of his companions, turned as if he would speak when Morgan started to leave. Morgan checked his horse to hear what the fellow might have to say, but nothing came out of the ugly mouth but a grin of such derision, such mockery, such hate, that Morgan felt as if the bright day contracted to shadows and a chill crept into the pelting heat of the sun. He thought, gravely and soberly, that he would be sparing the world at large, and himself specifically, future pain and trouble by putting this scoundrel out of the way as a man would remove a vicious beast.

Whatever justification the past, the present, or the future might plead for this course, Morgan was too much himself again to yield. He turned from them, giving the Dutchman his life to make out of it what he might.

From the top one of the ridges such as billowed like swells of the sea that gray-green, treeless plain, Morgan looked back. All of them but the Dutchman were either lying or sitting on the ground, beaten and winded by the torture of their bonds and the hard drive of more than three miles in the burning sun. The Dutchman still kept his feet, although the drag of the pole upon him must have been sore and heavy, as if he must stand to send his curse out after the man who had bent him to his humiliation.

And Morgan knew that the Dutchman was not a conquered man, nor bowed in his spirit, nor turned one moment away from his thought of revenge. Again the bright day seemed to contract and grow chill around him, like the oncoming shadow and breath of storm. He felt that this man would return in his day to trouble him, low-devising, dark and secret and meanly covert as a wolf prowling in the night.

The last look Morgan had of the Dutchman he was gazing that way still, his face peculiarly white, the weight of the pole and his fallen comrades dragging down on his bound arms. Morgan could fancy still, even over the distance between them, the small teeth, wide set in the red gums like a pup's, and the loathsome glitter of his sneering eyes.

CHAPTER XII

IN PLACE OF A REGIMENT

Morgan rode back to town in thoughtful, serious mood after conducting the six desperadoes across the small trickle of the Arkansas River. He was not satisfied with the morning's adventure, no matter to what extent it reflected credit on his manhood and competency in the public mind of Ascalon. He would have been easier in all conscience and higher in his own esteem if it had not happened at all.

He thought soberly now of getting his trunk over to Conboy's from the station and changing back into the garb of civilization before meeting that girl again, that wonderful girl, that remarkable woman who could play a tune on him to suit her caprice, he thought, as she would have fingered a violin.

Judge Thayer's little office, with the white stakes behind it marking off the unsold lots like graves of a giant race, reminded Morgan of his broken engagement to look at the farm. He hitched his horse at the rack running out from one corner of the building, where other horses had stood fighting flies until they had stamped a hollow like a buffalo wallow in the dusty ground.

Judge Thayer got up from the accumulated business on his desk at the sound of Morgan's step in his door, and came forward with welcome in his beaming face, warmth of friendliness and admiration in every hair of his beard, where the gray twinkled like laughter among the black.

"I asked the governor for a company of militia to put down the disorder and outlawry in this town--I didn't think less than a company could do it," said the judge.

"Is he sending them?" Morgan inquired with polite interest.

"No, I'm glad to say he refused. He referred me to the sheriff."

"And the sheriff will act, I suppose?"

"Act?" Judge Thayer repeated, turning the word curiously. "Act!"--with all the contempt that could be centered in such a short expression--"yes, he'll act like a forsworn and traitorous coward, the friend to thieves that he's always been! We don't need him, we don't need the governor's petted, stall-fed militia, when we've got one man that's a regiment in himself!"

The judge must shake hands with Morgan again, and clap him on the shoulder to further express his admiration and the feeling of security his single-handed exploit against the oppressors of Ascalon had brought to the town.

"I and the other officers and directors sat up in the bank four nights, lights out and guns loaded, sweatin' blood, expecting a raid by that gang. They had this town buffaloed, Morgan. I'm glad you came back here today and showed us the pattern of a real, old-fashioned man."

"I guess I was lucky," Morgan said, with modest depreciation of his valor, exceedingly uncomfortable to stand there and hear this loud-spoken praise of a deed he would rather have the public forget.

"Maybe you call it luck where you came from, but we've got another name for it here in Ascalon."

"I'm sorry I couldn't keep my engagement to look at that farm, Judge Thayer. You must have heard my reason for it."

"Stilwell told me. It's a marvel you ever came back at all."

"If the farm isn't sold----"

"No," said the judge hastily, as if to turn him away from the subject. "Come in and sit down--there's a bigger thing than farming on hand for you if you can see your interests in it as I see them, Mr. Morgan. A man's got to trample down the briars before he makes his bed sometimes, you know--come on in out of this cussed sun.

"Morgan, the situation in Ascalon is like this," Judge Thayer resumed, seated at his desk, Morgan between him and the door in much the same position that Seth Craddock had sat on the day of his arrival not long before; "we've got a city marshal that's bigger than the authority that created him, bigger than anything on earth that ever wore a star. Seth Craddock's enlarged himself and his authority until he's become a curse and a scourge to the citizens of this town."

"I heard something of his doings from Fred Stilwell. Why don't you fire him?"

"Morgan, I approached him," said the judge, with an air of injury. "I believe on my soul the old devil spared my life only because I had befriended him in past days. There's a spark of gratitude in him that the drenching of blood hasn't put out. If it had been anybody else he'd have shot him dead."

"Hm-m-m-m!" said Morgan, grunting his sympathy, eyes on the floor.

"Morgan, that fellow's killed eight men in as many days! He's got a regular program--a man a day."

"It looks like something ought to be done to stop him."

"The old devil's shrewd, he's had legal counsel from no less illustrious source than the county attorney, who's so crooked he couldn't lie on the side of a hill without rollin' down it like a hoop. Seth knows he fills an elective office, he's beyond the power of mayor and council to remove. The only way he can be ousted is by proceedings in court, which he could wear along till his term expired. We can't fire him, Morgan. He'll go on till he depopulates this town!"

"It's a remarkable situation," Morgan said.

"He's a jackal, which is neither wolf nor dog. He's never killed a man here yet out of necessity--he just shoots them down to see them kick, or to gratify some monstrous delight that has transformed him from the man I used to know."

"He may be insane," Morgan suggested.

"I don't know, but I don't think so. I can't abase my mind low enough to fathom that man."

"It's a wonder somebody hasn't killed him," Morgan speculated.

"He never arrests anybody, there hasn't been a prisoner in the calaboose since he took charge of this town. Notoriety has turned his head, notoriety seems to put a halo around him that makes a troop of sycophants look up to him as a saint. Look here--look at this!"

The judge held out a newspaper, shaking it viciously, his face clouded with displeasure.

"Here's a piece two columns long about that scoundrel in the Kansas City Times--the notoriety of the town is obscured by the bloody reputation of its marshal."

"It must be gratifying to a man of his ambitions," Morgan commented, glancing curiously over the story, his mind on the first victim of Craddock's gun in that town.

"It's a disgrace that some of us feel, whatever it may be to him. I expected him to confine his gun to gamblers and crooks and these vermin that hang around the women of the dance houses, but he's right-hand man with them, they're all on his staff."

Morgan looked up in amazement, hardly able to believe what he heard.

"It's enough to wind any decent man," Judge Thayer nodded. "You remember his first case--that fool cowboy he killed at the hotel?"

"I was just thinking of him," Morgan said.

"That's the kind he goes in for, cowboys from the range, green, innocent boys, harmless if you take 'em right. Yesterday afternoon he killed a young fellow from Glenmore. It's going to bring retaliation and reprisal on us, it's going to hurt us in this contest over the county seat."

"I shouldn't wonder," said Morgan, hoping the reprisal would be swift and severe.

"I think the man's blood mad," Judge Thayer speculated, in a hopeless way. "It must be the outcome of all that slaughter among the buffalo. He's not a brave man, he lacks the bearing and the full look of the eye of a courageous man, but he carries two guns now, Morgan, and he can sling out and shoot a man with incredible speed. And we've got him quartered on us for nearly two years unless somebody from Glendora comes over and nails him. We can't fire him, we don't dare to approach him to suggest his abdication. Morgan, we're in a three-cornered hell of a fix!"

"Can't the fellow be prosecuted for some of these murders? Isn't there some way the law can reach him?"

"The coroner's jury absolves him regularly," the judge replied wearily. "At first they did it because it was the routine, and now they do it to save their hides. No, there's just one quick and sure way of heading that devil off in his red trail that I can see, Morgan, and that's for me to act while he's away. He's gone on some high-flyin' expedition to Abilene, leaving the town without a peace officer at the mercy of bandits and thieves. I have the authority to swear in a deputy marshal, or a hundred of them."

Morgan looked up again quickly from his speculative study of the boards in Judge Thayer's floor, to meet the elder man's shrewd eyes with a look of complete understanding. So they sat a moment, each reading the other as easily as one counts pebbles at the bottom of a clear spring.

"I don't believe I'm the man you're looking for," Morgan said.

"You're the only man that can do it, Morgan. It looks to me like you're appointed by Providence to step in here and save this town from this reign of murder."

"Oh!" said Morgan, impatiently, discounting the judge's fervid words.

"You can supplant him, you can strip him of his badge of office when he steps from the train, and you're the one man that can do it!"

Morgan shook his head, whether in denial of his attributed valor and prowess, or in declination to assume the proffered honor, Judge Thayer could not tell.

"I believe you'd do it without ever throwing a gun down on him," Judge Thayer declared.

"I know he could!" said a clear, hearty, confident voice from the door.

"Come in and help me convince him, Rhetta," Judge Thayer said, his gray-flecked beard twinkling with the pleasure that beamed from his eyes. "Mr. Morgan, my daughter. You have met before."

Morgan rose in considerable confusion, feeling more like an abashed and clumsy cowboy than he ever had felt before in his life. He stood with his battered hat held flat against his body at his belt, turning the old thing foolishly like a wheel, so unexpectedly confronted by this girl again, before whom he desired to appear as a man, and the best that was in the best man that he could ever be. And she stood smiling before him, mischief and mastery in her laughing eyes, confident as one who had subjugated him already, playing a tune on him, surely--a tune that came like a little voice out of his heart.

"I didn't know, I didn't suspect," he said.

"Of course not. She isn't anything like me." Judge Thayer laughed over it, mightily pleased by this evidence of confusion in a man who could heat his branding iron to set his mark on half a dozen desperadoes, yet turned to dough before the eyes of a simple maid.

"No more than a bird is like a bear," said Morgan, thinking aloud, racing mentally the next moment to snatch back his words and shape them in more conventional phrase. But too late; their joint laughter drowned his attempt to set it right, and the world lost a compliment that might have graced a courtier's tongue, perhaps. But, not likely.

Morgan proffered the chair he had occupied, but Rhetta knew of one in reserve behind the display of wheat and oats in sheaf on the table. This she brought, seating herself near the door, making a triangle from which Morgan had no escape save through the roof.

Judge Thayer resumed the discussion of the most vital matter in Ascalon that hour, pressing Morgan to take the oath of office then and there.

"I wouldn't ask Mr. Morgan to take the office," said Rhetta when Judge Thayer paused, "if I felt safe to stay in Ascalon another day with anybody else as marshal."

"That's a compelling reason for a man to take a job," Morgan told her, looking for a daring moment into the cool clarity of her honest brown eyes. "But I might make it worse instead of better. Trouble came to this town with me; it seems to stick to my heels like a dog."

"You got rid of most of it this morning--that gang will never come back," she said.

Morgan looked out of the open door, a thoughtfulness in his eyes that the nearer attraction could not for the moment dispel. "One of them will," he replied.

"Oh, one!" said she, discounting that one to nothing at all.

"The gamblers and saloon men are right about it," Morgan said, turning to the judge; "this town will dry up and blow away as soon as it loses its notorious name. If you want to kill Ascalon, enforce the law. The question is, how many people here want it done?"

"The respectable majority, I can assure you on that."

"Nearly everybody you talk to say they'd rather have Ascalon a whistling station on the railroad, where you could go to sleep in peace and get up feeling safe, than the awful place it is now," Rhetta said. She removed her sombrero as she spoke, and dropped it on the floor at her feet, as though weary of the turmoil that vexed her days.

Morgan noted for the first time that she was not dressed for the saddle today as on the occasion of their first meeting, but garbed in becoming simplicity in serge skirt and brown linen waist, a little golden bar with garnets at her throat. Her redundant dark hair, soft in its dusky shade as summer shadows in a deep wood, was coiled in a twisted heap to fit the crown of her mannish sombrero. It came down lightly over the tips of her ears in pretty disorder, due to the excitement of the morning, and she was fair as a camelia blossom and fresh as an evening primrose of her native prairie land.

"I wouldn't like to be the man that killed Ascalon, after all its highly painted past," Morgan said, trying to turn it off lightly. "It might be better for all the respectable people to go away and leave it wholly wicked, according to its fame."

"That might work to the satisfaction of all concerned, Mr. Morgan, if we had wagons and tents, and nothing more," said the judge. "We could very well pick up and pull out in that case. But a lot of us have staked all we own on the future of this town and the country around it. We were here before Ascalon became a plague spot and a by-word in the mouths of men; we started it right, but it went wrong as soon as it was able to walk."

"It seems to have wandered around quite a bit since then," Morgan said, sparing them a grin.

"It's been a wayward child," Rhetta sighed. "We're ashamed of our responsibility for it now."

"It would mean ruination to most of us to pull out and leave it to these wolves," said the judge. "We couldn't think of that."

"Of course not, I was only making a poor joke when I talked of a retreat," Morgan said. "Things will begin to die down here in a year or two--I've seen towns like this before, they always calm down and take up business seriously in time, or blow away and vanish completely. That's what happens to most of them if they're let go their course--change and shift, range breaking up into farms, cowboys going on, take care of that."

"I don't think Ascalon will go out that way--not if we can keep the county seat," Judge Thayer said. "If you were to step into the breach while that killer's away and rub even one little white spot in the town----"

Morgan seemed to interpose in the manner of throwing out his hand, a gesture speaking of the fatuity and his unwillingness to set himself to the task.

"Not just temporarily, we don't mean just temporarily, Mr. Morgan, but for good," Rhetta urged. "I want to take over editing the paper and be of some use in the world, but I couldn't think of doing it with all this killing going on, and a lot of wild men shooting out windows and everything that way."

"No, of course you couldn't," Morgan agreed.

"The railroad immigration agent has been trying to locate a colony of Mennonites here," Judge Thayer said, "fifty families or more of them, but the notoriety of the town made the elders skittish. They were out here this spring, liked the country, saw its future with eyes that revealed like telescopes, and would have bought ten sections of land to begin with if it hadn't been for two or three killings while they were here."

"It was the same way with those people from Pennsylvania," said Rhetta.

"We had a crowd of Pennsylvania Dutch out here a week or two after the Mennonites," the judge enlarged, "smellin' around hot-foot on the trail as hounds, but this atmosphere of Ascalon and its bad influence on the country wouldn't be good for their young folks, they said. So they backed off. And that's the way it's gone, that's the way it will go. The blight of Ascalon falls over this country for fifty miles around, the finest country the Almighty ever scattered grass seed over.

"You saw the possibilities of it from a distance, Mr. Morgan; others have seen it. Wouldn't you be doing humanity a larger service, a more immediate and applicable service, by clearing away the pest spot, curing the repulsive infection that keeps them away from its benefits and rewards, than by plowing up eighty acres and putting in a crop of wheat? A man's got to trample down his bed-ground, as I've said already, Morgan, before he can spread his blankets sometimes. This is one of the places, this is one of the times."

Morgan thought it over, hands on his thighs, head bent a little, eyes on his boots, conscious that the girl was watching him anxiously, as one on trial at the bar watches a doubtful jury when counsel makes the last appeal.

"There's a lot of logic in what you say," Morgan admitted; "it ought to appeal to a man big enough, confident enough, to undertake and put the job through."

He looked up suddenly, answering directly Rhetta Thayer's anxious, expectant, appealing brown eyes. "For if he should fail, bungle it, and have to throw down his hand before he'd won the game, it would be Katy-bar-the-door for that man. He'd have to know how far the people of this town wanted him to go before starting, and there's only one boundary-- the limit of the law. If they want anything less than that a man had better keep hands off, for anything like a compromise between black and white would be a fizzle."

Rhetta nodded, her bosom quivering with the pounding of her expectant heart, her throat throbbing, her hands clenched as if she held on in desperate hope of rescue. Judge Thayer said no more. He sat watching

Morgan's face, knowing well when a word too many might change the verdict to his loss.

"The question is, how far do they want a man to go in the regeneration of Ascalon? How many are willing to put purity above profit for a while? Business would suffer; it would be as dead here as a grasshopper after a prairie fire while readjustment to new conditions shaped. It might be a year or two before healthy legitimate trade could take the place of this flashy life, and it might never rebound from the operation. A man would want the people who are calling for law and order here to be satisfied with the new conditions; he wouldn't want any whiners at the funeral."

"New people would come, new business would grow, as soon as the news got abroad that a different condition prevailed in this town," Judge Thayer said. "I can satisfy you in an hour that the business men want what they're demanding, and will be satisfied to take the risk of the result."

"I came out here to farm," Morgan said, unwilling to put down his plans for a questionable and dangerous service to a doubtful community.

"There'll not be much sod broken between now and late fall, from the present look of things," the judge said. "We've had the longest dry spell I've ever seen in this country--going on four weeks now without a drop of rain. It comes that way once every five or seven years, but that also happens back in Ohio and other places men consider especially favored," he hastened to conclude.

"I didn't intend to break sod," Morgan reflected, "a man couldn't sow wheat in raw sod. That's why I wanted to look at that claim down by the river."

"It will keep. Or you could buy it, and hire your crop put in while you're marshal here in town."

"And I could edit the paper. Between us we could save the county seat."

Rhetta spoke quite seriously, so seriously, indeed, that her father laughed.

"I had forgotten all about saving the county seat--I was considering only the soul of Ascalon," he said.

"If you refuse to let father swear you in, Mr. Morgan, Craddock will say you were afraid. I'd hate to have him do that," said Rhetta.

"He might," Morgan granted, and with subdued voice and thoughtful manner that gave them a fresh rebound of hope.

And at length they had their will, but not until Morgan had gone the round of the business men on the public square, gathering the assurance of great and small that they were weary of bloodshed and violence, notoriety and unrest; that they would let the bars down to him if he would undertake cleaning up the town, and abide by what might come of it without a growl.

When they returned to Judge Thayer's office Morgan took the oath to enforce the statutes of the state of Kansas and the ordinances of the city of Ascalon, Rhetta standing by with palpitating breast and glowing eyes, hands behind her like a little girl waiting her turn in a spelling class. When Morgan lowered his hand Rhetta started out of her expectant pose, producing with a show of triumph a short piece of broad white ribbon, with CITY MARSHAL stamped on it in tall black letters.

Judge Thayer laughed as Morgan backed away from her when she advanced to pin it on his breast.

"I set up the type and printed it myself on the proof press," she said, in pretty appeal to him to stand and be hitched to this sign of his new office.

"It's so--it's rather--prominent, isn't it?" he said, still edging away.

"There isn't any regular shiny badge for you, the great, grisly Mr. Craddock wore away the only one the town owns. Please, Mr. Morgan-- you'll have to wear something to show your authority, won't he, Pa?"

"It would be wiser to wear it till I can send for another badge, Morgan, or we can get the old one away from Seth. Your authority would be questioned without a badge, they're strong for badges in this town."

So Morgan stood like a family horse while Rhetta pinned the ribbon to the pocket of his dingy gray woolen shirt, where it flaunted its unmistakable proclamation in a manner much more effective than any police shield or star ever devised. Rhetta pressed it down hard with the palm of her hand to make the stiff ribbon assume a graceful hang, so hard that she must have felt the kick of the new officer's heart just under it. And she looked up into his eyes with a glad, confident smile.

"I feel safe now," she said, sighing as one who puts down a wearing burden at the end of a toilsome journey.

CHAPTER XIII

THE HAND OF THE LAW

The stars came out over a strange, silent, astonished, confounded, stupefied Ascalon that night. The wolf-howling of its revelry was stilled, the clamor of its obscene diversions was hushed. It was as if the sparkling tent of the heavens were a great bowl turned over the place, hushing its stridulous merriment, stifling its wild laughter and dry-throated feminine screams.

The windows of Peden's hall were dark, the black covers were drawn over the gambling tables, the great bar stood in the gloom without one priest of alcohol to administer the hilarious rites across its glistening altar boards.

As usual, even more than usual, the streets around the public square were lively with people, coming and passing through the beams of light from windows, smoking and talking and idling in groups, but there was no movement of festivity abroad in the night, no yelping of departing rangers. It was as if the town had died suddenly, so suddenly that all within it were struck dumb by the event.

For the new city marshal, the interloper as many held him to be, the tall, solemn, long-stepping stranger who carried a rifle always ready like a man looking for a coyote, had put the lock of his prohibition on everything within the town. Everything that counted, that is, in the valuation of the proscribed, and the victims who came like ephemera on the night wind to scorch and shrivel and be drained in their bright, illusive fires. The law long flouted, made a joke of, despised, had come to Ascalon and laid hold of its alluring institutions with stern and paralyzing might.

Early in the first hours of his authority the new city marshal, or deputy marshal, to be exact, had received from unimpeachable source, no less than a thick volume of the statutes, that the laws of the state of Kansas, which he had sworn to enforce, prohibited the sale of intoxicating liquors; prohibited gambling and games of chance; interdicted the operation of immoral resorts--put a lock and key in his hand, in short, that would shut up the ribald pleasures of Ascalon like a tomb. As for the ordinances of the city, which he also had obligated himself to apply, Morgan had not found time to work down to them. There appeared to be authority in the thick volume Judge Thayer had lent him to last Ascalon a long time. If he should find himself running short from that source, then the city ordinances could be drawn upon in their time and place.

Exclusive of the mighty Peden, the other traffickers in vice were inconsequential, mere retailers, hucksters, peddlers in their way. They were as vicious as unquenchable fire, certainly, and numerous, but small, and largely under the patronage of the king of the proscribed, Peden of the hundred-foot bar.

And this Peden was a big, broad-chested, muscular man, whose neck rose like a mortised beam out of his shoulders, straight with the back of his head. His face was handsome in a bold, shrewd mold, but dark as if his blood carried the taint of a baser race. He went about always dressed in a long frock coat, with no vest to obscure the spread of his white shirt front; low collar, with narrow black tie done in exact bow; broad-brimmed white sombrero tilted back from his forehead, a cigar that always seemed fresh under his great mustache.

This mustache, heavy, black, was the one sinister feature of the man's otherwise rather open and confidence-winning face. It was a cloud that more than half obscured the nature of the man, an ambush where his passions and dark subterfuges lay concealed.

Peden had met the order to close his doors with smiling loftiness, easy understanding of what he read it to mean. Astonished to find his offer of money silently and sternly ignored, Peden had grown contemptuously defiant. If it was a bid for him to raise the ante, Morgan was starting off on a lame leg, he said. Ten dollars a night was as much as the friendship of any man that ever wore the collar of the law was worth to him. Take it or leave it, and be cursed to him, with embellishments of profanity and debasement of language which were new and astonishing even to Morgan's sophisticated ears. Peden turned his back to the new officer after drenching him down with this deluge of abuse, setting his face about the business of the night.

And there self-confident defiance, fattened a long time on the belief that law was a thing to be sneered down, met inflexible resolution. The substitute city marshal had a gift of making a few words go a long way; Peden put out his lights and locked his doors. In the train of his darkness others were swallowed. Within two hours after nightfall the town was submerged in gloom.

Threats, maledictions, followed Morgan as he walked the round of the public square, rifle ready for instant use, pistol on his thigh. And the blessing of many a mother whose sons and daughters stood at the perilous crater of that infernal pit went out through the dark after him, also; and the prayers of honest folk that no skulking coward might shoot him down out of the shelter of the night.

Even as they cursed him behind his back, the outlawed sneered at Morgan and the new order that seemed to threaten the world-wide fame of Ascalon. It was only the brief oppression of transient authority, they said; wait till Seth Craddock came back and you would see this range wolf throw dust for the timber.

They spoke with great confidence and kindling pleasure of Seth's return, and the amusing show that would attend his resumption of authority. For it was understood that Seth would not come alone. Peden, it was said, had attended to that already by telegraph. Certain handy gunslingers would come with him from Kansas City and Abilene, friends of Peden who had made reputations and had no scruples about maintaining them.

As the night lengthened this feeling of security, of pleasurable anticipation, increased. This little break in its life would do the town good; things would whirl away with recharged energy when the doors were opened again. Money would simply accumulate in the period of stagnation to be thrown into the mill with greater abandon than before by the fools who stood around waiting for the show to resume.

And the spectacle of seeing Seth Craddock drive this simpleton clear over the edge of the earth would be a diversion that would compensate for many empty days. That alone would be a thing worth waiting for, they said.

Time began to walk in slack traces, the heavy wain of night at its slow heels, for the dealers and sharpers, mackerels and frail, spangled women to whom the open air was as strange as sunlight to an earthworm. They passed from malediction and muttered threat against the man who had brought this sudden change in their accustomed lives, to a state of indignant rebellion as they milled round the square and watched him tramp his unending beat.

A little way inside the line of hitching racks Morgan walked, away from the thronged sidewalk, in the clear where all could see him and a shot from some dark window would not imperil the life of another. Around and around the square he tramped in the dusty, hoof-cut street, keeping his own counsel, unspeaking and unspoken to, the living spirit of the mighty law.

It was a high-handed piece of business, the bleached men and kalsomined women declared, as they passed from the humor of contemplating Seth Craddock's return to fretful chafing against the restraint of the present hour. How did it come that one man could lord it over a whole town of free and independent Americans that way? Why didn't somebody take a shot at him? Why didn't they defy him, go and open the doors and let this thirsty, money-padded throng up to the gambling tables and bars?

They asked to be told what had become of the manhood of Ascalon, and asked it with contempt. What was the fame of the town based upon but a bluff when one man was able to shut it up as tight as a trunk, and strut around that way adding the insult of his tyrannical presence to the act of his oppressive hand. There were plenty of questions and suggestions, but nobody went beyond them.

The moon was in mid-heaven, untroubled by a veil of cloud; the day wind was resting under the edge of the world, asleep. Around and around the public square this sentinel of the new moral force that had laid its hand over Ascalon tramped the white road. Rangers from far cow camps, disappointed of their night's debauch, began to mount and ride away, turning in their saddles as they went for one more look at the lone sentry who was a regiment in himself, indeed.

The bleached men began to yawn, the medicated women to slip away. Good citizens who had watched in anxiety, fearful that this rash champion of the new order would find a bullet between his shoulders before midnight, began to breathe easier and seek their beds in a strange state of security. Ascalon was shut up; the howling of its wastrels was stilled. It was incredible, but true.

By midnight the last cowboy had gone galloping on his long ride to carry the news of Ascalon's eclipse over the desolate gray prairie; an hour later the only sign of life in the town was the greasy light of the Santa Fé café, where a few lingering nondescripts were supping on cove oyster stew. These came out at last, to stand a little while like stranded mariners on a lonesome beach watching for a rescuing sail, then parted and went clumping their various ways over the rattling board walks.

Morgan stopped at the pump in the square to refresh himself with a drink. A dog came and lapped out of the trough, stood a little while when its thirst was satisfied, turning its head listening, as though it missed something out of the night. It trotted off presently, in angling gait like a ferry boat making a crossing against an outrunning tide. It was the last living thing on the streets of the town but the weary city marshal, who stood with hat off at the pump to feel the cool wind that came across the sleeping prairie before the dawn.

At that same hour another watcher turned from her open window, where she had sat a long time straining into the silence that blessed the town. She had been clutching her heart in the dread of hearing a shot, full of upbraidings for the peril she had thrust upon this chivalrous man. For he would not have assumed the office but for her solicitation, she knew well. She stretched out her hand into the moonlight as if she wafted him her benediction for the peace he had brought, a great, glad surge of something more tender than gratitude in her warm young bosom.

In a little while she came to the window again, when the moonlight was slanting into it, and stood leaning her hands on the sill, her dark hair coming down in a cloud over her white night dress. She strained again into the quiet night, listening, and listening, smiled. Then she stood straight, touched finger tips to her lips and waved away a kiss into the moonlight and the little timid awakening wind that came out of the east like a young hare before the dawn.

CHAPTER XIV

SOME FOOL WITH A GUN

Morgan was roused out of his brief sleep at the Elkhorn hotel shortly after sunrise by the night telegrapher at the railroad station, who came with a telegram.

"I thought you'd like to have it as soon as possible," the operator said, in apology for his early intrusion, standing by Morgan's bed, Tom Conboy attending just outside the door with ear primed to pick up the smallest word.

"Sure--much obliged," Morgan returned, his voice hoarse with broken sleep, his head not instantly clear of its flying clouds. The operator lingered while Morgan ran his eye over the few words.

"Much obliged, old feller," Morgan said, warmly, giving the young man a quick look of understanding that must serve in place of more words, seeing that Conboy had his head within the door.

Morgan heard the operator denying Conboy the secret of the message in the hall outside his door. Conboy had lived long enough in Ascalon to know when to curb his curiosity. He tiptoed away from Morgan's door, repressing his desire behind his beard.

Knowing that he could not sleep again after that abrupt break in his rest, Morgan rose and dressed. Once or twice he referred again to the message that lay spread on his pillow.

Craddock wired Peden last night that he would arrive on number seven at 1:20 this afternoon.

That was the content of the message, not a telegram at all, but a friendly note of warning from the night operator, who had come over to the hotel to go to bed. The young man had shrewdly adopted this means to cover his information, knowing that Peden's wrath was mighty and his vengeance far-reaching. Nobody in town could question the delivery of a telegram.

Morgan had expected Craddock to hasten back and attempt to recover his scepter and resume his sway over Ascalon, where the destructive sickle of his passion for blood could be plied with safety under the shelter of his prostituted office. But he did not expect him to return so soon. It pleased him better that the issue was to be brought to a speedy trial between them. While he had his feet wet, he reasoned, he would just as well cross the stream.

Conboy was sweeping the office, having laid the thick of the dust with a sprinkling can. He paused in his work to give Morgan a shrewd, sharp look.

"Important news when it pulls a man out of bed this early," Conboy ventured, "and him needin' sleep like you do."

"Yes," said Morgan, going on to the door.

Conboy came after him, voice lowered almost to a whisper as he spoke, eyes turning about as if he expected a spy to bob up behind his counter.

"I heard it passed around late last night that Craddock was comin' back."

"Wasn't he expected to?" Morgan inquired, indifferently, wholly undisturbed.

Conboy watched him keenly, standing half behind him, to note any sign of panic or uneasiness that would tell him which side he should support with his valuable sympathy and profound philosophy.

"From the way things point, I think they're lookin' for him back today," he said.

"The quicker the sooner," Morgan replied in offhand cowboy way.

Conboy was left on middle ground, not certain whether Morgan would flee before the arrival of the man whose powers he had usurped, or stand his ground and shoot it out. It was an uncomfortable moment; a man must be on one side or the other to be safe. In the history of Ascalon it was the neutral who generally got knocked down and trampled, and lost his pocketbook and watch, as happens to the gaping nonparticipants in the squabbles of humanity everywhere.

"From what I hear goin' around," Conboy continued, dropping his voice to a cautious, confidential pitch, "there'll be a bunch of bad men along in a day or two to help Craddock hold things down. It looks to me like it's goin' to be more than any one man can handle."

"It may be that way," Morgan said, lingering in the door, Conboy doing his talking from the rear. Morgan was thinking the morning had a freshness in it like a newly gathered flower.

"It'll mean part closed and part open if that man takes hold of this town again," Conboy said. "Him and Peden they're as thick as three in a bed. Close all of 'em, like you did last night, or give everybody a fair whack. That's what I say."

"Yes," abstractedly from Morgan.

"It was kind of quiet and slow in town last night, slowest night I've ever had since I bought this dump. I guess I'd have to move away if things run along that way, but I don't know. Maybe business would pick up when people got used to the new deal. Goin' to let 'em open tonight?"

"Night's a long way off," Morgan said, leaving the question open for Conboy to make what he could out of it.

Conboy was of the number who could see no existence for Ascalon but a vicious one, yet he was no partisan of Seth Craddock, having a soreness in his recollection of many indignities suffered at the hands of the city marshal's Texas friends, even of Craddock's overriding and sardonic disdain. Yet he would rather have Craddock, and the town open, than Morgan and stagnation. He came to that conclusion with Morgan's evasion of his direct question. The interests of Peden and his kind were Conboy's interests. He stood like a housemaid with dustpan and broom to gather up the wreckage of the night.

"When can I get breakfast?" Morgan inquired, turning suddenly, catching Conboy with his new resolution in his shifty, flickering eyes, reading him to the marrow of his bones.

"It's a little early--not half-past five," Conboy returned, covering his confusion as well as he could by referring to his thick silver watch. "We don't begin to serve till six, the earliest of 'em don't come in before then. If you feel like turnin' in for a sleep, we'll take care of you when you get up."

Morgan said he had sleep enough to carry him over the day. Dora, yawning, disheveled, appeared in the dining-room door at that moment, tying her all-enveloping white apron around her like Poor Polly Bawn. She blushed when she saw Morgan, and put up her hands to smooth her hair.

"I had the best sleep last night I can remember in a coon's age--I felt so safe," she said.

"You always was safe enough," Conboy told her, not in the best of humor.

"Safe enough! I can show you five bullet holes in the walls of my room, Mr. Morgan--one of 'em through the head of my bed!"

"Pretty close," Morgan said, answering the animation of her rosy, friendly face with a smile.

"Never mind about bullet holes--you go and begin makin' holes in a piece of biscuit dough," her father commanded.

"When I get good and ready," said Dora, serenely. "You wouldn't care if we got shot to pieces every night as long as we could get up in the morning and make biscuits!"

"Yes, and some of you'd be rootin' around somebody else's kitchen for biscuits to fill your craws if this town laid dead a little while longer," Conboy fired back, his true feeling in the matter revealed.

"I can get a job of biscuit shooter any day," Dora told him, untroubled by the outlook of disaster that attended upon peace and quiet. "I'd rather not have no guests than drunks that come in stagger blind and shoot the plaster off of the wall. It ain't so funny to wake up with your ears full of lime! Ma's sick of it, and I'm sick of it, and it'd be a blessin' if Mr. Morgan would keep the joints all shut till the drunks in this town dried up like dead snakes!"

"You, and your ma!" Conboy grumbled, bearing on an old grievance, an old theme of servitude and discontent.

Morgan recalled the gaunt anxiety of Mrs. Conboy's eyes, hollow of every emotion, as they seemed, but unrest and straining fear. Dora had gone unmarked yet by the cursed fires of Ascalon; only her tongue discovered that the poison of their fumes had reached her heart.

"I'd like to put strickenine in some of their biscuits!" Dora declared, with passionate vehemence.

"Tut-tut! no niggers----"

"How's your face, Mr. Morgan?" Dora inquired, out of one mood into another so quickly the transition was bewildering.

"Face?" said Morgan, embarrassed for want of her meaning. "Oh," putting his hand to the forgotten wound--"about well, thank you, Miss Dora. I guess my good looks are ruined, though."

Dora half closed her eyes in arch expression, pursing her lips as if she meant to give him either a whistle or a kiss, laughed merrily, and ran off to cut patterns in a sheet of biscuit dough. She left such a clearness and good humor in the morning air that Morgan felt quite light at heart as he started for a morning walk.

Morgan was still wearing the cowboy garb that he had drawn from the bottom of his trunk among the things which he believed belonged to a past age and closed period of his life's story. He had deliberated the question well the night before, reaching the conclusion that, as he had stepped out of his proper character, lapsed back, in a word, to raw-handed dealings with the rough edges of the world, he would better dress the part. He would be less conspicuous in that dress, and it would be his introduction and credentials to the men of the range.

Last night's long vigil, tramping around the square in his high-heeled, tight-fitting boots, had not hastened the cure of his bruised ankles and sore feet. This morning he limped like a trapped wolf, as he said to himself when he started to take a look around and see whether any of the outlawed had made bold to open their doors.

Few people were out of bed in Ascalon at that hour, although the sun was almost an hour high. As Morgan passed along he heard the crackling of kindling being broken in kitchens. Here and there the eager smoke of fresh fires rose straight toward the blue. No stores were open yet; the doors of the saloons remained closed as the night before. Morgan paused at the bank corner after making the round of the square.

Ahead of him the principal residence street of the town stretched, the houses standing in exclusive withdrawal far apart on large plots of ground, a treeless, dusty, unlovely lane. Here the summer sun raked roof and window with its untempered fire; here the winds of winter bombarded door and pane with shrapnel of sleet and charge of snow, whistling on cornice and eaves, fluttering in chimney like the beat of exhausted wings.

Morgan knew well enough how the place would appear in that bitter season; he had lived in the lonely desolation of a village on the bald, unsheltered plain. How did Rhetta Thayer endure the winter, he wondered, when she could not gallop away into the friendly solitude of the clean, unpeopled prairie? Where did she live? Which house would be Judge Thayer's among the bright-painted dwellings along that raw lane? He favored one of the few white ones, a house with a wide porch screened by morning-glory vines, a gallant row of hollyhocks in the distance.

Lawn grass had been sown in many of the yards, where it had flourished until the scorching summer drouth. Even now there were little rugs of green against north walls where the noonday shadows fell, but the rest of the lawns were withered and brown. Some hardy flowers, such as zinnias and marigolds, stood clumped about dooryards; in the kitchen gardens tasseled corn rose tall, dust thick on the guttered blades.

Morgan turned from this scene in which Ascalon presented its better side, to skirmish along the street running behind Peden's establishment. It might be well, for future exigencies, to fix as much of the geography of the place in his mind as possible. He wondered if there had been a back-door traffic in any of the saloons last night as he passed long strings of empty beer kegs, concluding that it was very likely something had been done in that way.

Across the street from Peden's back door was a large vacant piece of ground, a wilderness of cans, bottles, packing boxes, broken barrels. On one corner, diagonally across from where Morgan stood, facing on the other street, a ragged, weathered tent was pitched. Out of this the sound of contending children came, the strident, commanding voice of a woman breaking sharply to still the commotion that shook her unstable home. Morgan knew this must be the home of the cattle thief whose case Judge Thayer had undertaken. He wondered why even a cattle thief would choose that site at the back door of perdition to pitch his tent and lodge his family.

A bullet clipping close past his ear, the sharp sound of a pistol shot behind him, startled him out of this speculation.

Morgan did not believe at once, even as he wheeled gun in hand to confront the careless gun-handler or the assassin, as the case might prove, that the shot could have been intended for him, but out of caution he darted as quick as an Indian behind a pyramid of beer kegs. From that shelter he explored in the direction of the shot, but saw nobody.

There was ample barrier for a lurking man all along the street on Peden's side. From behind beer cases and kegs, whisky barrels, wagons, corners of small houses, one could have taken a shot at him; or from a window or back door. There was no smoke hanging to mark the spot.

Morgan slipped softly from his concealment, coming out at Peden's back door. Bending low, he hurried back over the track he had come, keeping the heaps of kegs, barrels, and boxes between him and the road. And there, twenty yards or so distant, in a space between two wagons, he saw a man standing, pistol in hand, all set and primed for another shot, but looking rather puzzled and uncertain over the sudden disappearance of his mark.

Morgan was upon him in a few silent strides, unseen and unheard, his gun raised to throw a quick shot if the situation called for it. The man was Dell Hutton, the county treasurer. His face was white. There was the look in his eyes of a man condemned when he turned and confronted Morgan.

"Who was it that shot at you, Morgan?" he inquired, his voice husky in the fog of his fright. He was laboring hard to put a face on it that would make him the champion of peace; he peered around with simulated caution, as if he had rushed to the spot ready to uphold the law.

Morgan let the pitiful effort pass for what it was worth, and that was very little.

"I don't know who it was, Hutton," he replied, with a careless laugh, putting his pistol away. "If you see him, tell him I let a little thing like that pass--once."

Morgan did not linger for any further words. Several shock-haired children had come bursting from the tent, their contention silenced. They stood looking at Morgan as he came back into the road, wonder in their muggy faces. Heads appeared at windows, back doors opened cautiously, showing eyes at cracks.

"Some fool shootin' off his gun," Morgan heard a man growl as he passed under a window of a thin-sided house, from which the excited voices of women came like the squeaks of unnested mice.

"What was goin' on back there?" Conboy inquired as Morgan approached the hotel. The proprietor was a little way out from his door, anxiety, rather than interest, in his face.

"Some fool shootin' off his gun, I guess," Morgan replied, feeling that the answer fitted the case very well.

He gave Dora the same explanation when she met him at the blue door of the dining-room, trouble in her fair blue eyes. She looked at him with keen questioning, not satisfied that she had heard it all.

"I hope he burnt his fingers," she said.

CHAPTER XV

WILL HIS LUCK HOLD?

Dora escorted Morgan to a table apart from the few heavy feeders who were already engaged, indicating to the other two girls who served with her in the dining-room that this was her special customer and guest of honor. She whirled the merry-go-round caster to bring the salt and pepper to his hand; just so she placed his knife and fork, and plate overturned to keep the flies off the business side of it. Then she hurried away for his breakfast, asking no questions bearing on his preferences or desires.

A plain breakfast in those vigorous times was unvarying--beefsteak, ham or bacon to give it a savor, eggs, fried potatoes, hot biscuits, coffee. It was the same as dinner, which came on the stroke of twelve, and none of your six-o'clock pretenses about that meal, except there was no pie; identical with supper, save for the boiled potatoes and rice pudding. A man of proper proportions never wanted any more; he could not thrive on any less. And the only kind of a liver they ever worried about in that time on the plains of Kansas was a white one. That was the only disease of that organ known.

Dora was troubled; her face reflected her unrest as glass reflects firelight, her blue eyes were clouded by its gloom. She made a pretense of brushing crumbs from the cloth where there were no crumbs, in order to furnish an excuse to stoop and bring her lips nearer Morgan's ear.

"He's comin' on the one-twenty this afternoon--I got it straight he's comin'. I thought maybe you'd like to know," she said.

Morgan lifted his eyes in feigned surprise at this news, not having it in his heart to cloud her generous act by the revelation of a suspicion that it was no news to him.

"You mean----?"

"I got it straight," Dora nodded.

"Thank you, Miss Dora."

"I hope to God," she said, for it was their manner to speak ardently in Ascalon in those days, "you'll beat him to it when he gets off of the train!"

"A man can only do his best, Dora," he said gently, moved by her honest friendship, simple wild thing though she was.

"If I was a man I'd take my gun and go with you to meet him," she declared.

"I know you would. But maybe there'll not be any fuss at all."

"There'll be fuss enough, all right!" Dora protested. "If he comes alone--

but maybe he'll not come alone."

A man who rose from a near-by table came over to shake hands with Morgan, and express his appreciation for the good beginning he had made as peace officer of the town. Dora snatched Morgan's cup and hastened away for more coffee. When she returned the citizen was on his way to the door.

"Craddock used to come in here and wolf his meals down," she said, picking up her theme in the same troubled key, "just like it didn't amount to nothing to kill a man a day. I looked to see blood on the tablecloth every time his hand touched it."

"It's a shame you girls had to wait on the brute," Morgan said.

"Girls! he wouldn't let anybody but me wait on him." Dora frowned, her face coloring. She bent a little, lowering her voice. "Why, Mr. Morgan, what do you suppose? He wanted me to marry him!"

"That old buffalo wrangler? Well, he is kind of previous!"

"He's too fresh to keep, I told him. Marry him! He used to come in here, Mr. Morgan, and put his hat down by his foot so he could grab it and run out and kill another man without losin' time. He never used to take his guns off and hang 'em up like other gentlemen when they eat. He just set there watchin' and turnin' his mean old eyes all the time. He's afraid of them, I know by the way he always tried to look behind him without turnin' his head, never sayin' a word to anybody, he's afraid."

"Afraid of whom, Dora?"

"The ghosts of them murdered men!"

Morgan shook his head after seeming to think it over a little while. "I don't believe they'd trouble him much, Dora."

"I'd rather wait on a dog!" she said, scorn and rebellion in her pretty eyes.

"You can marry somebody else and beat him on that game, anyhow. I'll bet there are plenty of them standing around waiting."

"O Mr. Morgan!" Dora was drowned in blushes, greatly pleased. "Not so many as you might think," turning her eyes upon him with coquettish challenge, "only Mr. Gray and Riley Caldwell, the printer on the Headlight."

"Mr. Gray, the druggist?"

"Yes, but he's too old for me!" Dora sighed, "forty if he's a day. He's got money, though, and he's perfec'ly grand on the pieanno. You ought to hear him play The Maiden's Prayer!"

"I'll listen out for him. I saw him washing his window a while ago--a tall man with a big white shirt."

"Yes," abstractedly, "that was him. He's an elegant fine man, but I don't give a snap for none of 'em. I wish I could leave this town and never come back. You'll be in for dinner, won't you?" as Morgan pushed back from the repletion of that standard meal.

"And for supper, too, I hope," he said, turning it off as a joke.

"I hope to God!" said Dora fervently, seeing no joke in the uncertainty at all.

Excitement was laying hold of Ascalon even at that early hour. When Morgan went on the street after breakfast he found many people going about, gathering in groups along the shady fronts, or hastening singly in the manner of men bound upon the confirmation of unusual news. The pale fish of the night were out in considerable numbers, leaking cigarette smoke through all the apertures of their faces as they grouped according to their kind to discuss the probabilities of the day. Seth Craddock was coming back with fire in his red eyes; their deliverer was on his way.

There was no secret of Seth's coming any longer. Even Peden leered in triumph when he met Morgan as he sauntered outside his closed door in the peculiar distinction of his black coat, which the strong sun of that summer morning was not powerful enough to strip from his broad back.

None of the saloons or resorts made an attempt to open their doors to business. The proprietors appeared to have, on the other hand, a secret pleasure in keeping them closed, perhaps counting on the gain that would be theirs when this brief prohibition should come to its end.

Opposed to this pleasurable expectancy of the proscribed was the uneasiness and doubt of the respectable. True, this man Morgan had taken Seth Craddock's gun away from him once, but luck must have had much to do with his preservation in that perilous adventure. Morgan had rounded up the Texas men quartered on the town under Craddock's patronage, also, but they were sluggish from their debauch, and he had approached them with the caution of a man coming up on the blind side of a horse. Yesterday that had looked like a big, heroic thing for one man to accomplish, but in the light of reflection today it must be admitted that it was mainly luck.

Yes, Morgan had closed up the town last night, defying even Peden in his own hall, where defiance as a rule meant business for the undertaker. But the glamour of his morning's success was still over him at that time; Peden and his bouncers were a little cautious, a little cowed. He could not close the town up another night; murmurs of defiance were beginning to rise already.

And so the people who had applauded his drastic enforcement of the law last night, became of no more support to Morgan today than a furrow of sand. Luck was a great thing if a man could play it forever, they said, but it was too much to believe that luck would hold even twice with Morgan when he confronted Seth Craddock that afternoon.

Morgan walked about the square that morning like a stranger. Few spoke to him, many turned inward from their doors when they saw him coming, afraid that a little friendship publicly displayed might be laid up against them for a terrible reckoning of interest by and by. Morgan was neither offended nor downcast by this public coldness in the quarter where he had a right to expect commendation and support. He understood too well the lengths that animosities ran in such a town as Ascalon. A living coward was more comfortable than a dead reformer, according to their philosophy.

It was when passing the post-office, about nine o'clock in the morning, that Morgan met Rhetta Thayer. She saw him coming, and waited. Her face was flushed; indignation disturbed the placidity of her eyes.

"They don't deserve it, the cowards!" she burst out, after a greeting too serious to admit a smile.

"Deserve what?" he inquired, looking about in mystification, wondering if something had happened in the post-office to fire this indignation.

"The help and protection of a brave man!" she said.

Morgan was so suddenly confused by this frank, impetuous appreciation of his efforts, for there was no mistaking the application, that he could not find a word. Rhetta did not give him much time, to be sure, but ran on with her denunciation of the citizenry of the town.

"I wouldn't turn a hand for them again, Mr. Morgan--I'd throw up the whole thing and let them cringe like dogs before that murderer when he comes back! It's good enough for them, it's all they deserve."

"You can't expect them to be very warm toward a stranger," he said, excusing them according to what he knew to be their due.

"They're afraid you can't do it, they're telling one another your luck will fail this time. Luck! that's all the sense there is in that bunch of cowards."

"They may be right," he said, thoughtfully.

"You know they're not right!" she flashed back, defending him against himself as though he were another.

"I don't expect any generosity from them," he said, gentle in his tone and undisturbed. "They're afraid if my luck should happen to turn against me they'd have to pay for any friendship shown me here this morning. Business is business, even in Ascalon."

"Luck!" she scoffed. "It's funny you're the only lucky man that's struck this town in a long time, then. If it's all luck, why don't some of them try their hands at rounding up the crooks and killers of this town and showing them the road the way you did that gang yesterday? Yes, I know all about that kind of luck."

Morgan walked with her toward Judge Thayer's office, whither she was bound with the mail. Behind them the loafers snickered and passed quips of doubtful humor and undoubted obscenity, but careful to present the face of decorum until Morgan was well beyond their voices. No matter what doubt they had of his luck holding with Seth Craddock, they were not of a mind to make a trial of it on themselves.

"I think the best thing to do with this town is just let it go till it dries up and blows away," she said, with the vindictive impatience of youth. "What little good there is in it isn't worth the trouble of cleaning up to save."

"Your father's got everything centered here, he told me. There must be a good many honest people in the same boat."

"Maybe we could sell out for something, enough to take us away from here. Of course we expected Ascalon to turn out a different town when we came here, the railroad promised to do so much. But there's nothing to make a town when the cattle are gone. We might as well let it begin to die right now."

"You're gloomy this morning, Miss Thayer. You remember the Mennonites that wanted to settle here and were afraid?"

"There's no use for you to throw your life away making the country safe for them."

"Of course not. I hadn't thought of them."

"Nor any of these cold-nosed cowards that turn their backs on you for fear your luck's going to change. Luck! the fools!"

"They don't figure in the case at all, Miss Thayer."

"If it's on account of your own future, if you're trampling down a place in the briars to make your bed, as pa called it, then I think you can find a nicer place to camp than Ascalon. It never will repay the peril you'll run and the blood you'll lose--have lost already."

"I'm further out of the calculation than anybody, Miss Thayer."

"I don't see what other motive there can be, then," she reflected, eyes bent to the ground as she walked slowly by his side.

"A lady asked me to undertake it. I'm doing it for her," he replied.

"She was a thoughtless, selfish person!" Rhetta said, her deep feeling stressed in the flush of her face, her accusation as vehement as if she laid charges against another. "Last night she thought it over; she had time to realize the danger she'd asked a generous stranger to assume. She wants to withdraw the request today--she asks you to give it up and let Ascalon go on its wicked way."

"Tell her," said he gently, holding her pleading, pained eyes a moment with his assuring gaze, "that a man can't drop a piece of work like this and turn his back on it and walk away. They'd say in Ascalon that he was a coward, and they'd be telling the truth."

"Oh! I oughtn't have argued you into it!" she regretted, bitter in her self-blame. "But the thought of that terrible, cruel man, of all he's killed, all he will kill if he comes back--made a selfish coward of me. We had gone through a week of terror--you can't understand a woman's terror of that kind of men, storming the streets at night uncurbed!"

"A man can only guess."

"I was so grateful to you for driving them away from here, for purifying the air after them like a rain, that I urged you to go ahead and finish the job, just as if we were conferring a great favor! I didn't think at the time, but I've thought it all over since."

"You mustn't worry about it any more. It is a great favor, a great honor, to be asked to serve you at all."

"You're too generous, Mr. Morgan. There are only a few of us here who care about order and peace--you can see that for yourself this morning--no matter what assurance they gave you yesterday. Let it go. If you don't want to get your horse and ride away, you can at least resign. You've got justification enough for that, you've seen the men that promised to support you yesterday turn their backs on you when you came up the street today. They don't want the town shut up, they don't want it changed--not when it hits their pocketbooks. You can tell pa that, and resign--or I'll tell him--it was my fault, I got you into it."

"You couldn't expect me to do that--you don't expect it," he chided, his voice grave and low.

"I can want you to do it--I don't expect it."

"Of course not. We'll not talk about it any more."

They continued toward her father's office in silence, crossing the stretch of barren in which the little catalpa tree stood. Rhetta looked up into his face.

"You've never killed a man, Mr. Morgan," she said, more as a positive statement than as a question.

"No, I never have, Miss Thayer," Morgan answered her, as ingenuously sincere as she had asked it.

"I think I know it by the touch of a man's hand," she said, her face growing pale from her deep revulsion. "I shudder at the touch of blood. If you could be spared that in the ordeal ahead of you!"

"There's no backing out of it. The challenge has passed," he said.

"No, there's no way. He's coming--he knows you're waiting for him. But I hope you'll not have to--I hope you'll come out of it clean! A curse of blood falls on every man that takes this office. I wish--I hope, you can keep clear of that."

CHAPTER XVI

THE MEAT HUNTER COMES

The few courageous and hopeful ones who remained loyal to Morgan were somewhat assured, the doubtful ones agitated a bit more in their indecision, when he appeared on horseback a little past the turn of day. These latter people, whose courage had leaked out overnight, now began to weigh again their business interests and personal safety in the balance of their wavering judgment.

Morgan, on horseback, looked like a lucky man; they admitted that. Much more lucky, indeed, than he had appeared that morning when he went limping around the square. It was a question whether to come over to his side again, openly and warmly, or to hold back until he proved himself to be as lucky as he looked. A man might as well nail up his door and leave town as fall under the disfavor of Seth Craddock. So, while they wavered, they were still not quite convinced.

Prominent among the business men who had revised their attitude on reform as the shadow of Seth Craddock approached Ascalon was Earl Gray, the druggist, one of the notables on Dora Conboy's waiting list. Druggist Gray was a man who wore bell-bottomed trousers and a moleskin vest without a coat. His hair had a fetching crinkle to it, which he prized above all things in bottles and out, and wore long, like the man on the label.

There was so much hair about Mr. Gray, counting mustache and all, that his face and body seemed drained and attenuated by the contribution of sustenance to keep the adornment flourishing in its brown abundance.

For Gray was a tall, thin, bony-kneed man, with long flat feet like wedges of cheese. His eyes were hollow and melancholy, as if he bore a sorrow; his nose was high and bony, and bleak in his sharp, thin-cheeked face.

Gray expressed himself openly to the undertaker, in whom he found a cautious, but warm supporter of his views. There would be fevers and ills with Ascalon closed up, Gray said he knew very well, just as there would be deaths and burials in the natural course of events under the same conditions. But there would be neither patches for the broken, stitches for the cut nor powders for the headaches of debauchery called for then as now; and all the burying there would be an undertaker might do under his thumb nail.

They'd go to drugging themselves with boneset tea, and mullein tea, and bitter-root powders and wahoo bark, said Gray. Likewise, they'd turn to burying one another, after the ways of pioneers, who were as resourceful in deaths and funerals as in drugs and fomentations. Pioneers, such as would be left in that country after Morgan had shut Ascalon up and driven away those who were dependent on one another for their skinning and fleecing, filching and plundering, did not lean on any man. Such as came there to plow up the prairies would be of the same stuff, rough-barked men and women who called in neither doctor to be born nor undertaker to be buried.

It was a gloomy outlook, the town closed up and everybody gone, said Gray. What would a man do with his building, what would a man do with his stock?

"Maybe Craddock ain't no saint and angel, but he makes business in this town," said Gray.

"Makes business!" the undertaker echoed, with abstraction and looking far away as if he already saw the train of oncoming, independent, self-burying pioneers over against the horizon.

"If this feller's luck don't go ag'in' him, you might as well ship all your coffins away but one--they'll need one to bury the town in. What do you think of him ridin' around the depot down there, drawin' a deadline that no man ain't goin' to be allowed to cross till the one-twenty pulls out? Kind of high-handed deal, I call it!"

"I've got a case of shrouds comin' in by express on that train, two cases layin' in my place waitin' on 'em," the undertaker said, resentfully, waking out of his abstraction and apparent apathy.

"You have!" said Gray, eying him suddenly.

"He stopped me as I was goin' over to wait around till the train come in, drove me back like I was a cow. He said it didn't make no difference how much business I had at the depot, it would have to wait till the train was gone. When a citizen and a taxpayer of this town can't even cross the road like a shanghai rooster, things is comin' to a hell of a pass!"

"Well, I ain't got no business at the depot this afternoon, or I bet you a cracker I'd be over there," Gray boasted. "I think I'll close up a while and go down to the hotel where I can see better--it's only forty minutes till she's due."

"Might as well, everybody's down there. You won't sell as much as a pack of gum till the train's gone and this thing's off of people's minds."

Gray went in for his hat, to spend a good deal of time at the glass behind his prescription case setting it at the most seductive slant upon his luxuriant brown curls. This was an extremely enticing small hat, just a shade lighter brown than the druggist's wavy hair. It looked like a cork in a bottle placed by a tipsy hand as Druggist Gray passed down the street toward the hotel, to post himself where he might see how well Morgan's luck was going to hold in this encounter with the meat hunter of the Cimarron.

As the undertaker had said, nearly everybody in Ascalon was already collected in front and in the near vicinity of the hotel, fringing the square in gay-splotched crowds. Beneath the canopy of the Elkhorn hotel many were assembled, as many indeed, as could conveniently stand, for that bit of shade was a blessing on the sun-parched front of Ascalon's bleak street.

Business was generally suspended in this hour of uncertainty, public feeling was drawn as tight as a banjo head in the sun. In the courthouse the few officials and clerks necessary to the county's business were at the windows looking upon the station, all expecting a tragedy of such stirring dimensions as Ascalon never had witnessed.

The stage was set, the audience was in waiting, one of the principal actors stood visible in the wings. With the rush of the passenger train from the east Seth Craddock would make his dramatic entry, in true color with his violent notoriety and prominence in the cast.

Unless friends came with Craddock, these two men would hold the stage for the enactment of that swift drama alone. Morgan, silent, determined, inflexible, had drawn his line around the depot, across which no man dared to pass. No friend of Craddock should meet him for support of warning word or armed hand; no innocent one should be jeopardized by a curiosity that might lead to death.

The moving question now was, had Peden's gun-notable friends joined Craddock? If so, it would call for a vast amount of luck to overcome their combined numbers and dexterity.

Morgan was troubled by this same question as he waited in the saddle where the sun bore hot upon him at the side of the station platform. About there, at that point, the station agent had told him, the smoking-car would stand when the train came to a stop, the engine at the water tank. When Craddock came down out of the train, would he come alone?

Morgan was mounted on the horse borrowed from Stilwell, an agile young animal, tractable and intelligent. A yellow slicker was rolled and tied at the cantle of the saddle; at the horn a coil of brown rope hung, pliant and smooth from much use upon the range among cattle. Morgan's rifle was slung on the saddle in its worn scabbard, its battered stock, from which the varnish had gone long ago in the hard usage of many years, close to the rider's hand.

It needed no announcement of wailing whistle or clanging bell to tell Ascalon of the approach of a train from the east. In that direction the fall of the land toward the Arkansas River began many miles distant from the town, seeming to blend downward from a great height which dimmed out in blue haze against the horizon. A little way along this high pitch of land, before it turned down the grade that led into the river valley, the railroad ran transversely.

The moment a train mounted this land's edge and swept along the straight transverse section of track, it was in full sight of Ascalon, day or night, except in stormy weather, although many miles away. A man still had ample time to shine his shoes, pack his valise, put on his collar and coat--if he wore them--walk to the depot and buy his ticket, after the train came in sight on top of this distant hill.

Once the train headed straight for Ascalon it dropped out of sight, and one unused to the trend of things might wonder if it had gone off on another line. Presently it would appear again, laboring up out of a dip, rise the intervening billow of land, small as a toy that one could hold in the hand, and sink out of sight again. This way it approached Ascalon, now promising, now denying, drawing into plainer sight with every rise.

On this particular afternoon when the sun-baked people of Ascalon stood waiting in such tensity of expectation that their minds were ready to crack like the dry, contracting earth beneath their feet, it seemed that nature had laid off that land across which the railroad ran with the sole view of adding to the dramatic value of Seth Craddock's entry in this historic hour. Certainly art could not have devised a more effective means of whetting the anxiety, straining the suspense, than this.

When the train first came in sight over the hill there was a murmur, a movement of feet as people shifted to points believed to be more advantageous for seeing the coming drama; watches clicked, comments passed on the exactness to the schedule; breaths were drawn with fresh tingling of hope, or falling of doubt and despair.

Morgan was watching that far skyline for the first smoke, for the first gleam of windows in the sun as the train swept round the curve heading for a little while into the north. He noted the murmur and movement of the watchers as it came in sight; wondered if any breast but one was agitated by a pang of friendly concern, wondered if any hand loosed weapon in its sheath to strike in his support if necessity should call for such intervention. He knew that Rhetta Thayer stood in the shade of the bank with her father and others; he was cheered by the support of her presence to witness his triumph or fall.

Now, as the train swept into the first obscuring swale, Morgan rode around the depot again to see that none had slipped through either in malice or curiosity. Only the station agent was in sight, pulling a truck with three trunks on it to the spot where he estimated the baggage-car would stop. Morgan rode back again to take his stand at the point where arrivals by train crossed from depot into town. His left hand was toward the waiting crowd, kept back by his injunction fifty yards or more from the station; his right toward the track on which the train would come.

Conversation in the crowd fell away. Peden, garbed in his long coat, was seen shouldering through in front of the hotel, the nearest point to the set and waiting stage. As always, Peden wore a pistol strapped about him on ornate belt, the holster carrying the weapon under the skirt of his coat. His presence on the forward fringe of the crowd seemed to many as an upraised hand to strike the waiting horseman in the back.

Morgan saw Peden when he came and took his stand there, and saw others in his employ stationed along the front of the line. He believed they were there to throw their weight on Craddock's beam of the balance the moment they should see him outmastered and outweighed.

Because he mistrusted these men, because he did not know, indeed, whether there was a man among all those who had pledged their moral support who would lift a hand to aid him even if summoned to do so, Morgan kept his attention divided, one eye on the signs and portents of the crowd, one on keeping the depot platform clear.

Morgan did not know whether even Judge Thayer and the men who had guarded the bank with him would risk one shot in his defense if the outlawed forces should sweep forward and overwhelm him. He doubted it very much. It was well enough to delegate this business to a stranger, one impartial between the lines, but they could not be expected to turn their weapons on their fellow-townsmen and depositors in the bank, no matter how their money came, no matter how much the law might lack an upholding hand.

The train came clattering over the switch, safety valve roaring, bell ringing as gaily as if arriving in Ascalon were a joyous event in its day. Conductor and brakeman stood on the steps ready to swing to the platform; the express messenger lolled with bored weariness in the door of his car, scorning the dangerous notoriety of the town by exposing to the eye all the boxed treasure that it contained. Passengers crowded platforms, leaning and looking, ready to alight for a minute, so they might be able to relate the remainder of their lives how they braved the perils of Ascalon one time and came out unsinged.

A movement went over the watching people of the town, assembled along its business front, as wind ripples suddenly a field of grain. Nobody had breath for a word; dry lips were pressed tightly in the varying emotions of hope, fear, expectancy, desire. Morgan was seen to be busy for a moment with something about his saddle; it was thought he was drawing his rifle out of its case.

Nearly opposite where Morgan waited, the first coach of the train stopped. Instantly, like children freed from school, the eager passengers poured off for their adventurous breath of this most wicked town's intoxicating air. Morgan's whole attention was now fixed on the movement around the train. He shifted his horse to face that way, risking what might develop behind him, one hand engaged with the bridle rein, the other seemingly dropped carelessly on his thigh.

And in that squaring of expectation, that pause of breathless waiting, Seth Craddock descended from the smoking-car, his alpaca coat carried in the crook of his left elbow, his right hand lingering a moment on the guard of the car step. The hasty ones who had waited on the car platform were down ahead of him, standing a little way from the steps; others who wanted to get off came pressing behind him, in their ignorance that they were handling a bit of Ascalon's most infernal furnishing, pushing him out into the timid crowd of their fellows.

A moment Craddock stood, taller than the tallest there, sweeping his quick glance about for signs of the expected hostility, the trinkets of silver on the band of his costly new sombrero shining in the sun. Then he came striding among the gaping passengers, like a man stalking among tall weeds, something unmistakably expressive of disdain in his carriage.

There he paused again, and put on his coat, plainly mystified and troubled by the absence of townspeople from the depot, and the sight of them lined up across the square as if they waited a circus parade. All that he saw between himself and that fringe of puzzling, silent people was a cowboy sitting astraddle of his bay horse at the end of the station platform.

And as Craddock started away from the crowd of curious passengers who were whispering and speculating behind him, pointing him out to each other, wondering what notable he might be; as Craddock started down the platform away from there, the voice of the conductor warning all to clamber aboard, the waiting cowboy tightened the reins a little, causing his horse to prick up its ears and start with a thrill of expectancy which the rider could feel ripple over its smooth hide under the pressure of his knees.

Craddock came on down the platform, turning his head on his long neck in the way of a man entirely mystified and suspicious, alone, unsupported by even as much as the shadow of a strange gun-slinger or local friend.

TRAIL'S END

What was passing through the fellow's head Morgan could pretty well guess. There was a little break of humor in it, for all the tight-drawn nerves, for all the chance, for all the desperation of the gathering moment. The grim old killer couldn't make out whether it was through admiration of him the people had gathered to welcome him home, or in expectation of something connected with the arrival of the train. Two rods or so from where Morgan waited him, Craddock stopped to look back at the train, now gathering slow headway, and around the deserted platform, down which the station agent came dragging a mail sack.

It was when he turned again from this suspicious questioning into things which gave him back no reply, that Craddock recognized the hitherto unsuspected cowboy. In a start he stiffened to action, flinging hand to his pistol. But a heartbeat quicker, like a flash of sunbeam from a mirror, the coiled rope flew out from Morgan's high-flung arm.

As the swift-running noose settled over Craddock's body, the horse leaped at the pressure of its rider's knees. Craddock fired as the flying rope snatched him from his feet, the noose binding his arms impotently to his sides; in his rage he fired again and again as he dragged in ludicrous tangle of long, thrashing legs from the platform into the dust.

There, in a cloud of obscuring dust from the trampled road, the horse holding the line taut, Morgan flung from the saddle in the nimble way of a range man, bent over the fallen slayer of men a little while. When the first of the crowd came breaking across the broad space intervening and drew up panting and breathless in admiration of the bold thing they had witnessed, Seth Craddock lay hog-tied and harmless on the ground, one pistol a few feet from where he struggled in his ropes, the other in the holster at his side.

And there came Judge Thayer, in his capacity as mayor, officious and radiant, proud and filled with a new feeling of safety and importance, and took the badge of office from Craddock's breast, in all haste, as if it were the most important act in this spectacular triumph, this bloodless victory over a bloody man.

CHAPTER XVII

WITH CLEAN HANDS

Seth Craddock was a defiant, although a fallen man. He refused to resign the office of marshal of the third-class city of Ascalon when Morgan released his feet at Judge Thayer's direction, allowing him to stand. Somebody brought his hat and put it down harshly on his small, turtle-like head, flaring out his big red ears. There he stood, glowering, dusty, blood on his face from an abrasion he had got in the rough handling at the end of Morgan's rope.

Judge Thayer said it made no difference whether he gave up the office willingly, he was without a voice in the matter, anyhow. He was fired, and that's all there was to it. But no, said Seth; not at all. The statutes upheld him, the constitution supported him, and hell and damnation and many other forces which he enumerated in his red-tongued defiance, could not move him out of that office. He demanded to be allowed to consult his lawyer, he glared around and cursed the curious and unawed public which laughed at his plight and the figure he cut, ordering somebody to go and fetch the county attorney, on pain of death when he should come again into the freedom of his hands.

But nobody moved, except to shift from one foot to the other and laugh. The terror seemed to have departed out of Seth Craddock's name and presence; a terrible man is no longer fearful when he has been dragged publicly at the end of a cow rope and tied up in the public place like a calf for the branding iron.

The county attorney was discreet enough to keep his distance. He did not come forward with advice on habeas corpus and constitutional rights. Only Earl Gray, the druggist, with seven kinds of perfumery on his hair, came out of the crowd with smirking face, ingratiating, servile, offering Morgan a cigar. The look that Morgan gave him would have wilted the tobacco in its green leaf. It wilted Druggist Gray. He turned back into the crowd and eliminated himself from the day's adventure like smoke on the evening wind.

Peden was seen, soon after Craddock's dusty downfall, making his way back to the shelter of his hall, a cloud on his dark face, a sneer of contempt in his eyes. His bearing was proclamation that he had expected a great deal more of Seth Craddock, and that the support of his influence was from that moment withdrawn. But there was nothing in his manner of a disturbed or defeated man. Those who knew him best, indeed, felt that he had played only a preliminary hand and, finding it weak, had taken up the deck for a stronger deal.

Seth Craddock stood with his back to the station platform, hands bound behind him, his authority gone. A little way to one side Morgan waited beside his horse, his pistol under his hand, rifle on the saddle, not so confident that all was won as to lay himself open to a surprise. Judge Thayer was holding a session with Craddock, the town, good and bad, looking on with varying emotions of mirth, disappointment, and disgust.

Judge Thayer unbuckled Craddock's belt and remaining pistol, picked up the empty weapon from the ground, sheathed it in the holster opposite its once terrifying mate, and gave them to Morgan. Morgan hung them on his saddle horn, and the wives and mothers of Ascalon who had trembled for their husbands and sons when they heard the roar of those guns in days past, drew great breaths of relief, and looked into each other's faces and smiled.

"We can't hold you for any of the killings you've done here, Seth, though some of them were unjustified, we know," Judge Thayer said. "You've been cleared by the coroner's jury in each case, there's no use for us to open them again. But you'll have to leave this town. Your friends went yesterday, escorted by Mr. Morgan across the Arkansas River. You can follow them if you want to--you might overtake 'em somewhere down in the Nation--you'll have to go in the same direction, in peace if you will, otherwise if you won't."

"I'm marshal of this town," Seth still persisted, in the belief that forces were gathering to his rescue, one could see. "The only way I'll ever leave till I'm ready to go'll be in a box!"

Certainly, Seth did not end the defiance and the declaration that way, nor issue it from his mouth in such pale and commonplace hues. Judge Thayer argued with him, after his kindly disposition, perhaps not a little sorry for the man who had outgrown his office and abused the friend who had elevated him to it.

Seth remained as obdurate as a trapped wolf. He roved his eyes around, craned his long, wrinkled neck, looking for the succor that was so long in coming. He repeated, with blasting enlargement, that the only way they could send him out of Ascalon would be in a box.

Judge Thayer drew apart to consult Morgan, in low tones. Morgan was undisturbed by Craddock's unbending opinion that he had plenty of law behind him to sustain his contention that he could not be removed from office. It did not matter how much ammunition a man had if he couldn't shoot it. It was Morgan's opinion, given with the light of humor quickening in his eyes, that they ought to take Craddock at his word.

"Ship him out?" said Judge Thayer.

"In a box," Morgan nodded, face as sober as judgment, the humor growing in his eyes.

"But we can't butcher the fellow like a hog!" Judge Thayer protested.

"Live hogs are shipped in boxes, right along," Morgan explained.

Judge Thayer saw the light; his pepper-and-salt whiskers twinkled and spread around his mouth, and rose so high in their bristling over his silent laughter that they threatened his eyes. He turned to Craddock, forcing a sober front.

"All right, Seth, we'll take you up on it. You're going out of town in a box," he said.

Judge Thayer ordered the undertaker to bring over a coffin box, the longest one he had. The word ran like a prairie fire from those who heard the order given, that they were going to shoot Craddock for his crimes and bury him on the spot.

There was not a little disappointment, but more relief, in the public mind when it became understood that Craddock was not to be shot. As a mockery of his past oppression and terrible name, he was to be nailed up in a box and shipped out like a snake. And so it turned out again in Ascalon that comedy came in to end the play where tragedy had begun it.

Morgan bore no part in this unexpected climax to his hard-straining and doubt-clouded day. He stood by watchful and alert, a great peace in his mind, a great lightness. He had come through it according to Rhetta Thayer's wish, according to his own desire, with no man's blood upon his hands.

There were many willing ones who came forward to make light the labor of Seth Craddock's packing. They unbound his hands with derision and bundled him into the capacious long box against his strivings and curses with scorn. Morgan suggested the enclosure of a jug of water. Let him frizzle and fry, they said. They'd bore an auger hole or two in the box to give him air, and that was greater humanity than he deserved. Morgan insisted on at least a bottle of water, and had his way, against grumbling.

The undertaker officiated, as if it were a regular funeral, putting the long screws in the stout lid while citizens sat on it to hold the explosive old villain down. They fastened him in as securely as if he were a dead man, in all sobriety, boxed up againt the worms of the grave.

Then the question rose of where to send him, and how. On the first part of it the public was of undivided mind. No matter where he went, or in what direction, let it be far. On the second division there was some argument. Some held for shipping him by freight, as livestock, and some were for express as the quickest way to the end of a long journey. For the farther out of sight he could be carried in the shortest possible time, they said, the better for all concerned.

There the station agent was called in to lend the counsel of his official position. A man could not be shipped by freight if alive, he said. He could be sent as a corpse is sent, by paying the rate of a fare and a half and stowing him in the baggage-car with trunks and dogs. The undertaker was of the same opinion, which he expressed gravely, with becoming sadness and gloom.

Judge Thayer wrote the address on the shipping tag, the undertaker tacked it on Seth Craddock's case, and then the amazed people of Ascalon came forward surrounding the case, and read:

Chief of Police, Kansas City, Missouri.

That was the consignee of the strangest shipment ever billed out of Ascalon. People wondered what the chief of police would do with his gift. They wished him well of it, with all their hearts.

Meantime Seth Craddock, with the blood of eight men on his hands, was making more noise in the coffin box than a sack of cats. It was a most undignified way for a man of his sanguinary reputation to accept this humiliation at the hands of a public that he had outraged. A mule in a box stall could not have made a greater clatter with heels against planks than the fallen city marshal of Ascalon drummed up with his on the stout end of the coffin box. He cursed as he kicked, and called in muffled voice on the friends of his brief day of power to come and set him free.

But the sycophants who had hung to his heels like hand-fed dogs when power glorified him like a glistening garment and exalted him high above other men, turned out as all time-servers and cowardly courtiers always finish when the object of their transitory adulation falls with his belly in the dust. They sneered, they jeered, they turned white-shirted coatless backs upon his box with derisive, despising laughter on their night-pale faces. Seth Craddock was a mighty man as long as he had a license to walk about and slay, but fastened up in a box like a corpse for shipment at the rate of the dead, he was only a hull and an empty husk of a man.

They said he was a coward; they had known it all along. It called for a coward to shoot men down like rabbits. That was not the way of a brave and worthy man. This great moral conclusion they reached readily enough, Seth Craddock securely caged before them. If Morgan's rope had missed its mark, if a snarl had shortened it a foot; if Craddock had been a second sooner in starting to draw his gun, this wave of moral exaltation would not have descended upon Ascalon that day.

There was some concern over the holding quality of the box. People feared Craddock might burst out of it before going far, and return against them for the reckoning so volubly threatened. The undertaker quieted these fears by tapping the box around with his hammer, pointing out its reenforced strength with melancholy pride. A ghost might get out of it if some other undertaker put the lid on, he said, but even that thin and vaporous thing would have to call for help if he screwed him shut in that most competent container of the mortal remains of man.

Thus assured, the citizens carried the box in festive spirit, with more charity and kindness toward old Seth than he deserved, and stood it on end in the shadow of the depot. There was an auger hole on a level with Seth's eye, through which he could glower out for his last look on Ascalon, and the people who gathered around to deride him and triumph in his overthrow.

Through this small opening Seth cursed them, checking such of them off by name as he recognized, setting them down in his memory for the vengeance he declared he would return speedily and exact. There he stood, like Don Quixote in his cage, his red eye to the hole, swearing as terribly as any man that marched in that hard-boiled army in Flanders long ago.

Those who had been awed by his grim silence in the days when he ruled above all law in Ascalon, were surprised now by his volubility. Under provocation Craddock could say as much as the next man, it appeared. Unquestionably, he could express his limited thoughts in words luridly strange. He wearied of this arraignment at last, and subsided. Long before the train came he lapsed into his natural blue sulkiness, remaining as quiet behind his auger hole as one ready for the grave.

They loaded Craddock on a truck when the train from the west whistled, trundled him down the platform and posted him ready to load in the baggage-car, attended by a large, jubilant crowd. There was so much hilarity in this gathering for a funeral, indeed, and so much profanity, denunciation, and threat issuing out of the coffin box--for Seth broke out again the minute they moved him--that the baggage-man aboard the train demurred on receiving the shipment. He closed the door against the eager citizens who mounted the truck to shove the box aboard, leaving only opening enough for him to stand flatwise in and shout up the platform to the conductor.

This conductor was a notable man in his day on that pioneer railroad. He was a bony, irascible man, fiery of face, with a high hook nose that had been smashed to one side in some battle when he was construction foreman in his days of lowly beginning. He wore a pistol strapped around his long coat, which garment was braided and buttoned like an ambassador's, and he was notable throughout the land of cattle and cards as a man who could reach far and hit hard. If Seth Craddock had applied to him for instruction in invective and profanity, veteran that he was he would have been put at the very foot of the primer class.

Now this mighty man came striding down the platform, thrusting his way through the crowd with no gentle elbow, hand on his gun, displeasure ready to explode from his mouth. The baggage-man asked advice on accepting the proffered box, with fare and a half ticket attached as in the case of a corpse.

The conductor remarked, with terrible sarcasm, that the corpse was the noisiest one he ever had encountered, even in that cursed and benighted and seven times outcast hole. He knocked on the box and demanded of the occupant an account of himself, and the part he was bearing in this pleasant little episode, this beautiful little joke.

Seth lifted up his muffled voice to say that it was no joke, at least to him. He explained his identity and denounced his captors, swearing vengeance to the last eyebrow. The conductor faced the crowd with disdainful severity.

What were they trying to play off on him, anyhow? Who did they suppose he was? Maybe that was fun in Ascalon, but his company wasn't going to carry no man from nowhere against his will and be sued for it. Burn him and box up the ashes, boil him and bottle the soup; reduce him by any comfortable means they saw fit, according to their humane way, fetch him there in any guise but that of a living man, and the company would haul him to Hades if they billed him to that destination.

But not in his present shape and form; not as a living, swearing, suit-threatening man. Take him to hell out of there, the conductor ordered in rising temper. Don't insult him and his road by coming around there to make them a part in their idle, life-wasting, time-gambling, blasted to the seventh depth of Hades tricks.

The baggage-man closed the door, the conductor gave the signal to pull out, and the train departed, leaving Seth Craddock on the truck, the rather shamed and dampened citizens standing around. They concluded they would have to hang him, after all their trouble for a more romantic, picturesque, and unusual exit. And hanging was such a common, ordinary way of getting rid of a distasteful man that the pleasure was taken out of their day.

Judge Thayer was firmly against hanging. He ordered the undertaker to open the box, which he did with fear and trembling, seeing in a future hour the vengeance of Seth Craddock descending on his solemn head. Craddock, sweat-drenched and weak from his rebellion and the heat of his close quarters, sat up with scarcely a breath left in him for a curse. Judge Thayer delivered him to Morgan, with instructions to lock him up.

The city calaboose was an institution apart from the county jail. Due to some past rivalry between the county and city officials, the palatial jail was closed to offenders against the lowly and despised-by-the-sheriff town ordinances. So, out of its need, the city had built this little house with bars across the one small window, and a barred door formed of wagon tires to close outside the one of wood.

No great amount of business ever had been done in this calaboose, for minor infractions of the law were not troubled with in that town. If there ever was anybody left over from a shooting he usually went along about his business or his pleasure until the coroner's jury assembled and let him off. The last man confined in the calaboose had stolen a bottle of whisky, a grave and reprehensible offense which set all the town talking and speculating on the proper punishment. This poor bug had made a fire of his hay bedding in the night, and perished as miserably as everybody said he deserved. The charred boards in one corner still attested to his well-merited end.

Morgan was not at all confident of the retaining powers of the calaboose, neither was he greatly concerned. He believed that if Craddock could break out he would make a streak away from Ascalon, hooked up at high speed, never to return. It was not in the nature of a man humbled from a high place, mocked by the lowly, derided by those whom he had oppressed, contemned by the false friends he had favored, to come back on an errand of revenge. The job was too general in a case like Craddock's. He would have to exterminate most of the town.

They left him in the calaboose with whatever reflections were his. The window was too high in the wall for anybody on the outside to see in, or for Craddock, tall as he was, to see anything out of it but the sky. Public interest had fallen away since he was neither to be shipped out nor hanged, only locked up like a whisky thief. Only a few boys hung around the calaboose, which stood apart in the center of at least half an acre of ground, as if ashamed of its office in a community that used it so seldom when it was needed so often.

Morgan returned to the square for his horse, rather dissatisfied now with the day's developments. It was going to be troublesome to have this fellow on his hands. Judge Thayer should not have interfered with the last decree of public justice. It would have been over with by now.

Rhetta Thayer was in the door of the newspaper office. She came to the edge of the sidewalk as Morgan approached, leading his horse. She did not reflect the public satisfaction from her handsome face and troubled eyes that Ascalon in general enjoyed over Craddock's humiliation. Morgan wondered why.

"I asked too much of you, Mr. Morgan," she said, coming at once to the matter that clouded her honest eyes.

"You couldn't ask too much of me," he returned, with no unction of flattery, but the cheerfully frank expression of an ingenuous heart.

"I didn't realize the disadvantage you would be under, I didn't know what I expected of you when I urged you into this. Meeting that desperate man with a rope instead of a gun!"

"You didn't know I was going to meet him with a rope," he said.

He stood before her, hat in hand, wholesomely honest in his homely ruggedness, a flush of embarrassment tinging his face. The sun in his short hair seemed laughing, picking out little flecks of gold as mica flakes in the sea waves turn and flash.

"You might have been killed! When I saw him throw his hand to his gun! Oh! it was terrible!"

"So you're the editor now?" he said, cheerfully, trying to turn her from this disturbing subject.

"My heart jumped clear out of my mouth when you threw your rope!"

"It came over and helped me," he said, in manner sincere and grave.

A little flame of color lifted in her pale cheek. She looked at the dusty road, her hand pressed to her bosom as if to make certain that the truant heart had come back to her like a dove to its cote out of the storm. She looked up presently, and smiled a bit; looked down again, the hot blood writing a confession in her face.

"I hope it did," she said.

Morgan felt himself in such a suffocation of strange delight he could find no word that seemed the right word, and left it to silence, which, perhaps was best. He looked at the road, also, as if he would search with her there for grains of gold, or for lost hearts which leap out of maidens' breasts, in the white dust marked by many feet.

Together they looked up, faces white, breath faltering on dry lips. So the fire leaps in a moment such as this and enwraps the soul. It is no mystery, it is no process of long distillation. In a moment; so.

"Here are his guns," said he, his voice trembling as if it strained in leaping the subject that lay in its door to go back to the business of the day.

"His guns!" she repeated after him, shuddering at the thought.

"Hang them over your desk--you might need them, now you're the editor."

She accepted them from his hand, but dubiously, holding them far out from contact with her dress as something unclean. Morgan reproached himself for offering her these instruments which had sent so many men to sudden, undefended death. He reached to relieve her hand.

"Let me do it for you, Miss Thayer."

"No," she denied him, putting down her qualm, clutching the heavy belt firmly. "It is a notable trophy, a great distinction you're giving me, Mr. Morgan. I'm afraid you'll think I'm a coward," smiling wanly as she lifted her face.

"You're not afraid to edit the paper. That seems to me the most dangerous job in town."

"Most dangerous job in town!" she reproved him, giving him to understand very plainly that she could name one attended by greater perils. "They've only killed one editor, so far."

"Can you shoot?" he asked, as seriously concerned as if the fate of editors in Ascalon darkened over her already.

"Everybody in this town can shoot," she sighed. "It's every boy's ambition to own and carry a pistol, and most of them do."

"I hope you'll never have to defend the independence of the press with arms," he said, making a small pleasantry of it. "More than likely they're gentlemen enough to let you say whatever you want to, and make no kick."

"The Headlight is going to be an awful joke with Riley Caldwell and me getting it out. But I'm not going to try to please anybody. That way I may please them all."

"It sounds like the sensible way. Have you edited before?"

"I used to help Mr. Smith, the editor they killed. That was in the summer vacation, just. I taught school the rest of the time."

"You must have been the busiest person in town," he said, with pride in her activities as if they had touched his own life long ago.

"I'm a poor stick of an editor, I'm afraid, though--I seem to be all mussed up with legal notices and this sudden flood of news. And I can't set type worth a cent!"

"Just let the news go," he suggested, not without concern for the part he might bear in her chronicle of late events in Ascalon.

"Let the news go!" She censured him with her softly chiding eyes. "I wish I could write like Mr. Smith--I'd wake this town up! Poor man, his coat is hanging in the office by the desk, so suggestive of him it makes me cry. I haven't had the heart to take it away--it would seem like expelling his spirit from the place. He was a slender, gentle little man, more like a minister than an editor. It took an awful coward to shoot him down that way."

"You're right; I met him," Morgan said, remembering Dell Hutton among the wagons, his smoking gun in his hand.

"Sneaking little coward!"

"Well, he'll hardly sling his gun down on you," Morgan reflected, as if he communed with himself, yet thinking that Hutton scarcely would be beyond even that.

"Hardly," she replied, in abstraction. "What are you going to do with that old brigand you've got locked in the calaboose?"

"I expect we'll turn him loose in the morning. There doesn't seem to be anything we can hold him for, guilty as he is."

"If he'll leave, and never come back," doubtfully. "I'm glad now it turned out the way it did, I'm so thankful you didn't have to--that you came through without blood on your hands!"

"It would have been a calamity the other way," he said.

When Morgan went his way presently, leaving her in the door of the little boxlike newspaper office, from where she gave him a parting smile, it was with a revised opinion of the day's achievements. He felt peculiarly exalted and satisfied. He had accomplished something, after all.

Whatever this was, he did not confess, but he smiled, and felt renewed with a lifting gladness, as he went on to the livery barn, his horse at his heels.

CHAPTER XVIII

A BONDSMAN BREATHES EASIER

There was a little ripple, more of mirth than excitement or concern, in Ascalon next morning when it became known that Seth Craddock had kicked a hole in the burned corner of the calaboose and leaked out of it into the night.

Let him go; it was as well that way as any, they said, since it relieved them at once of the charge of his keep and the trouble of disposing of him in the end. He never would come back to that town, let him ravage in other parts of the world as he might. What the town had lost in notoriety by his going would be offset by the manner of his degradation, already written at length by the local correspondent of the Kansas City Times and sent on to be printed with a display heading in a prominent position in that paper and copied by other papers all over the land.

Seth Craddock and his reign were behind the closed door of the past, through which he was not likely to kick a hole and emerge again, after his manner of going from the calaboose. That matter off the town's mind, it ranged itself along the shady side of the street to watch the present contest between the law and those who lived beyond it.

Up to this point it appeared that the law was going to have it according to its mandate. Peden made no attempt to open his place on the night following Craddock's deposition, the lesser lights following his virtuous example.

But there was in this quiescent confidence, in this lull almost threatening, something similar to the impertinent repression of an incorrigible child who yields to authority immediately above him, knowing that presently it will be overruled. Something was clouding up to break over Ascalon; the sleepiest in the town was aware of that.

How much more keenly, then, was this charged atmosphere sensed and explored with the groping hand of trepidation by Rhetta Thayer, finely tuned as a virtuoso's violin. She knew something was hatching in that Satan's nest of iniquity that would result in an outbreak of defiance, but what form it would take, and when, she could not determine, although friends tried to sound for her the bottom of this pit.

Morgan knew it; all the scheme was as plain to him as the line of hitching racks around the square. They were waiting to gather force, when they meant to rise up and crush him, fling wide their doors, invite the outlawed of the world in, and proceed as in the past. All there was to be done was wait the uncovering of their hands.

Meantime, there was a breathing spell between, a spell of pleasant hours in the little newspaper office, reading the exchanges, helping on the arrangement of such news as the town and country about it yielded, and having many a good laugh over their bungling of the job, himself and the pretty, brown-eyed editor, that was better for their bodies and souls than all the physic on Druggist Gray's shelves. And not one line concerning Morgan's adventures appeared in the Headlight during that time.

In this manner, Ascalon enjoyed as it might three days of peace out of this summer solstice. The drouth was aggravating in its duration and growing hardships. Many families in town were without water, and obliged to carry it from the deep well in the public square. Numberless cattle were being driven to the loading pens for shipment to market, weeks ahead of their day of doom, unfattened, unfit. The range was becoming a barren; disaster threatened over that land with a torch in its blind-striking hand.

On the evening of this third day, between sunset and twilight, Rhetta Thayer stopped Morgan as he was passing the Headlight office at the beginning of his nightly patrol. She was disturbed by an agitation that she could not conceal; her eyes stood wide as if some passing terror had opened their windows.

"He shot at you, and you didn't tell me!" she said, reproachfully, facing him just inside the door.

"Well, he isn't much of a shot," Morgan told her, cheerful assurance in his words. "I can assure you I was at no time in any danger."

"Oh! you didn't tell me!" she said, her voice little above a whisper on her quick-coming breath.

"It didn't amount to anything," Morgan discounted, wondering how she had heard of it. "All that puzzled me was why the little rat did it--I never stepped in front of him anywhere."

"That woman in the tent--the rustler's wife--told me--she told me just a little while ago. Oh! if he--if he'd have hit you!"

"The kids all came running out of the tent--I thought he'd hit one of them," Morgan said, humorously, thinking only to calm her great agitation and quiet her friendly--if there could be no dearer interest--concern.

"It was Peden got him to do it," she declared.

"Peden? Why should Hutton go out to do that fellow's gunning?"

"Dell Hutton's gambling the county's money, he killed Mr. Smith because he charged him with it! Pa knows it, pa's on his bond, and if he keeps on losing the county funds there on Peden's game we'll have to make it good. It will take everything we've got--if he keeps on."

"That's bad, that's mighty bad," Morgan said, deeply concerned, curiously awakened to the inner workings of things in Ascalon. "Still, I don't see what connection I have in it, why he'd want to take a shot at me on the quiet that way."

"He shoots from behind, he shot Mr. Smith in the back, and it was at night, besides. Don't you see how it was? Peden must have bribed him to do it, promised to make good his losses, or something like that."

"Plain as a wagon track," Morgan said.

"I don't know why I ever got you into this tangle," she lamented, "I don't know what made me so selfish and so blind."

"It's just one more little complication in Ascalon's sickness," he comforted her, "it doesn't amount to beans. The poor little fool was so scared that morning he could hardly lift his gun. He'll never make another break."

"If I only thought he wouldn't! He's as treacherous as a snake, you can't tell where he's sneaking to bite you. Give it up, Mr. Morgan, won't you, please?" She turned to him suddenly, appealing with her eyes, with her wistful lips, with every line of her sympathetic, anxious face.

"Give it up?" he repeated, her meaning not quite clear.

"The office, I mean. Surely, as I coaxed you into taking it, I've got a right to ask you to give it up. You've done what you took the place to do, you've got Craddock out of it and away from here. Your work's done, you can quit now with a good conscience and no excuse to anybody."

"Why," said Morgan, reflectively, "I don't believe I could quit right now, Miss Rhetta. There's something more to come, it isn't quite finished yet."

"There's a great deal more to come, the end of all this fighting and killing and grinning treachery never will come!" she said, in great bitterness. "What's the use of one man putting his life against all this viciousness? There's no cure for the curse of Ascalon but time. Let it go, Mr. Morgan--I beg you to give it up."

Morgan took the hand that she reached out to him in her appeal. The great fervor of her earnest heart had drawn the blood away from it, leaving it cold. He clasped it, tightly, to warm it in his big palm, and spoke comfortingly, yet he would not, could not, tell her that he would give over the office and leave the town to its devices. The work he had begun on her account, at her appeal, was not finished. He wanted to give her a peace that would make permanent the placidity of her eyes such as had warmed his heart during those three days. But he could not tell her that.

"If it goes on," she said, sad that he would not yield to her appeal, "you'll have to--you'll have to--do what the rest of them have done. And I don't want you to do that, Mr. Morgan. I want you to keep clean."

"As it must be, so it will be," he said. "But I don't see any reason why I can't keep on the way I've started. There's nobody doing any shooting here now."

"They're only waiting," she said.

"I'll have to watch them a little longer, then," he told her; "somebody might shoot your windows out."

He led her away from the subject of Ascalon's dangers and unrest, its sinister ferment and silent threat, but she would come back to it in a little while, and to Dell Hutton, who shot men in the back.

"He's over there in the courthouse now--that's his office where you see the light--trying to doctor up his books to hide his stealing, I know," she declared.

Morgan left her, his rifle in his hand, to go on his patrol of the town according to his nightly program. As he tramped around the square, he watched the light in the courthouse window, thinking of the account on his own books against the old-faced young man who labored there alone to hide his peculations for a little while longer. And so, watching and considering, thinking and devising, the night came down over him, guardian of the peace of Ascalon, where there was no peace.

Rhetta Thayer, leaving the Headlight office at nine o'clock, saw two men come down the courthouse steps, shadowy and indistinct in the dusk of starlight and early night. She paused on her way, wondering, and her wonder and mystification grew when she saw them cut across the square in the direction of Peden's dark and silent hall. One of them was Dell Hutton. The other she had no need to name.

When Dell Hutton, county treasurer, deposited three thousand dollars of the county's funds in the bank next morning, a certain man who stood surety on his bond wiped the sweat of vast relief from his forehead. And when Rhetta heard of it, she smiled, and the incense of gratitude rose out of her heart for the strong-handed man who had stopped this leak in the slender finances of the county, a thing which he believed he was holding secret in the simplicity of his honest soul.

CHAPTER XIX

THE CURSE OF BLOOD

Sensitive as a barometer to every variation, every shading, in public sentiment and sympathy, Morgan patroled the town nightly until the streets were deserted. Night by night he felt, rather than saw, the growing insolence of the pale feeders on the profits of vice, the confidence in some approaching triumph gleaming in their furtive eyes.

None of the principals, few of the attendant vultures, had left Ascalon. The sheriff had returned from his excursion after cattle thieves, and, contrary to the expectation of anybody, had brought one lean and hungry, hound-faced man with him and locked him up in jail.

But the sheriff was taking no part in the new city marshal's campaign in the town, certainly not to help him. If he worked against him in the way his fat, big-jowled face proclaimed that it was his habit to work, no evidence of it was in his manner when he met Morgan. He was a friendly, puffy-handed man, loud in his hail and farewell to the riders who came in from the far-off cow camps to see for themselves this wide-heralded reformation of the godless town of Ascalon.

These visitors, lately food for the mills of the place, walked about as curiously as fowls liberated in a strange yard after long confinement in a coop. They looked with uncomprehending eyes on the closed doors of Peden's famous temple of excesses; they turned respectful eyes on Morgan as he passed them in his silent, determined rounds. And presently, after meeting the white-shirted, coatless dealers, lookout men, macquereaux, they began to have a knowing look, an air of expectant hilarity. After a little they usually mounted and rode away, laughing among themselves like men who carried cheerful tidings to sow upon the way.

In that manner Ascalon remained closed five nights, nobody contesting the authority of the new marshal, not a shot fired in the streets. On the afternoon of the sixth day an unusual tide of visitors began to set in to this railroad port of Ascalon. By sundown the hitching rack around the square was packed with horses; Dora Conboy told Morgan she never had waited on so many people before in her hotel experience.

At dusk Morgan brought his horse from the livery stable, mounted with his rifle under the crook of his knee. At nine o'clock Peden threw open his doors, the small luminaries which led a dim existence in his effulgence following suit, all according to their preconcerted plan.

There was a shout and a break of wild laughter, a scramble for the long bar with its five attendants working with both hands; a scrape of fiddles and a squall of brass; a squeaking of painted and bedizened drabs, who capered and frisked like mice after their long inactivity. And on the inflow of custom and the uprising of jubilant mirth, Peden turned his quick, crafty eyes as he stood at the head of the bar to welcome back to his doors this golden stream.

Close within Peden's wide door, one on either hand, two vigilant strangers stood, each belted with two revolvers, each keeping a hand near his weapons. One of these was a small, thin-faced white rat of a man; the other tall, lean, leathery; burned by sun, roughened by weather. A shoot from the tree that produced Seth Craddock he might have been, solemn like him, and grim.

Dell Hutton, county treasurer, cigar planted so far to one corner of his wide thin mouth that wrinkles gathered about it like the leathery folds of an old man's skin, came to Peden where he stood at the bar.

"All's set for him," he said, drawing his eyes small as he peered around through the fast-thickening smoke.

"Let him come!" said Peden, watching the door with expectant, vindictive eyes.

The news of Peden's defiance swept over the town like a taint on the wind. Not only that Peden had opened his doors to the long-thirsting crowd gathered by the advertised news of a big show for that night, but that he had posted two imported gun-fighters inside his hall with instructions to shoot the city marshal if he attempted to interfere. With the spread of this news men began to gather in front of Peden's to see what the city marshal was going to do, how he would accept this defiance, if he meant to accept it, and what the result to him would be.

Judge Thayer came down to the square without his alpaca coat, his perturbation was so great, looking for Morgan, talking of swearing in a large number of deputies to uphold the law.

This was received coldly by the men of Ascalon. Upholding the law was the city marshal's business, they said. If he couldn't do it alone, let the law drag; let it fall underfoot, where it seemed the best place for it in that town, anyhow. So Judge Thayer went on, looking around the square for Morgan, not finding him, nor anybody who had seen him within the last half hour.

Rhetta was working late in the Headlight office, preparing for the weekly issue of the paper. This disquieting news had come in at her door like the wave of a flood. She had no thought of work from that moment, only to stand at the door listening for the dreaded sound of shooting from the direction of Peden's hall.

Judge Thayer found her standing in the door when he completed his search around the square, his heart falling lower at every step.

"He's gone! Morgan's deserted us!" he said.

"Gone!" she repeated in high scorn. "He'll be the last to go."

"I can't find him anywhere--I've hunted all over town. Nobody has seen him. I tell you, Rhetta, he's gone."

"I wish to heaven he would go! What right have we got to ask him to give his life to stop the mean, miserable squabbles of this suburb of hell!"

"I think you'd better run along home now--Riley will go with you. Why, child, you're cold!"

He drew her into the office, urging her to put on her bonnet and go.

"I'll stay here and see it out," she said. "Oh, if he would go, if he would go! But he'll never go."

She threw herself into the chair beside her littered desk, hands clenched, face white as if she bore a mortal pain, only to leap up again in a moment, run to the door, and listen as if she sought a voice out of the riotous sound.

Judge Thayer had none of this poignant concern for Morgan's welfare. He was not a little nettled over his failure to find the marshal, and that officer's apparent shunning of duty in face of this mocking challenge to his authority.

"Why, Rhetta, you wanted him to take the office, you urged him to," he reminded her. "I don't understand this sudden concern for the man's safety in disregard of his oath and duty, this--this--unaccountable----"

"I didn't know him then--I didn't know him!" she said, in piteous low moan.

Judge Thayer looked at her with a sudden sharp turning of the head, as if her words had expressed something beyond their apparent meaning. He came slowly to the door, where he stood beside her a little while in silence, hand upon her shoulder tenderly.

"I'll look around again," he said, "and come back in a little while."

Meanwhile, in Peden's place the celebrants at the altar of alcohol were rejoicing in this triumph of personal liberty. Where was this man-eating city marshal? What had become of that knock-kneed horse wrangler from Bitter Creek they had heard so much about? They drank fiery toasts to his confusion, they challenged him in the profane emphasis of scorn. Upon what was his fame based? they wanted to be told. The mere corraling of certain stupid drunk men; the lucky throw of a rope. He never had killed a man!

With the mounting of their hastily swilled liquor the hilarious patrons of Peden's hall became more contemptuous of the city marshal. His apparent avoidance of trouble, his unaccountable absence, his failure to step up and meet this challenge from Peden, became a grievance against him in their inflamed heads.

They had counted on him to make some kind of a bluff, to add something either of tragedy or comedy to this big show. Now he was hiding out, and they resented it in the proper spirit of men deprived of their rights. They began to talk of going out to find him, of dragging him from his hole and starting a noise behind him that would scare him out of the country.

Peden encouraged this growing notion. If Morgan wouldn't bring his show there, go after him and make him stand on his hind legs like a dog. After a few more drinks, after a dance, after another stake on the all-devouring tables of chance. They turned to these diversions in the zest of long abstinence, in the redundant vitality of youth, mocking all restraint, insolent of any reckoning of circumstance or time.

Peden distended with satisfaction to see the free spending, the free flinging of money into his games. A little virtuous recess seemed to be profitable; it was like giving a horse a rest. His two guards waited at the door, his lookout at the faro table swept the hall from his high chair with eyes keen to mark any hostile invasion. Morgan never could come six feet inside his door.

Well satisfied with himself and the beginning of that night's business, exceedingly comfortable in the thought that this defiance of the law would bring a newer and wider notoriety to himself and the town of which he was the spirit, Peden sauntered among the boisterous merrymakers on his floor.

Dancers were worming and shuffling in close embrace, couples breaking out of the whirl now and then to rush to the bar; players stood deep around the tables; men reached over each other's shoulders to take their drinks from the bar. All was haste and hilarity, all a crowding of pleasure with hard-pursuing feet, a snatching at the elusive thing with rough boisterous hands, with loud laughter, with wild yells.

Pleasure, indeed, seemed on the flight before these coarse revelers, who pursued it blindfold down the steeps of destruction unaware.

Peden shouldered his way through the throng toward the farther end of the long bar, nodding here with a friendly smile, stopping now and then to shake hands with some specially favored patron, throwing commands among his female entertainers from his cold, hard, soulless eyes as he passed along.

And in that sociable progression down his thronging hall, ten feet from the farther end of his famous bar, Peden came face to face with Morgan, as grim as judgment among the crowd of wastrels and women of poisoned lips, who fell back in breathless silence to let him pass.

Morgan was carrying his rifle; his pistol hung at his side. The big shield of office once worn by Seth Craddock was pinned on the pocket of his shirt; his broad-brimmed hat threw a shadow over his stern face.

Peden stopped with a little start of withdrawal at sight of Morgan, surprised out of his poise, chilled, perhaps, at the thought of the long pistol shot between this unexpected visitor and the hired killers at his front door, the way between them blocked by a hundred revelers.

So, this was the cunning of this range wolf, to come in at his back door and fall upon him in surprise! Peden's resentment rose in that second of reflection with the dull fire that spread in his dark face. He flung his hand to his revolver, throwing aside the skirt of his long coat.

"Let your gun stay where it is," Morgan quietly advised him. "Get these people out of here, and close this place."

"Show me your authority!" Peden demanded, scouting for a moment of precious time.

The musicians in the little orchestra pit behind Morgan ceased playing on a broken note, the shuffle of dancing feet stopped short. Up the long bar the loud hilarity quieted; across the hall the clash of pool balls cut sharply into the sudden stillness. As quickly as wind makes a rift in smoke the revelers fell away from Morgan and Peden, leaving a fairway for the shooting they expected to begin at the door. Peden stood as he had stopped, hand upon his gun.

Morgan stepped up to him in one long, quick stride, rifle muzzle close against Peden's broad white shirt front. In that second of hesitant delay, that breath of portentous bluff, Morgan had read Peden to the roots. A man who had it in him to shoot did not stop at anybody's word when he was that far along the way.

"Clear this place and lock it up!" Morgan repeated.

The temperature of the crowded hall seemed to fall forty degrees in the second or two Morgan stood pushing his rifle against Peden's breastbone. Those who had talked with loud boasts, picturesque threats, high-pitched laughter, of going out to find this man but a little while before, were silent now and cold around the gills as fish.

Morgan was watching the two men at the front door while he held Peden up those few seconds. He knew there was no use in disarming Peden, to turn him loose where he could get fifty guns in the next two seconds if he wanted them. He believed, in truth, there was not much to fear from this fellow, who depended on his hired retainers to do his killing for him. So, when Peden, watching Morgan calculatively, shifted a little to get himself out of line so he would not stand a barrier between his gun-slingers and their target and longer block the opening of operations to clear the hall of this upstart, Morgan let him go. Then, with a sudden bound, Peden leaped across into the crowd.

A moment of strained waiting, quiet as the empty night, Morgan standing out a fair target for any man who had the nerve to pull a gun. Then a stampede in more of sudden fear than caution by those lined up along the bar, and the two hired killers at the front of the house began to shoot.

Morgan pitched back on his heels as if mortally hit, staggered, thrust one foot out to stay his fall. He stood bracing himself in that manner with out-thrust foot, shooting from the hip.

Three shots he fired, the roar of his rifle loud above the lighter sound of the revolvers. With the third shot Morgan raised his gun. In the smoke that was settling to the floor the taller of the gunmen lay stretched upon his face. The other, arms rigidly at his sides, held a little way from his body, head drooping to his chest, turned dizzily two or three times, spinning swiftly in his dance of death, gave at the knees, settled down gently in a strange, huddled heap.

Dead. Both of them dead. The work of one swift moment when the blood curse fell on this new, quick-handed marshal of Ascalon.

There was a choking scream, and a woman's cry. "Look out! look out!"

Peden, on the fringe of a crowd of shrinking, great-eyed women, ghastly in the painted mockery of their fear, fired as Morgan turned. Morgan blessed the poor creature who was woman enough in her debauched heart to cry out that warning, as the breath of Peden's bullet brushed his face. Morgan could not defend himself against this assault, for the coward stood with one shoulder still in the huddling knot of women, and fired again. Morgan dropped to the floor, prone on his face as the dead man behind him.

Peden came one cautious step from his shelter, leaning far over to see, a smile of triumph baring his gleaming teeth; another step, while the crowd broke the stifling quiet with shifted feet. Morgan, quick as a serpent strikes, raised to his elbow and fired.

Morgan had one clear look at Peden's face as he threw his arms high and fell. Surprise, which death, swift in its coming had not yet overtaken, bulged out of his eyes. Surprise: no other emotion expressed in that last look upon this life. And Peden lay dead upon his own floor, his hat fallen aside, his arms stretched far beyond his head, his white cuffs pulled out from his black coat sleeves, as if he appealed for the mercy that was not ever for man or woman in his own cold heart.

CHAPTER XX

TRAIL'S END

UNCLEAN

Earl Gray came down the street hatless, the big news on his tongue. Rhetta Thayer, in the door of the Headlight office, where she had stood in the pain of one crucified while the shots sounded in Peden's hall, stopped him with a gasped appeal.

Dead. Peden and the gun-slingers he had brought there to kill Morgan; any number of others who had mixed in the fight; Morgan himself--all dead, the floor covered with the dead. That was the terrible word that rolled from Gray's excited tongue. And when she heard it, Rhetta put out her hands as one blind, held to the door frame a moment while the blood seemed to drain out of her heart, staring with horrified eyes into the face of the inconsequential man who had come in such avid eagerness to tell this awful tale.

People were hastening by in the direction of Peden's, scattered at first, like the beginning of a retreat, coming then by twos and threes, presently overflowing the sidewalk, running in the street. Rhetta stood staring, half insensible, on this outpouring. Riley Caldwell, the young printer, rushed past her out of the shop, his roached hair like an Algonquin's standing high above his narrow forehead, his face white as if washed by death.

Impelled by a desire that was commanding as it was terrifying, moved by a hope that was only a shred of a raveled dream, Rhetta joined the moving tide that set toward Peden's door. Dead--Morgan was dead! Because she had asked him, he had set his hand to this bloody task. She had sent him to his death in her selfish desire for security, in her shrinking cowardice, in her fear of riot and blood. And he was dead, the light was gone out of his eyes, his youth and hope were sacrificed in a cause that would bring neither glory nor gratitude to illuminate his memory.

She began to run, out in the dusty street where he had marched his patrol that first night of his bringing peace to Ascalon; to run, her feet numb, her body numb, only her heart sentient, it seemed, and that yearning out to him in a great pain of pity and stifling labor of remorse. It was only a little way, but it seemed heavy and long, impeded by feet that could not keep pace with her anguish, swift-running to whisper a tender word.

The lights were bright in Peden's hall, a great crowd leaned and strained and pushed around its door. There were some who asked her kindly to go away, others who appealed earnestly against her looking into the place, as Rhetta pushed her way, panting like an exhausted swimmer, through the crowd.

Nothing would turn her; appeals were dim as cries in drowning ears. Gaining the door, she paused a moment, hands pressed to her cheeks, hair fallen in disorder. Her eyes were big with the horror of her thoughts; she was breathless as one cast by breakers upon the sand. She looked in through the open door.

Morgan was standing like a soldier a little way inside the door, his rifle carried at port arms, denying by the very sternness of his pose the passage of any foot across that threshold of tragedy. There was nothing in his bearing of a wounded man. Beyond him a few feet lay the bodies of the two infamous guards who had been posted at the door to take his life; along the glistening bar, near its farther end, Peden stretched with face to the floor, his appealing hands outreaching.

A gambling table had been upset, chairs strewn in disorder about the floor, when the rabble was cleared out of the place. Only Morgan remained there with the dead men, like a lone tragedian whose part was not yet done.

Rhetta looked for one terrifying moment on that scene, its tragic detail impressed on her senses as a revelation of lightning leaps out of the blackest night to be remembered for its surrounding terror. And in that moment Morgan saw her face; the horror, the revulsion, the sickness of her shocked soul. A moment, a glance, and she was gone. He was alone amidst the blood that the curse of Ascalon had led his hand to pour out in such prodigality in that profaned place.

Long after the fearful waste of battle had been cleared from Peden's floor, and the lights of that hall were put out; long after the most wakeful householder of Ascalon had sought his bed, and the last horseman had gone from its hushed streets, Morgan walked in the moonlight, keeping vigil with his soul. The curse of blood had descended upon him, and she whose name he could speak only in his heart, had come to look upon his infamy and flee from before his face.

Time had saved him for this excruciating hour; all his poor adventures, slow striving, progression upward, had been designed to culminate in the mockery of this night. Fate had shaped him to his bitter ending, drawing him on with lure as bright as sunrise. And now, as he walked slowly in the moonlight, feet encumbered by this tragedy, he felt that the essence had been wrung out of life. His golden building was come to confusion, his silver hope would ring its sweet chime in his heart no more. From that hour she would abhor him, and shrink from his polluted hand.

He resented the subtle indrawing of circumstance that had thrust him in the way of this revolting thing, that had thrust upon him this infamous office that carried with it the inexorable curse of blood. Softly, against the counsel of his own reason, he had been drawn. She who had stared in horror on the wreckage of that night had inveigled him with gentle word, with appeal of pleading eye.

This resentment was sharpened by the full understanding of his justification, both in law and in morals, for the slaying of these desperate men. Duty that none but a coward and traitor to his oath would have shunned, had impelled him to that deed. Defense of his life was a justification that none could deny him. But she had denied him that. She had fled from the lifting of his face as from a thing unspeakably unclean.

He could not chide her for it, nor arraign her with one bitter thought. She had hoped it would be otherwise; her last word had been on her best hope for him in a place where such hope could have no fruition--that he would pass untainted by the bloody curse that fell on men in this place. It could not be.

Because he had taken Seth Craddock's pistol away from him on that first day, she had believed him capable of the superhuman task of enforcing order in Ascalon without bloodshed. Sincere as she had been in her desire to have him assume the duties of peace officer, she had acted unconsciously as a lure to entangle him to his undoing.

Very well; he would clean up the town for her as she had looked to him to do, sweep it clear of the last iniquitous gun-slinger, the last slinking gambler, the last drab. He would turn it over to her clean, safe for her day or night, no element in it to disturb her repose. At what further cost of life he must do this, he could not then foresee, but he resolved that it should be done. Then he would go his way, leaving his new hopes behind him with his old.

Although it was a melancholy resolution, owing to its closing provision, it brought him the quiet that a perturbed mind often enjoys after the formation of a definite plan, no matter for its desperation. Morgan went to the hotel, where Tom Conboy was still on duty smoking his cob pipe in a chair tilted back against a post of his portico.

"Well, the light's out up at Peden's," said Conboy, feeling a new and vast respect for this man who had proved his luck to the satisfaction of all beholders in Ascalon that night.

"Yes," said Morgan, wearily, pausing at the door.

"They'll never be lit again in this man's town," Conboy went on, "and I'm one that's glad to see 'em go. Some of these fellers around town was sayin' tonight that Ascalon will be dead in the shell inside of three weeks, but I can't see it that way. Settlers'll begin to come now, that hall of Peden's'll make a good implement store, plenty of room for thrashin' machines and harvesters. I may have to put up my rates a little to make up for loss in business till things brighten up, but I'd have to do it in time, anyhow."

"Yes," said Morgan, as listlessly as before.

"They say you made a stand with that gun of yours tonight that beat anything a man ever saw--three of 'em down quicker than you could strike a match! I heard one feller say--man! look at that badge of yours!"

Conboy got up, gaping in amazement. Morgan had stepped into the light that fell through the open door, passing on his way to bed. The metal shield that proclaimed his office was cupped as if it had been held edgewise on an anvil and struck with a hammer. Morgan hastily detached the badge and put it in his pocket, plainly displeased by the discovery Conboy had made.

"Bullet hit it, square in the center!" Conboy said. "It was square over your heart!"

"Keep it under your hat!" Morgan warned, speaking crossly, glowering darkly on Conboy as he passed.

"No niggers in Ireland," said Conboy, knowingly; "no-o-o niggers in Ireland!"

Morgan regretted his oversight in leaving the badge in place. He had intended to remove it, long before. As he went up the complaining stairs he pressed his hand to the sore spot over his heart where the bullet almost had driven the badge into his flesh. Pretty sore, but not as sore as it was deeper within his breast from another wound, not as sore as that other hurt would be tomorrow, and the heavy years to come.

CHAPTER XXI

AS ONE THAT IS DEAD

"I feel like I share his guilt," said Rhetta, voice sad as if she had suffered an irreparable loss.

"He's not guilty," said Violet, stoutly, standing in his defense.

Rhetta had fled from Ascalon that morning, following the terrible night of Morgan's sanguinary baptism. Racked by an agony of mingled remorse for her part in this tragedy and the loss of some valued thing which she would not bring her heart to acknowledge, only moan over and weep, and bend her head to her pillow through that fevered night, she had taken horse at sunrise and ridden to Stilwell's ranch, for the comfort of Violet, whose sympathy was like balm to a bruise. Rhetta had come through the night strained almost to breaking. All day she had hidden like one crushed and shamed, in Stilwell's house, pouring out to Violet the misery of her soul.

Now, at night, she was calmer, the haunting terror of the scene which rose up before her eyes was drawing off, like some frightful thing that had stood a menace to her life. But she felt that it never would dim entirely from her recollection, that it must endure, a hideous picture, to sadden her days until the end.

The two girls had gone to the river, where the moonlight softened the desert-like scene of barren bars, and twinkled in the ripples of shallow water which still ran over against the farther shore. They were sitting near the spot where Morgan had laved his bruised feet in the river not many nights past. A whippoorwill was calling in the tangle of cottonwoods and grapevines that grew cool and dark on a little island below them, its plaint as sad as the mourner's own stricken heart.

"I begged him to give up the office and let things go," said Rhetta, pleading to mitigate her own blame, against whom no blame was laid.

"You'd have despised him for it if he had," said Violet.

"But he wouldn't do it, and now this has happened, and he's a man-killer like the rest of them. Oh it's terrible to think about!"

"Not like the rest of them," Violet corrected, in her firm, gentle way. "He had to stand up like a man for what he was sworn to do, or run like a dog. Mr. Morgan wouldn't run. Right or wrong, he wouldn't run from any man!"

"No," said Rhetta, sadly, "he wouldn't run."

"You talk like you wanted him to!"

"I don't think I would," said Rhetta.

"Then what do you expect of a man?" impatiently. "If he stands up and fights he's either got to kill or be killed."

"Don't--don't, Violet! It seems like killing is all I hear--the sound of those guns--I hear them all the time, I can't get them out of my ears!"

"Suppose," said Violet, looking off across the runlet sparkling, gurgling like an infant across the bar, "it was him you saw when you looked in there, instead of the others. You'd have been satisfied then, I suppose?"

"Violet! how can you say such awful things!"

"Well, somebody had to be killed. Do you suppose Mr. Morgan killed them just for fun?"

"They say, they were talking all over town that night--last night--and saying the same thing this morning, that he didn't give them a show, that he just turned his rifle on them and killed them before he knew whether they were going to shoot or not!"

"Well, they lie," said Violet, with the calmness of conviction.

"I suppose he had a right to do what he did, but he doesn't seem like the same man to me now. I feel like I'd lost something--some friendship that I valued, I mean, Violet--you know what I mean."

"I know as well as anything," said Violet, smiling to herself, head turned away, the moonlight on her good, kind face.

"I feel like somebody had died, and that he--they--that he----"

"And you ought to be thankful it isn't so!" said Violet, sharply, "but I don't believe you are."

"I never want to see him again, I'll always think of him standing there with that terrible gun in his hands, those dead men around him on the floor!"

"You may have to go to him on your knees yet, and I hope to God you will Rhetta Thayer!" Violet said.

"If you'd seen somebody--somebody that you--that was--if you'd seen him like I saw him, you wouldn't blame me so," Rhetta defended, beginning again to cry, and bend her head upon her hands and moan like a mother who had lost a child.

Violet was moved out of her harshness at once. She put her arm around the weeping girl, whose sorrow was too genuine to admit a doubt of its great depth, and consoled her with soft words.

"And he looked so big to me, and he was so clean, before that," Rhetta wailed.

"He's bigger than ever, he's as blameless as a lamb," said Violet. "After a little while you'll see it different, he'll be the same to you."

"I couldn't touch his hand!" said Rhetta, shuddering at the thought.

"Never mind," said Violet, soothingly; "never mind."

Violet said no more, but took Rhetta by the hand, and it was wet with tears from her streaming cheeks. There was peace in the night around them, for all the turmoil there might be in human hearts, for night had eased the throbbing, drouth-cursed earth of its burning, and called the trumpeters of the greenery out along the riverside.

"I'm afraid he'll come," said Rhetta by and by.

"Why should he come?" asked Violet, stroking back the other's hair.

"He's got one of your horses--I'm afraid he'll come to bring it home."

"You only hope he will," said Violet, in her assured, calm way.

"Violet!" But there was not so much chiding in the word as a cry of pain, a confession of despair. He would not come; and she knew he would not come.

CHAPTER XXII

WHINERS AT THE FUNERAL

Joe Lynch, the bone man, stopped at the well in the public square to pour water on his wagon tires. A man was pestered clean out of his senses by his tires coming off, his felloes shrinking up like a fried bacon rind in that dry weather, Joe said. It beat his time, that drouth. He had been through some hot and dry spells in the Arkansaw Valley, but never one as dry and hot as this.

He told Morgan this as he poured water slowly on his wheels to swell the wood and tighten the tires, there at the town well in the mid-morning of that summer day. It was so hot already, the ceaseless day wind blowing as if it trailed across a fire, that one felt shivers of heat go over the skin; so hot that the heat was bitter to the taste, and shade was only an aggravation.

This was almost a week after Morgan's forceful assertion of the law's supremacy in Ascalon, when Peden and his assassins fell in their insolence. It seemed that day as if Ascalon itself had fallen with Peden, and the blood of life had drained out of its body. There was a quietude over it that seemed the peace of death.

"I never thought, the day I hauled you into this town," said Joe, his high rasping voice harmonizing well with his surroundings, like a katydid on a dead limb, "you'd be the man to put the kibosh on 'em and close 'em up like you done. I never saw the bottom drop out of no place as quick as it's fell out of this town, and I've saw a good many go up in my day. The last of them gamblers pulled out a couple of days ago, I hauled his trunk over to the depot. He went a cussin', and he pulled the hole in after him, I guess, on all the high-kickin' this town'll ever do. Well, I ain't a carin'; I've been waitin' my time."

"You were wiser than some of them, you knew it would come," Morgan said, glad to meet this bone-gathering philosopher in the desert he had made of Ascalon, and stand talking with him, foot on his hub in friendly way.

"Not so much bones," said Joe reflectively, as if he had weighed the possibilities long ago and now found them coming out according to calculation, "as bottles. Thousands of bottles, every boy in this town's out a pickin' up bottles for me. I reckon I'll have a couple of carloads of nothing but bottles. Oh-h-h, they'll be some bones, but the skeleton of this town is bottles. That's why I tell 'em it never will pick up no more. You've got to build a town on something solider'n a bottle if you want it to stand up."

"I believe you," Morgan said.

"You've worked yourself out of a job. They won't no more need a marshal here'n they will a fish net."

Morgan shook his head, got out his pipe, struck a match on the bleached forehead of a buffalo skull in Joe's wagon.

"No. I'm leaving town in a week or two--when I make sure it is dead, that they'll never come back and start the games again."

"They never will," said Joe, shaking a positive head. "Peden was the guts of this town; it can't never be what it was without him. So you're goin' to leave the country, air you?"

"Yes."

"Give up that fool notion you had about raising wheat out here on this pe-rairie, heh?"

"Gave it up," Morgan replied, nodding in his solemn, expressive way.

"Well, you got some sense hammered into you, anyhow. I told you right at the jump, any man that thought he could farm in this here country should be bored for the simples. Look at that range, look at them cattle that's droppin' dead of starvation and want of water all over it. Look at them cattlemen shippin' out thousands of head that ain't ready for market all along this railroad every day. This range'll be as bare of stock by fall, I tell you, as the pa'm of my hand's bare of hairs. Bones? I'll have more bones to pick up than ever was in this country before. Ascalon ain't all that's dead--the whole range's gone up. This'll clean 'em all out. It's the hottest summer and the longest dry spell that ever was."

"It couldn't be much worse."

"Worse!" Joe looked up from his pouring in his reprovingly surprised way, stopping his dribbling stream on the wagon wheel. "You hang around here a month longer and see what worse is! I'm goin' to begin pickin' up bones over on Stilwell's range in about a week; I'm givin' them wolves and buzzards time to clean 'em up a little better. About then you'll see the cattlemen begin to fight for range along the river where their stock can eat the leaves off of the bushes and find a bunch of bluestem once in a while that ain't frizzled and burnt up. You'll begin to see the wolf side to some of these fellers in this country then."

Joe rumbled on to the car that he was loading, his tires being tight enough to hold him that far. Morgan sauntered down the shady side of the street, meeting few, getting what ease he could out of life with his pipe. He had put off his cowboy dress only that morning, feeling it out of place in the uneventful quiet of the town. He had not carried his rifle since the night of his battle in Peden's hall. Today he was beginning to consider leaving off his revolver. A pocketknife for whittling would be about all the armament a man would need in Ascalon from that time forward.

Earl Gray was leaning on one long leg in the door of his drug-store, oil on his fluffy brown hair. He was melancholy and downcast, plainly resentful in his bearing toward Morgan as the contriver of this business stagnation. He swept his hand around the emptiness of the town as Morgan drew near, giving voice to his contemplation.

"Look at it--not a dime been spent around this square this morning! I ain't sold but one box of pills in two days! If it wasn't for the little trade in t'backer and cigars of a night when the cowboys come in, I'd have to lock up and leave. I will anyhow--I can see it a-comin'."

Morgan leaned against the building close by the door, the indolence of the day over him. There was nothing to do but hear the dying town's complaint. He was not a doctor; he had nothing to prescribe. He realized that the merchants had been hit hard by this sudden paralysis. It would not have been so much like disaster if the town had been left to die in its own way, as time and change would have attended to more slowly.

Morgan could not tell Druggist Gray, whose trade in pills had come to a standstill; he could not tell the hardware merchant, whose traffic in firearms and ammunition had fallen away; he could not explain to the proprietor of the Santa Fé café, or any of the other merchants of the town who had come to regret their one spasm of virtue, induced by fear, that he had not considered either their prosperity or their loss when he closed up the saloons and gambling-houses and drove the proscribed of the law away. They were squealing now, exactly as he had known they would squeal in spite of their assurance before the event. Let them squeal, let them stagnate, let dust settle on their wares that no man came to buy.

For the security of somebody's sleep, for the tranquillity of somebody's dreams; for the peace of two brown eyes, for the safety of a short little white hand, strong and comforting just to see--for these, for these alone, he had closed up the riotous places and swept away like a purging fire the chaff and pestilence of Ascalon. He could not tell them this. Even her he could not tell.

Earl Gray, giving off perfume to the hot winds, was pursuing his complaint.

"The undertaker's packin' up to leave, goin' to ship his stock today. I wish I could go with him, but a man's got to have a place to light before he starts out with a drug stock."

"I don't suppose anybody's sorry to see him go," Morgan said. "I think it's a good sign."

"They'll bury each other, as I told him, and they'll drug each other with mullein tea, as I told him the other day," Gray said, acrimoniously. "Yes, and they'll be eatin' each other before spring! I'd like to know what they're goin' to live on, the few that's left in this town--a little cow-punchin', a little clerkin' in the courthouse and gittin' jury and witness fees. That won't keep no town alive."

"Judge Thayer's got a big colonization project going that looks good, he says. If he puts it through things will begin to pick up."

"Them Mennonites, I guess. They ain't the kind of people a man wants to see come in here--whiskers all over 'em, never sell 'em a cake of shavin' soap or a razor from Christmas to doomsday. Them fellers don't shave, they never shave; they grow up from the cradle with whiskers all over 'em."

"They'll need horse liniment, and stuff like that."

"There might be a livin' here for a drug-store if settlers begun to come in," Gray admitted, picking up a little hope. "They say this sod gives off fevers and chills when it's broke up. Something poison in it."

Tom Conboy was on the sidewalk before his door, casting his eyes up and down the street as if on the lookout for somebody that owed him a bill. He was in bed when Morgan left the hotel on his early round, and there was a look about him still of fustiness and the cobwebs of sleep.

"If a man was to take a sack of meal and empty it, and spread the sack down flat, he'd have something like this man's town's got to be," Conboy complained. "Dead, not a breath left in it. I saw a couple of buzzards sailin' around over the square a while ago. I've been lookin' to see them light on the courthouse tower."

"It is a little quiet, but they all say it will begin to pick up in a day or two," Morgan prevaricated, with a view to reeling him out, having no other diversion.

"I don't know what it's goin' to pick up on," Conboy sighed. "Two for breakfast outside of the regulars. I used to have twenty to thirty-five up to a week ago."

"Court will convene next month," Morgan reminded him by way of cheer.

"It'll bring a few," Conboy allowed, "not many, and all of them big eaters. You don't make anything off of a man that rides thirty or forty miles before breakfast when you sit him down to a twenty-five cent meal."

Morgan said he was not a hotel man, but it seemed pretty plain even to him that there could be no wide border of profit in any such transaction.

"No, it was those night-working men, dealers, bartenders, and that crowd, that were the light and profitable eaters. A man that drinks heavy all night don't get up with a thirty-mile appetite in him next day. Well, they're gone; they'll never come back to this man's town."

TRAIL'S END

"You were one of the men that wanted the town cleaned up."

"No niggers in Ireland, now, Morgan--no-o-o niggers in Ireland!"

Conboy made a warning of his peculiar expression, as if he halted Morgan on ground that was dangerous to advance over as far as another word. It was impressive, almost threatening, given in his deep voice, with grave eye and face suddenly stern, but Morgan knew that it was all on the outside.

"Cowboys don't any more than hit the ground here till they hop on their horses and leave," Conboy continued. "Nothing to entertain them, no interest for a live man in a dead town, where the only drink he can get is out of the well. There was just three horses tied along the square last night, where there used to be fifty or a hundred. I'll have to leave this man's town; I can't stand the pressure."

"A man with a little nerve ought to swallow his present losses for his future gains," Morgan said, beginning to grow tired of this whining.

"If I could see any future gains comin' my way I'd gamble on them with any man," Conboy returned with some spirit. "I'm goin' over to Glenmore this afternoon and see what it looks like there. That's the comin' town, it seems to me; good crops over there in the valley, no cattle starvin'. They may bend the railroad around to touch that town, too--they're talkin' of it. That's sure to happen if Glenmore wins the county seat this fall. Then you'll see skids put under every house in this town and moved over there. Ascalon will be a name some of us old-timers will remember twenty years from now, and that's all."

"If Judge Thayer and the railroad colonization agent put through a big deal they've got going, I don't see why this town shouldn't pick up again on a healthy business foundation," Morgan said.

"Them Pennsylvania Dutch?" Conboy scoffed. "They're not the kind of people that ever stay in a hotel, they carry their blankets with 'em and flop down under their wagons like Indians. When they come to town they bring a basket of grub along, they don't spend money for a meal in any man's hotel. You put Pennsylvania Dutch into this country and there'll never be another coroner's jury called!"

Morgan knocked the ashes out of his short, clubby little pipe, put it in his shirt pocket behind his badge, and went on. He paused at the door of the Headlight office to look within, hoping to see a face that had been missing since the night of his great tragedy. Only Riley Caldwell, the printer, was there, working furiously, as if fired by an ambition that Ascalon, dead or alive, could not much longer contain. The droop-shouldered alpaca coat once worn by the editor now dead, hung beside the desk, like the hull he had cast when he took flight away from the troubles of his much-harassed life.

cxli

Only the day before Judge Thayer had told Morgan that Rhetta was still at Stilwell's ranch, whither she had gone to compose herself after the strain of so much turmoil. Morgan could only feel that she had gone there to avoid him, shrinking from the sight of his face.

There was not much warmth in Morgan's reception by the business men of Ascalon around the square that morning, hot as the weather was. It seemed as if some messenger had gone before him crying his coming, as a jaybird goes setting up an alarm from tree to tree before the squirrel hunter in the woods.

Earnest as their solicitations had been for him to assume the office of marshal, voluble as their protestations in the face of fear and insecurity of life and property that they would accept the result without a whimper, there were only a few who stood by their pledges like men. These were the merchants of solider character, whose dealings were with the cattlemen and homesteaders. The hope of these merchants was in the coming of more homesteaders, according to Judge Thayer's dream. They were the true patriots and pioneers.

While these few commended Morgan's stringent application of the letter and spirit of the state and town laws, their encouragement was only a flickering candle in the general gloom of the place. Morgan knew the grunters were saying behind his back that he had gone too far, farther than their expectations or instructions. All they had expected of him was that he knock off the raw edges, suppress the too evident, abate the promiscuous banging around of guns by every bunch of cowboys that arrived or left, and to cut down a little on the killing, at least confine it to the unprofitable class.

They admitted they didn't want the cowboys killed off the way Craddock had been doing it, giving the town a bad name. But to shut the saloons all up, to go and shoot Peden down that way and kill the town with him, that was more than they had given him license for. So they growled behind his back, afraid of him as they feared lightning, without any ground for such fear in the world.

Judge Thayer appeared to be the only man in town who was genuinely happy over the result of Morgan's sweeping out the encumbering rubbish that blocked the country's progress by its noisome notoriety. But through all the judge's glow of gratitude for duty well done, Morgan was conscious of a peculiar aloofness, not exactly fear such as was unmistakable in many others, but a withdrawing, as if something had fallen between them and changed their relations man to man.

Morgan knew that it was the blood of slain men. He was to this man, and to another of far greater consequence to Morgan's peace and happiness, like a pitcher that had been defiled.

Judge Thayer's friendliness was unabated, but it was the sort of friendliness that did not offer the hand, or touch the arm when walking by Morgan's side, as in the early hours of their acquaintance. Useful this man, to the work that must be done in this place to make it fit, and safe, and secure for property and life, but unclean. That was what Judge Thayer's attitude proclaimed, as plainly as printed words.

This morning when Judge Thayer encountered Morgan on the street, not far from the little catalpa tree that was having a bitter struggle against wind and drouth, he invited the city marshal to accompany him to his office. News that would tickle his ears, he said; big news.

The biggest of this big news was that the railroad company was going to establish a division point there at once. The railroad officials had given Judge Thayer to understand, directly, that this decision had come as a result of the town waking up and shedding its leprous skin. They felt that it would be a safe place for their employees to live now, with the pitfalls closed, the temptations removed. And the credit, Judge Thayer owned, was Morgan's alone.

But there was more news. The eastern immigration agents of the railroad were spreading the news of Ascalon's pacification with gratifying result. Already parties of Illinois and Indiana farmers, who had been looking to that country for a good while, were preparing to come out and scout for locations.

"They're getting tired of farming that high-priced land, Morgan. They're wearing it out, it costs them more for fertilizers than they take off of it. They're coming here, where a man can plow a furrow forty miles long, we tell them--and it's the gospel truth, a hundred miles, or two hundred if he wanted to--and never hit a stump."

Judge Thayer got up at that point, and stood in his door looking at the dull sky sullen with heat; looking at the glimmer that rose like impalpable smoke from the hard surface of the cracked, baked earth.

"But I wish we could get a good rain before they begin to come," he sighed, "and I think--" cautiously, with a sly wink at Morgan--"we're going to get it. I've got a man here right now working on it, along scientific principles, Morgan--entirely scientific."

"A rainmaker?" said Morgan, his incredulity plain in his tone.

"He came to me highly recommended by bankers and others in Nebraska, where he undoubtedly brought rain, and in Texas, where the proof is indisputable. But I'm doing it solely on my own account," Judge Thayer hastened to explain, "carrying the cost alone. He's under contract to bring a copious rain not later than seven days from today."

"What's the bill?" Morgan asked, amused by this man's eager credulity.

"One hundred dollars on account, four hundred to be paid the day he delivers the rain--provided that he delivers it within the specified time.

I've bound him up in a contract."

"I think he'll win," said Morgan, drily, looking meaningly at the murky sky.

"It's founded on science, pure science, Morgan," Judge Thayer declared, warmly. "I'm telling you this in confidence, not another soul in town knows it outside of my own family. We'll keep it a pleasant secret--I want to give the farmers and cattlemen of this valley the present of a surprise. When the proper time comes I'll announce the responsible agency, I'll show that crowd over at Glenmore where the progressive people of this county live, I'll prove to the doubters and knockers where the county seat belongs!"

"It's a great scheme," Morgan admitted. "How does the weather doctor work?"

"Chemicals," Judge Thayer whispered, mysteriously; "sends up vapors day and night, invisible, mainly, but potent, causing, as near as I can come to it from his explanation--which is technical and thoroughly scientific, Morgan--" this severely, as if to rebuke the grin that dawned on Morgan's face. "Causing, as near as I can come to it, a dispersion of the hot belt of atmosphere, this superheated belt that encircles the globe in this spot like a flame of fire, causing a break in this belt, so to speak, drilling a hole in it, bringing down the upper frigid air."

Judge Thayer looked with triumph at Morgan when he delivered this, sweating a great deal, as if the effort to elucidate this scientific man's methods of conspiring against nature to beat it out of a rain were equal to a ten-mile walk in the summer sun.

"Yes, sir," said Morgan, with more respect in his voice and manner than he felt. "And then what happens?"

"Why, when the cold and the hot currents meet, condensation is the natural result," said the judge. "Plain, simple, scientific as a fiddle."

"Just about," said Morgan.

Judge Thayer passed it, either ignoring it as a fling beneath the notice of a scientific man, or not catching the note of ridicule.

"He's at work in my garden now," he said, "sending up his invisible vapors. I want to center the downpour from the heavens over this God-favored spot, right over this God-favored spot of Ascalon."

CHAPTER XXIII

ASCALON CURLS ITS LIP

TRAIL'S END

It was the marvel and regret of people who made their adventures vicariously, and lived the thrill of them by reading the newspapers, that Ascalon had come to a so sudden and unmistakable end of its romance. For a little while there was hope that it might rise against this Cromwell who had reached out a long arm and silenced it; for a few days there was satisfaction in reading of this man's exploits in this wickedest of all wicked towns, for newspapers sent men to study him, and interview him, and write of his conquest of Ascalon on the very battle ground.

Little enough they got out of Morgan, who met them kindly and talked of the agricultural future of the country lying almost unpeopled beyond the notorious little city's door. Such as they learned of his methods of taming a lawless community they got from looser tongues than the city marshal's.

Even from Chicago and St. Louis these explorers among the fallen temples of adventure came, some of them veterans who had talked with Jesse James in his day but recently come to a close. They waited around a few days for the shot that would remove this picturesque crusader, not believing, any more than the rest of the world, including Ascalon itself, believed that this state of quiescence could prevail without end.

While they waited, sending off long stories by telegraph to their papers every night, they saw the exodus of the proscribed begin, increase, and end. The night-flitting women went first, urged away by the necessities of the flaccid fish which lived upon their shame. The gamblers and gamekeepers followed close behind.

A little while the small saloon-keepers who had nosed the floor and licked up the crumbs which fell from Peden's bar hung around, hoping that it was a flurry that would soon subside. They had big eyes for future prosperity, the overlord being now out of the way, and talked excitedly among themselves, even approached Morgan through an emissary with proposals of a handsome subsidy.

But when they saw a Kansas City gambler come and strip Peden's hall of its long bar and furnishings, of its faro tables and doctored roulette wheels, load them all on a car and ship them to his less notorious but safer town, they knew it was the end. Ascalon had fallen with its most notable man, never to rise up again.

The last of the correspondents left on the evening of the day that Judge Thayer set the rainmaker to work. He sent the obituary of Ascalon, as he believed, ahead of him by wire.

Not that Ascalon was as dead as it appeared on the surface, or the gamblers would make it out to be. True, the undertaker's business had gone, and he with it; Druggist Gray's trade in the bromides and restoratives in demand after debauches, and repairs for bunged heads after the nightly carousels, had fallen away to nothing; the Elkhorn hotel and the Santa Fé café were feeding few, and the dealers in vanities and fancies, punctured hosiery, lacy waists, must pack up and follow those upon whom they had prospered.

But there was as much business as before in lumber and hardware, implements, groceries, and supplies for the cattle ranches and the many settlers who were arriving without solicitation or proclamation and establishing themselves to build success upon the ruins of failure left by those who had gone before.

It was only the absence of the wastrels and those who preyed upon them, and the quiet of nights after raucous revelry, that made the place seem dead. Ascalon was as much alive as any town of its kind that had no more justification for being in the beginning. It had more houses than it could use now, since so many of its population had gone; empty stores were numerous around the square, and more would be seen very soon. The fair was over, the holiday crowd was gone. That was all.

Rhetta Thayer came back the same evening the last correspondent faced away from Ascalon. Morgan saw her in the Headlight office, where she worked late that night to overtake her accumulated affairs, her pretty head bent over a litter of proofs. Her door stood open as he passed, but he hastened by softly, and did not return that way again.

He felt that she had gone away from Ascalon on his account, fearful that she would meet him with blood fresh upon his hands. The attitude of Judge Thayer was but a faint reflection of her own, he was sure. It was best that they should not meet again, for blood had blotted out what had seemed the beginning of a tender regard between them. That was at an end.

During the next few days little was seen of Morgan in Ascalon. When he was not riding on long excursions into the outlying country he could have been found, if occasion had arisen demanding his presence on the square, in the station agent's office at the depot. There he spent hours hearing the little agent, whose head was as bald as a grasshopper's, nothing but a pale fringe from ear to ear at the back of his neck, recount the experiences that had fallen in his way during his five-years' occupancy of that place.

This period covered the most notorious history of the town. In that time, according to the check the agent had kept on them, no fewer than fifty-nine men had met violent death on the street and in the caves of vice in Ascalon. This man also noted keenly every arrival in these slack days, duly reporting them all to Morgan, for whom he had a genuine friendship and respect. So there was little chance of anybody slipping in to set a new brewing of trouble over the dying embers of that stamped-out fire.

Morgan avoided the Headlight office, for there was a sensitive spot in his heart that Rhetta's abhorrence of him hurt keenly. But more than that he had the thought of sparing her the embarrassment of a meeting, even of his shadow passing her door.

Twice he saw her at a distance in the street, and once she stood waiting as if to speak to him. But the memory of her face at Peden's door that night was with him always; he could not believe she would seek a meeting out of a spontaneous and honest desire to see him. Only because their lives were thrown together for a little while in that dice-box of fate, and avoidance seemed studied and a thing that might set foolish tongues clapping, she paused and looked his way as if waiting for him to approach. She was serving convention, not with a wish of her heart. So he believed, and turned the other way.

Cattlemen from the range at hand, and several from Texas who had driven their herds to finish on the far-famed Kansas grass for the fall market, were loading great numbers of cattle in Ascalon every day. The drouth was driving them to this sacrifice. Lean as their cattle were, they would be leaner in a short time.

This activity brought scores of cowboys to town daily. Under the old order business would have been lively at night, when most of the herdsmen were at leisure. As it was, they trooped curiously around the square, some of them who had looked forward on the long drive to a hilarious blowout at the trail's end resentfully sarcastic, but the greater number humorously disposed to make the most of it.

Sober, these men of the range were very much like reservation Indians in town on a holiday. They walked slowly around and around the square, looking at everything closely, saying little, to dispose themselves along the edge of the sidewalk after a while and smoke. There were no fights, nobody let off a gun. When Morgan passed them on his quiet rounds, they nudged each other, and looked after him with low comments, for his fame had gone far in a little while.

These men had no quarrel with Morgan, disappointed of their revelry, thirsty after their long waiting, sour as some of them were over finding this oasis of their desert dry. They only looked on him with silent respect. Nobody cared to provoke him; it was wise to give the road when a fellow met that man. So they talked among themselves, somewhat disappointed to find that Morgan was not carrying his rifle about with him these peaceful days, unusual weapon for a gun-fighting man in that country.

In this way, with considerable coming and going through its doors, yet all in sobriety and peace, Ascalon passed the burning, rainless summer days. But not without a little cheer in the hard glare of the parching range, not without a laugh and a chuckle, and a grin behind the hand. The town knew all about the rainmaker at work behind the shielding rows of tall corn in Judge Thayer's garden. An undertaking of such scope was too big to sequester in any man's back yard.

Whether the rainmaker believed in his formula, or whether he was a plain fraud who was a little sharper on weather conditions than most men, and good on an estimate of a drouth's duration, he seemed to be doing something to earn his money. Day and night he kept something burning in a little tin stove with a length of pipe that came just above the corn, sending up a smoke that went high toward the cloudless sky before the wind began to blow in the early morning hours, and after it ceased at evening, after its established plan. During the day this smoke dispersed very generally over town, causing some coughing and sneezing, and not a little swearing and scoffing.

Sulphur, mainly, the doctor and Druggist Gray pronounced the chemical to be. It was a sacrilege, the Baptist preacher declared, an offering to Satan, from the smell of it, rather than a scientific assault upon the locked heavens to burst open the windows and let out a dash of rain. If the effort of the mysterious stranger brought anything at all, it would bring disaster, the preacher declared. A cyclone, very likely, and lightning, in expression of the Almighty's wrath.

Those who did not accept it wrathfully, as the preacher, or resentfully, as Druggist Gray, from whom the experimenter bought none of his chemicals, or humorously, as the doctor and many of higher intelligence, had a sort of sneaking hope that something might come of it. If the rain man could stir up a commotion and fetch a soaker, it would be the salvation of that country. The range would revive, streams would flow, water would come again into dry wells, and the new farmers who had come in would be given hope to hang on another year and by their trade keep Ascalon from perishing utterly.

But mainly the disposition was to laugh. Judge Thayer was a well-meaning man, but easy. He believed he was bringing a doctor in to cure the country's sickness, where all of his hopes were staked out in town lots, when he had brought only a quack. A hundred dollars, even if the faker made no more, was pretty good pay for seven days' work, they said. A dollar's worth of sulphur would cover his expenses. And if it happened to turn out a good guess, and a rain did blow up on time, Judge Thayer was just fool enough to give the fellow a letter that would help him put his fraud through in another place.

It did not appear, as the days passed, that the rainmaker was driving much of a hole in the hot air that pressed down upon that tortured land. No commotion was apparent in the upper regions, no cloud lifted to cut off for an hour the shafts of the fierce sun. Ascalon lay panting, exhausted, dry as tow, the dust of driven herds blowing through its bare, bleak streets.

Gradually, as dry burning day succeeded the one in all particulars like it that had gone before, what little hope the few had in Judge Thayer's weather doctor evaporated and passed away. Those who had scoffed at the beginning jeered louder now, making a triumph of it. The Baptist preacher said the evil of meddling in the works of the Almighty was becoming apparent in the increasing severity of the hot wind. Ascalon, for its sins past and its sacrilege of the present, was to writhe and scorch and wither from the face of the earth.

TRAIL'S END

For all this, interest in the rainmaker's efforts did not lax. People sniffed his smoke, noting every change in its flavor, and pressed around Judge Thayer's garden fence trying to get a look at the operations. Judge Thayer was not a little indignant over the scoffings and denunciations, and this impertinent curiosity to pry upon what he gave them to understand was his own private venture.

Keep off a safe distance from this iniquitous business, he warned with sarcasm; don't lean on the fence and risk the wrath of the Almighty. Let the correction of Providence fall on his own shoulders, which had been carrying the sins of Ascalon a long time; don't get so close as to endanger their wise heads under the blow. At the same time he gave them to understand that if any rain came of the efforts of his weather doctor it would be his, the judge's, own private and individual rain, wrung from denying nature by science, and that science paid for by the judge's own money.

The scoffers laughed louder at this, the sniffers wrinkled their noses a little more. But the Baptist preacher only shook his head, the hot wind blowing his wide overalls against his thin legs.

Morgan stood aloof from doubters, hopers, scoffers, and all, saying no word for or against the rainmaker. Every morning now he took a ride into the country, to the mystification of the town, coming back before the heat mounted to its fiercest, always on hand at night to guard against any outbreak of violence among the visitors.

There were not a few in town who watched him away each morning in the hope that something would overtake him and prevent his return; many more who felt their hearts sink as he rode by their doors with the fear that each ride would be his last. Out there in the open some enemy might be lying behind a clump of tangled briars. These women's prayers went with the city marshal as he rode.

On a certain morning Morgan overtook Joe Lynch, driving toward town with his customary load of bones. Morgan walked his horse beside Joe's wagon to chat with him, finding always a charm of originality and rather more than superficial thinking about the old fellow that was refreshing in the intellectual stagnation of the town.

"Is that rain-crow feller still workin' over in town?" Joe inquired as soon as greetings had passed.

"I suppose he is, I don't believe his seven days are up yet."

"This is his sixth, I'm keepin' notches on him. I thought maybe he'd skinned out. Do you think he'll be able to fetch it?"

"I hope he can, but I've got my doubts, Joe."

"Yes, and I've got more than doubts. Science is all right, I reckon, as fur as I ever heard, but no science ain't able to rake up clouds in the sky like you'd rake up hay in a field and fetch on a rain. Even if they did git the clouds together, how're they goin' to split 'em open and let the rain out?"

"That would be something of a job," Morgan admitted.

"You've got to have lightnin' to bust 'em, and no science that ever was can't make lightnin', I'm here to tell you, son. If some feller did happen on how it was done, what do you reckon'd become of that man?"

"Why, they do make it, Joe--they make it right over at Ascalon, keep it in jars under that table at the depot. Didn't you ever see it?"

"That ain't the same stuff," Joe said, with high disdain, almost contempt. "Wire lightnin' and sky lightnin' ain't no more alike than milk's like whisky. Well, say that science did make up a batch of sky lightnin'--but I ain't givin' in it can be done--how air they goin' to git up to the clouds, how're they goin' to make it do the bustin' at the right time?"

"That's more than I can tell you, Joe. It's too deep for me."

"Yes, or any other man. They'd let it go all at once and cause a waterspout, that's about what they'd do, and between a waterspout and a dry spell, give me the dry spell!"

"I never was in one, but I've seen 'em tearin' up the hills."

"Then you know what they air. It'd suit me right up to the han'le if this feller could bring a rain, for I tell you I never saw so much sufferin' and misery as these settlers are goin' through out here on this cussid pe-rairie right now. Some of these folks is haulin' water from the river as much as thirty mile!"

"I notice all the creeks and branches are dry. But it's only a little way to plenty of water all over this country if they'll dig. Some of them have put down wells during this dry spell and hit all the water they need. There's a sheet of water flowing under this country from the mountains in Colorado."

"Oh, you git out!"

"Just the same as the Arkansas River, only spread out for miles," Morgan insisted. "A drouth here doesn't mean anything to that water supply; I've been riding around over this country trying to show people that. Most of them think I'm crazy--till they dig."

"I don't guess you're cracked yit," Joe allowed, "but you will be if you stay in this country. If it wasn't for the bones you wouldn't find me hangin' around here--I'd make for Wyoming. They tell me there's any amount of bones that's never been touched up in that country."

"I noticed several other wagons out gathering bones. They'll soon clean them up here, Joe."

"They're all takin' to it," Joe said, with the resentment of a man who feels competition, "hornin' in on my business, what's mine by rights of bein' the first man to go into it in this blame country. Let 'em--let 'em run their teams down scourin' around after bones--I'll be here to pick up the remains of 'em all. I was here first, I've stuck through the rushes of them fellers that's come into this country and dried up, and I'll be here when this crowd of 'em dries up. Them fellers haul in bones and trade 'em at the store for flour and meal, they don't git half out of 'em what I do out of mine, and they're hurtin' the business, drivin' it down to nothin'."

"Hotter than usual this morning," Morgan remarked, not so much interested in bones and the competition of bones.

"Wind's dying down; I noticed that some time ago. Goin' to leave us to sizzle without any fannin'. Ruther have it that way, myself. This eternal wind dries a man's brains up after a while. I'd say, if I was anywhere else, it was fixin' up to rain."

"Or for a cyclone."

"Too late in the season for 'em," Joe declared, not willing to grant even that diversion to the drouth-plagued land of bones.

Joe reverted to the bones; he could not keep away from bones. There was not much philosophy in him today, not much of anything but a plaint and a denunciation of competition in bones. Morgan thought the wind must be having its effect on Joe's brains; they seemed to be so hydrated that morning they would have rattled against his skull. Morgan considered riding on and leaving him, at the risk of giving offense, dismissing the notion when they rose a hill and looked down on Ascalon not more than a mile away.

"I believe there's a cloud coming up over there," said Morgan, pointing to the southwest.

"Which?" said Joe, rousing as briskly as if he had been doused with a bucket of water. "Cloud? No, that ain't no cloud. That's dust. More wind behind that, a regular sand storm. Ever been through one of 'em?"

"In Nebraska," Morgan replied, with detached attention, watching what he still believed to be a cloud lifting above the hazy horizon.

"Nothin' like the sand storms in this country," Joe discounted, never willing to yield one point in derogative comparison between that land and any other. "Feller told me one time he saw it blow sand so hard here it started in wearin' a knot hole in the side of his shanty in the evenin', and by mornin' the whole blame shack was gone. Eat them boards up clean, that feller said. Didn't leave nothin' but the nails. But I always thought he was stretchin' it a little," Joe added, not a gleam of humor to be seen anywhere in the whole surface of his wind-dried face.

"That's a cloud, all right," Morgan insisted, passing the reduction by attrition of the settler's shack.

"Cloud?" said Joe, throwing up his head with renewed alertness. He squinted a little while into the southwest. "Bust my hub if it ain't a cloud! Comin' up, too--comin' right along. Say, do you reckon that rain-crow feller brought that cloud up from somewheres?"

"He didn't have anything to do with it," Morgan assured him, grinning a little over the quick shift in the old man's attitude, for there was awe in his voice.

"No, I don't reckon," said Joe thoughtfully, "but it looks kind of suspicious."

The cloud was lifting rapidly, as summer storms usually come upon that unprotected land, sullen in its threat of destruction rather than promise of relief. A great dark fleece rolled ahead of the green-hued rain curtain, the sun bright upon it, the hush of its oncoming over the waiting earth. No breath of wind stirred, no movement of nature disturbed the silent waiting of the dusty land, save the lunging of foolish grasshoppers among the drooping, withered sunflowers beside the road as the travelers passed.

"I'm goin' to see if I can make it to town before she hits," said Joe, lashing out with his whip. "Lordy! ain't it a comin'!"

"I think I'll ride on," said Morgan, feeling a natural desire for shelter against that grim-faced storm.

The oncoming cloud had swept its flank across the sun before Morgan rode into town, and in the purple shadow of its threat people stood before their houses, watching it unfold. In Judge Thayer's garden--it was the house Morgan had fixed on that first morning of his exploration--the rainmaker was firing up vigorously, sending up a smoke of such density as he had not employed in his labors before. This black column rose but a little way, where it flattened against the cool current that was setting in ahead of the storm, and whirled off over the roofs of Ascalon to mock the scoffers who had laughed in their day.

Morgan stabled his horse and went to the square, where many of the town's inhabitants were gathered, all faces tilted to watch the storm. Judge Thayer was there, glorifying in the success of his undertaking, sparing none of those who had mocked him for a sucker and a fool. A cool breath of reviving wind was moving, fresh, sweet, rain-scented; as hopeful, as life-giving, as a reprieve to one chained among faggots at the stake of intolerance.

"It looks like you're going to win, Judge," Morgan said.

"Win? I've won! Look at it, pourin' rain over at Glenmore, the advance of it not three miles from here! It'll be here inside of five minutes, rainin' pitchforks."

But it did not happen so. The rain appeared to have taken to dallying on the way, in spite of the thickening of clouds over Ascalon. Straining faces, green-tinted in the gloomy shadow of the overhanging cloud, waited uplifted for the first drops of rain; the dark outriders of the storm wheeled and mingled, turned and rolled, low over the dusty roofs; lightning rived the rain curtain that swept the famished earth, so near at hand that the sensitive could feel it in their hair; deep thunder sent its tremor through the ground, jarring the windows of Ascalon that had looked in their day upon storms of human passion which were but insect strife to this.

Yet not a drop of rain fell on roof, on trampled way, on waiting face, on outstretched hand, in all of Ascalon.

Judge Thayer was seen hurrying from the square, making for home and the weather doctor, who was about to let the rain escape.

"He's goin' to head it off," said one of the scoffers to Morgan, beginning to feel a return of his exultation.

"It's goin' to miss us," said Druggist Gray, his head thrown back, his Adam's apple like an elbow of stovepipe in his thin neck.

"We may get a good shower out of one end of it," Conboy still hoped, pulling for the rain as he might have boosted for a losing horse.

"Nothing more than a sprinkle, if that much," said the station agent, shaking his head, which he had bared to the cool wind.

"He's got him firin' up like he was tryin' to hive a swarm of bees," one reported, coming from the seat of scientific labors.

"It's breakin', it's passin' by us--we'll not get a drop of it!"

So it appeared. Overhead the swirling clouds were passing on; in the distance the thunder was fainter. The wind began to freshen from the track of the rain, the pigeons came out of the courthouse tower for a look around, light broke through the thinning clouds.

Not more than a mile or two southward of Ascalon the rain was falling in a torrent, the roar of it still quite plain in the ears of those whose thirst for its cooling balm was to be denied. The rain was going on, after soaking and reviving Glenmore, which place Judge Thayer would have given a quarter of his possessions to have had it miss.

A mockery, it seemed, a rebuke, a chastisement, the way nature conducted that rain storm. Judge Thayer urged the rainmaker to his greatest efforts to stop it, turn it, bring it back; smoke green and black went up in volumes, to stream away on the cool, refreshing wind. Sulphur and rosin and pitch were identified in that smoke as surely as the spectrum reveals the composition of the sun. But the wind was against the rainmaker; nature conspired to mock him before men as the quack that he was.

The gloom of storm cleared from the streets of Ascalon, the worn and tired look came back into faces that had been illumined for a little while with hope. Farther away, fainter, the thunder sounded, dimmer the murmur of the withdrawing rain.

The cool wind still blew like whispered consolation for a great, a pangful loss, but it could not soften the hard hearts of those who had stood with lips to the fountain of life and been denied. The people turned again to their pursuits, their planning, their gathering of courage to hold them up against the blaze of sun which soon must break upon them for a parching season again. The dust lay deep under their feet, gray on their roofs where shingles curled like autumn leaves in the sun. The rainmaker sent up his vain, his fatuous, foolish, infinitesimal breath of smoke. The rain went on its way.

"Aw, hell!" said Ascalon, in its derisive, impious way; "Aw, hell!"

CHAPTER XXIV

MADNESS OF THE WINDS

Ascalon's temper was not improved by the close passing of the rain, which had refreshed but a small strip of that almost limitless land. The sun came out as hot as before, the withering wind blew from the southwest plaguing and distorting the fancy of men. Everybody in town seemed sulky and surly, ready to snap at a word. The blight of contention and strife seemed to be its heritage, the seed of violence and destruction to be sown in the drouth-cursed soil.

The judgment of men warped in that ceaseless wind, untempered by green of bough overhead or refreshing turf under foot. There was no justice in their hearts, and no mercy. Morgan himself did not escape this infection of ill humor that rose out of the hard-burned earth, streamed on the hot wind, struck into men's brains with the rays of the penetrating sun. Not conscious of it, certainly, any more than the rest of them in Ascalon were aware of their red-eyed resentment of every other man's foot upon the earth. Yet Morgan was drilled by the boring sun until his view upon life was aslant. Resentment, a stranger to him in his normal state, grew in him, hard as a disintegrated stone; scorn for the ingratitude of these people for whom he had imperiled his life rose in his eyes like a flame.

More than that, Morgan brooded a great deal on the defilement of blood he had suffered there, and the alienation, real or fancied, that it had brought of such friends as he valued in that town. By an avoidance now unmistakably mutual, Morgan and Rhetta Thayer had not met since the night of Peden's fall.

One thing only kept Morgan there in the position that had become thankless in the eyes of those who had urged it upon him in the beginning. That was the threatened vengeance of Peden's friends. He was giving them time to come for their settlement; he felt that he could not afford to be placed in the light of one who had fled before a threat. But it seemed to him, on the evening of the second day after the rain storm's passing, that he had waited long enough. The time had come for him to go.

There were a few cowboys in town that evening, and these as quiet as buzzards on a fence as they sat along the sidewalk near the hotel smoking their cigarettes. The wind had fallen, leaving a peace in the ears like the cessation of a hateful turmoil. There was the promise of a cool night in the unusual clearness of the stars. Morgan rode away into the moonless night, leaving the town to take care of its own dignity and peace.

Morgan's thought was, as he rode away into the early night, to return Stilwell's horse, come back to Ascalon next day, resign his office and leave the country. Not that his faith in its resources, its future greatness and productivity when men should have learned how to subdue it, was broken or changed. His mind was of the same bent, but circumstances had revised his plans. There was with him always, even in his dreams, a white, horror-stricken face looking at him in the pain of accusation, repulsion, complete abhorrence, where he stood in that place of blood.

This was driving him away from the hopes he had warmed in his heart for a day. Without the sweet flower he had hoped to fend and enjoy, that land would be a waste to him. He could not forget in going away, but distance and time might exorcise the spirit that attended him, and dim away the accusing pain of that terrified face.

Ascalon's curse of blood had descended to him; it was no mitigation in her eyes that he had slain for her. But he had brought her security. Although he had paid the tremendous price, he had given her nights of peace.

Even as this thought returned to him with its comfort, as it came always like a cool breath to preserve his balance in the heat and turmoil of his regret and pain, Rhetta Thayer came riding up the dim road.

Her presence on that road at night was a greater testimonial to her confidence in the security he had brought to Ascalon and its borders than her tongue might have owned. She was riding unattended where, ten days ago, she would not have ventured with a guard. It gave Morgan a thrill of comfort to know how completely she trusted in the security he had given her.

"Mr. Morgan!" she said, recognizing him with evident relief. Then, quickly, in lively concern. "Who's looking after things in town tonight?"

"I left things to run themselves," he told her quietly, but with something in his voice that said things might go right or wrong for any further concern he had of them.

"Well," she said, after a little silence, "I don't suppose you're needed very much."

"That's what the business men are saying," he told her, sarcasm in his dry tone.

"I don't mean it that way," she hastened to amend. "You've done us a great service--we'll never be able to pay you----"

"There isn't any pay involved," he interposed, almost roughly. "That's what's worrying those nits around the square, they say they can't carry a marshal's pay with business going to the devil since the town's closed. Somebody ought to tell them. There never will be any bill."

"You're too generous," she said, a little spontaneous warmth in her voice.

"Maybe I can live it down," he returned.

"It's such a lovely cool night I couldn't stay in," she chatted on, still laboring to be natural and at ease, not deceiving him by her constraint at all, "after such a hard day fussing with that old paper. We missed an issue the week--last week--we're getting out two in one this time. Why haven't you been in? you seem to be in such a hurry always."

"I wanted to spare you what you can't see in the dark," he said, the vindictive spirit of Ascalon's insanity upon him.

"What I can't see in the dark?" she repeated, as if perplexed.

"My face."

"You shouldn't say that," she chided, but not with the hearty sincerity that a friend would like to hear. "Are you going back to town?"

"I'll ride with you," he granted, feeling that for all her friendly advances the shadow of his taint lay between them.

They were three miles or more from town, the road running as straight as a plumbline before them. A little way they jogged on slowly, nothing said.

TRAIL'S END

Rhetta was the first to speak.

"What made you run away from me that day I wanted to speak to you, Mr. Morgan?"

"Did you want to, or were you just--did you want to speak to me that day, Miss Thayer?" Morgan's heart began to labor, his forehead to sweat, so hard was the rebirth of hope.

"And you turned right around and walked off!"

"You can tell me now," he suggested, half choking on the commonplace words, the tremor of his springing hope was so great.

"I don't remember--oh, nothing in particular. But it looks so strange for us--for you--to be dodging me--each other--that way, after we'd started being friends before everybody."

"Only for the sake of appearances," he said sadly. "I hoped--but you ran away and hid for a week, you thought I was a monster."

Foolish, perhaps, to cut down the little shoot of hope again, when a gentle breath, a soft word, might have encouraged and supported it. But it was out of his mouth, the fruit of his brooding days, in his resentfulness of her injustice, her ingratitude for his sacrifice, as he believed. He saw her turn from him, as if a revulsion of the old feeling swept her.

"Don't judge me too harshly, Mr. Morgan," she appealed, still looking away.

Morgan was melted by her gentle word; the severity of the moment was dissolved in a breath.

"If we could go on as we began," he suggested, almost pleading in his great desire.

"Why, aren't we?" she asked, succeeding well, as a woman always can in such a situation, in giving it a discouraging artlessness.

"You know how they're kicking and complaining all around the square because I've shut up the town, ruined business, brought calamity to their doors as they see it?"

"Yes, I know."

"They forget that they came to me with their hats in their hands and asked me to do it. Joe Lynch says the hot wind has dried their reason up like these prairie springs. I believe he's right. But I didn't shut the town up for them, I didn't go out there with my gun like a savage and shoot men down for them, Miss Thayer. If you knew how much you were----"

"Don't--don't--Mr. Morgan, please!"

"I think there's something in what Joe Lynch says about the wind," he told her, leaning toward her, hand on the horn of her saddle. "It warps men, it opens cracks in their minds like the shrunk lumber in the houses of Ascalon. I think sometimes it's getting its work in on me, when I'm lonesome and disappointed."

"You ought to come in and talk with me and Riley sometimes."

"I've often felt like going to them, whining around about the town being killed," he went on, pursuing his theme as if she had not spoken, "and telling them they didn't figure in my calculations at the beginning nor come in for any of my consideration at the end--if this is the end. There was only one person in my thoughts, that one person was Ascalon, and all there was in it, and that was you. When I took the job that day, I took it for you."

"Not for me alone!" she hastened to disclaim, as one putting off an unwelcome responsibility, unfriendly denial in her voice.

"For you, and only you," he told her, earnestly. "If you knew how much you were to me----"

"Not for me alone--I was only one among all of them," she said, spurring her horse in the vehemence of her disclaimer, causing it to start away from Morgan with quick bound. She checked it, waiting for him to draw up beside her again. "I'd hate to think, Mr. Morgan--oh, you can't want me alone to take the responsibility for the killing of those men!"

Morgan rode on in silence, head bent in humiliation, in the sad disappointment that fell on him like a blow.

"If it could have been done, if I could have brought peace and safety to the women of Ascalon without bloodshed, I'd have done it. I wanted to tell you, I tried to tell you----"

"Don't--don't tell me any more, Mr. Morgan--please!"

She drew across the road, widening the space between them as she spoke. Perhaps this was due to the unconscious pressure on the rein following her shrinking from his side, from the thought of his touch upon her hand, but it wounded Morgan's humiliated soul deeper than a thousand unkind words.

"No, I'll never tell you," he said sadly, but with dignity that made the renunciation noble.

Rhetta seemed touched. She drew near him again, reaching out her hand as if to ease his hurt.

"It was different before--before that night! you were different, all of us, everything. I can't help it, ungrateful as I seem. You'll forgive me, you'll understand. But you were different to me before then."

"Yes, I was different," Morgan returned, not without bitterness in his slow, deep, gentle voice. "I never killed a man for--I never had killed a man; there was no curse of blood on my soul."

"Why is it always necessary to kill in Ascalon?" she asked, wildly, rebelliously. "Why can't anything be done without that horrible ending!"

"If I knew; if I had known," he answered her, sadly.

"Forgive me, Mr. Morgan. You know how I feel about it all."

"I know how you feel," he said, offering no word of forgiveness, as he had spoken no word of reminder where a less generous soul might have spoken, nor raised a word of blame. If he had a thought that she must have known when she urged him to the defense of the defenseless in Ascalon, what the price of such guardianship must be, he kept it sealed in his heart.

They rode on. The lights of Ascalon came up out of the night to meet their eyes as they raised the last ridge. There Morgan stopped, so abruptly that she rode on a little way. When he came up to her where she waited, he was holding out his hand.

"Here is my badge--the city marshal's badge," he said. "If you can bear the thought of touching it, or touch it without a thought, I wish you would return it to Judge Thayer for me. I'm not needed in Ascalon any longer, I'm quitting the job tonight. Good-bye."

Morgan laid the badge in her hand as he spoke the last word, turned his horse quickly, rode back upon their trail. Rhetta wheeled her horse about, a protest on her lips, a sudden pang in her heart that clamored to call him back. But no cry rose to summon him to her side, and Morgan, gloomy as the night around him, went on his way.

But the lights of Ascalon were blurred as if she looked on them through a rain-drenched pane when Rhetta faced again to go her way alone, the marshal's badge clutched in her hand. Remorse was roiling in her breast; the corrosive poison of regret for too much said, depressed her generous heart.

If he had known how to accomplish what he had wrought without blood, he had said; if he had known. Neither had she known, but she had expected it of him, she had set him to the task with an unreasonable condition. Blood was the price. Ascalon exacted blood, always blood.

The curse of blood, he had said, was on his soul, his voice trembling with the deep, sad vibration that might have risen from a broken heart. Yes, there was madness in the wind, in the warping sun, in the hard earth that denied and mocked the dearest desires of men. It had struck her, this madness that hollowed out the heart of a man like a worm, leaving it an unfeeling shell.

Rhetta had time for reflection when she reached home, and deeper reflection than had troubled the well of her remorse as she rode. For there in the light of her room she saw the bullet-mark on the dented badge, which never had come quite straight for all Morgan's pains to hammer out its battle scars. A little lead from the bullet still clung in the grooves of letters, unmistakable evidence of what had marred its nickled front.

Conboy had regarded Morgan's warning to keep that matter under his hat, for he had learned the value of silence at the right time in his long experience in that town. Nobody else knew of the city marshal's close escape the night of his great fight. The discovery now came to Rhetta Thayer with a cold shudder, a constriction of the heart. She stared with newly awakened eyes at the badge where it lay in her palm, her pale cheeks cold, her lips apart, shocked by the sudden realization of his past peril as no word could have expressed.

Hot thoughts ran in thronging turmoil through her brain, thoughts before repressed and chilled in her abhorrence of that flood of blood. For her he had gone into that lair of murderous, defiant men, for her he had borne the crash of that ball just over his heart. For there he had worn the badge--just over his honest heart. Perhaps because she had thought his terrible work had been unjustified, as the spiteful and vicious told, she had recoiled from him, and the recollection of him standing on grim guard among the sanguinary wreckage of that awful place. If he had known any other way, he had said; if he had known!

Not for the mothers of Ascalon, of whom he had spoken tenderly; not for the men who came cringing to beg their redemption from the terror and oppression of the lawless at his hand. Not for them. But for her. So he had said not half an hour past.

But he had said no word to remind her where reminder was needed, not an accusation had he uttered where accusation was so much deserved, that would bring back to her the plain, hard fact that it was at her earnest appeal he had undertaken the regeneration of that place.

On the other hand, he had spoken as if he had assumed the task voluntarily, to give her the security that she now enjoyed. She had sent him to this work, expecting him to escape the curse of blood that had fallen. But she had not shown him the means. And when it fell on him, saddening his generous heart, she had fled like an ingrate from the sight of his stern face. Now he was gone, leaving her to the consideration of these truths, which came rushing in like false reserves, too late.

She put out the light and sat by the open window, the scarred badge between her hands, warming it tenderly as if to console the hurt he had suffered, wondering if this were indeed the end. This evidence in her hand was like an absolution; it left him without a stain. The justification was there presented that removed her deep-seated abhorrence of his deed. In defense of his own life he had struck them down. His life; most precious and most dear. And he was gone.

Was this, indeed, the end? For her romance that had lifted like a bright flower in an unexpected place for a little day, perhaps; for Ascalon, not the end. Something of unrest, as an impending storm, something of the night's insecurity, troubled her as she sat by the window and told her this. The sense of peace that had made her nights sweet was gone; a vague terror seemed growing in the silent dark.

This feeling attended her when she went to bed, harassed her sleep like a fever, woke her at early dawn and drew her to the window, where she leaned and listened, straining to define in the stillness the thing that seemed to whisper a warning to her heart.

There was nothing in the face of nature to account for this; not a cloud was on the sky. The town, too, lay still in the mists of breaking morning, its houses dim, its ways deserted. Alarm seemed unreasonable, but her heart quivered with it, and shrunk within her as from a chilling wind. There was no warder at the gate of Ascalon; the sentry was gone.

Rhetta turned back to her bed, neither quieted of her indefinable uneasiness nor inclined to resume her troubled sleep. After a little while she rose again, and dressed. Dread attended her, dread had brooded on her bosom while she slept uneasily, like a cat breathing its poisoned breath into her face.

Dawn had widened when she went to the window again, the mist that clung to the ground that morning in the unusual coolness was lifting. A horseman rode past the corner at the bank, stopped his horse in the middle of the street, turned in his saddle and looked around the quiet square.

Other riders followed, slipping in like wolves from the range, seven or eight of them, their horses jaded as if they had been long upon the road. Cowboys in with another herd to load, she thought. And with the thought the first horseman, who had remained this little while in the middle of the street gazing around the town, rode up to the hitching rack beside the bank and dismounted. Rhetta gasped, drawing back from the window, her heart jumping in sudden alarm.

Seth Craddock!

There could be no mistaking the man, slow-moving when he dismounted, tall and sinewy, watchful as a battered old eagle upon its crag. With these ruffians at his back, gathered from the sweepings of no knowing how many outlawed camps, he had come in the vengeance that had gathered like a storm in his evil heart, to punish Ascalon and its marshal for his downfall and disgrace.

CHAPTER XXV

A SUMMONS AT SUNRISE

Three horses were standing in Stilwell's yard, bridle reins on the ground, as three horses had stood on the morning that Morgan first found his tortured way to that hospitable door. In the house the Stilwell family and Morgan were at breakfast, attended by Violet, who bore on biscuits and ham to go with the coffee that sent its cheer out through the open door as if to find a traveler and lead him to refreshment. Behind the cottonwoods along the river, sunrise was about to break.

"I'm gittin' so I can't wake up of a morning when I sleep in a house," Stilwell complained, his broad face radiating humor. "I guess I'll have to take the blankets ag'in, old lady."

"I guess you can afford to sleep till half-past three in the morning once in a while," Mrs. Stilwell said complacently. "Why, Mr. Morgan, that man didn't sleep under a roof once a month the first five or six years we were on this range! He just laid out like a coyote anywhere night overtook him, watchin' them cattle like they were children. Now, what's come of it!"

This last bitter note, ranging back to their recent loss from Texas fever, took the cheer out of Stilwell's face. A brooding cloud came over it; his merry chaff was stilled.

"Yes, and Drumm'll pay for them eight hundred head of stock he killed for us, if I have to trail him to his hole in Texas!" Fred declared. "Suit or no suit, that man's goin' to pay."

"I don't like to hear you talk that way, honey," his mother chided.

"Suit!" Fred scoffed; "what does that man care about a suit? He'll never show his head in this country any more, the next drive he makes he'll load west of here and we'll never know anything about it. There's just one way to fix a man like him, and I know the receipt that'll cure his hide!"

"If he ever drives another head of stock into this state I'll hear of it, and I'll attach him. It'll be four or five years before the railroad's built down into that country, he'll have to drive here or nowheres. I'll set right here on this range till he comes."

"Did the rain strike any of your range?" Morgan inquired, eager to turn them away from this gloomy matter of loss and revenge.

"Yes, we got a good soakin' over the biggest part of it. Plenty of water now, grass jumpin' up like spring. It's the purtiest country, Cal, a man ever set eyes on after a rain."

"And in the spring," said Mrs. Stilwell, wistfully.

"And when the wild roses bloom along in May," said Violet. "There's no place in the world as pretty as this country then."

"I believe you," Morgan told them, nodding his head in undivided assent. "Even dry as it is around Ascalon and that country north, it gets hold of a man."

"You buy along on the river here somewhere, Cal, and put in a nice little herd. It won't take you long to make a start, and a good start. This country ain't begun to see the cattle it will----"

"Somebody comin'," said Violet, running to the door to see, a plate of hot biscuits in her hand.

"Seems to be in a hurry for this early in the day," Stilwell commented, listening to the approach of a galloping horse. He was not much interested; horsemen came and went past that door at all hours of the day and night, generally in a gallop.

"It's Rhetta!" Violet announced from the door, turning hurriedly to put the plate of biscuits on the table, where it stood before unheeding eyes.

"Rhetta?" Mrs. Stilwell repeated, getting up in excitement. "I wonder what----"

Rhetta was at the door, the dust of her arrival making her indistinct to those who hurried from the unfinished breakfast to learn the cause of this precipitous visit. Morgan saw her leaning from the saddle, her loosely confined hair half falling down.

"Is Mr. Morgan here?" she inquired.

The girl's voice trembled, her breath came so hard Morgan could hear its suspiration where he stood. It was evident that she labored under a tremendous strain of anxiety, arising out of a trouble that Morgan was at no loss to understand. Yet he remained in the background as Stilwell and Fred crowded to the door.

"Why, Rhetty! what's happened?" Stilwell inquired, hurrying out, followed by his wife and son. Violet was already beside her perturbed visitor, looking up into her terror-blanched face.

"Oh, they've come, they've come!" Rhetta gasped.

"Who?" Stilwell asked, mystified, laying hold of her bridle, shaking it as if to set her senses right. "Who's come, Rhetty?"

"I came for Mr. Morgan!" she panted, as weak, it seemed, as a wounded bird. "I thought he came here--he had your horse."

"He's here, honey," Mrs. Stilwell told her, consoling her like a hurt child.

Morgan did not come forward. He stood as he had risen from his chair at the table, one hand on the cloth, his head bent as if in a travail of deepest thought. The shaft of tender new sunlight reaching in through the open door struck his shoulders and breast, leaving his face in the shadow that well suited the mood darkening over his soul like a storm. A thousand thoughts rose up and swirled within him, a thousand harsh charges, a thousand seeds of bitterness. Rhetta, leaning to peer under the lintel of the low door, could see him there, and she reached out her hand, appealing without a word.

"He is here, honey," Mrs. Stilwell repeated, assuringly, comfortingly.

"Tell him--tell him--Craddock's come!" Rhetta said.

"Craddock?" said Stilwell, pronouncing the name with inflection of surprise. "Oh, I thought something awful had happened to somebody." He turned with the ease of indifference in his manner, to go back and finish his meal. "Well, didn't you look for him to come back? I knew all the time he'd come."

Morgan lifted his head. The sun, broken by Rhetta's shadow, brightened on the floor at his feet, and spread its beam upon his breast like a golden stole. The old wound on his check bone was a scar now, irregular, broad from the crude surgery that had bound it but illy. Its dark disfigurement increased the somber gravity of his face, sunburned and wind-hardened as any ranger's who rode that prairie waste. From where he stood Morgan could not see the girl's face, only her restless hand on the bridle rein, the brown of her riding skirt, the beginning of white at her waist.

"There ought to be men enough in Ascalon to take care of Craddock," Violet said.

"He's not alone, some of those Texas cowboys are with him," Rhetta explained, her voice firmer, her words quicker. "Mr. Morgan is still marshal--he gave me his badge, but please tell him I didn't--I forgot to turn it in with his resignation."

"I don't see that it's Cal's fight this time, Rhetty," Stilwell said. "He's done enough for them yellow pups over in Ascalon, to be yelped at and cussed for savin' their dirty hides."

"They're looking for him, they think he's hiding!"

"Well, let 'em look. If they come over here they'll find him--Cal ain't makin' no secret of where he's at. And they'll find somebody standin' back to back with him, any time they want to come." Stilwell's

TRAIL'S END

resentment of Ascalon's ingratitude toward his friend was plainer in his mouth than print.

"They're going to burn the town to drive him out!" Rhetta said, gasping in the terror that shook her heart.

"I guess it'll be big enough to hold all the people that's in it when they're through," said Stilwell, unfeelingly.

"Here's his badge," said Rhetta, offering it frantically. "Tell him he's still marshal!"

"Yes, you can come for him--now!" said Violet, accusingly. "I told you-- you remember now what I told you!"

"O Violet, Violet! If you knew what I've paid for that--if you knew!"

"Not as much as you owe him, if it was the last drop of blood in your heart!" said Violet. And she turned away, and went and stood by the door.

"They'll burn the town!" Rhetta moaned. "Oh, isn't anybody going to help me--won't you call him, Violet?"

"No," said Violet. "He can hear you--he'll come if he wants to--if he's fool enough to do it again!"

"Violet!" her mother cautioned.

"How many are with him?" Fred inquired.

"Seven or eight--I didn't see them all. Pa's collecting a posse to guard the bank--they're going to rob it!"

"They're welcome to all I've got in it," Stilwell said. "You better come in and have a cup of coffee, Rhetty, before----"

"The one they call the Dutchman's there, and Drumm----"

"Drumm?" Fred and his father spoke like a chorus, both of them jumping to alertness.

"And some others of that gang Mr. Morgan drove out of town. They were setting the hotel afire when I left!"

Stilwell did not wait for all of it. He was in the house at a jump, reaching down his guns which hung beside the door. Close after him Fred came rushing in, snatching his weapons from the buffalo horns on the wall.

"I'm goin' to git service on that man!" Stilwell said. "Are you goin' with us, Cal?"

But Cal Morgan did not reply. He went to the bedroom where he had slept, took up his gun, stood looking at it a moment as if considering something, snatched his hat from the bedpost and turned back, buckling his belt. Mrs. Stilwell and Violet were struggling with husband and brother to restrain them from rushing off to this battle, raising a turmoil of pleading and protesting at the door.

As Morgan passed Stilwell, who was greatly impeded in his efforts to buckle on his guns by his wife's clinging arms and passionate pleadings to remain at home, Fred broke away from his sister and ran for the kitchen door.

"Let Drumm go--let all of them go--let the cattle go, let everything go! none of it's worth riskin' your life for!" Stilwell's affectionate good wife pleaded with him.

"Now, Mother, I'm not goin' to git killed," Morgan heard Stilwell say, his very assurance calming. But the poor woman, who perhaps had recollections of past battles and perils which he had gone through, burst out again, weeping, and clung to him as if she could not let him go.

Morgan paused a moment at the threshold, as if reconsidering something. Violet, who had stood leaning her head on her bent arm, weeping that Fred was rushing to throw his life away, lifted her tearful face, reached out and touched his arm.

"Must you go?" she asked.

For reply Morgan put out his hand as if to say farewell. She took it, pressed it a moment to her breast, and ran away, choked on the grief she could not utter. Morgan stepped out into the sun.

Rhetta Thayer stood at the door, a little aside, as if waiting for him, as if knowing he would come. She was agitated by the anxious hope that spoke out of her white face, but restrained by a fear that could not hide in her wide-straining eyes. She moved almost imperceptibly toward him, her lips parted as if to speak, but said nothing.

As Morgan lifted his hand to his hat in grave salute, passing on, she offered him the badge of his office which she had held gripped in her hand. He took it, inclining his head as in acknowledgment of its safe keeping through the night, and hastened on to one of the horses that stood dozing on three legs in the early sun.

As he left her, Rhetta followed a few quick steps, a cry rising in her heart for him to stay a moment, to spare her one word of forgiveness out of his grim, sealed lips. But the cry faltered away to a great, stifling sob, while tears rose hot in her eyes, making him dim in her sight as he threw the rein over the horse's head, starting the animal out of its sleep with a little squatting jump. She stood so, stretching out her hands to him, while he, unbending in his stern answer to the challenge of duty, unseeing in the hard bitterness of his heart, swung into the saddle and rode away.

Rhetta groped for her saddle, blind in her tears. Morgan was hidden by the dust that hung in the quiet morning behind him as she mounted and followed.

Half a mile or so along the road, Fred passed her, bending low as he rode, as if his desire left the saddle and carried him ahead of his horse; a little while, and Stilwell thundered by, leaving her last and alone on that road leading to what adventures her heart shrunk in her bosom to contemplate.

Ahead of her the smoke of Ascalon's destruction rose high.

CHAPTER XXVI

IN THE SQUARE AT ASCALON

Morgan had time for a bitter train of reflection as he rode, never looking behind him to see who came after. Whether Stilwell would yield to his wife's appeal and remain at home, whether Fred could be bent from his fiery desire to be avenged on the author of their calamity, he took no trouble to surmise. He only knew that he, Calvin Morgan, was rushing again to combat at the call of this girl whose only appeal was in the face of dreadful peril, whose only service was that of blood.

She had come again, this time like a messenger bearing a command, to call him back to a duty which he believed he had relinquished and put down forever. And solely because it would be treasonable to that duty which still clung to him like a tenacious cobweb, he was riding into the smoke of the burning town.

So he told himself as he galloped on, but never believing for a moment in the core of his heart that it was true. Deep within him there was a response to a more tender call than the stern trumpeting of duty--the answer to an appeal of remorseful eyes, of a pleading heart that could not bear the shame of the charge that he was hiding and afraid. For her, and his place of honor in her eyes, he was riding to Ascalon that hour. Not for Ascalon, and those in it who had snarled at his heels. For her, not the larger duty of a sworn officer of the law riding to defend and protect the lives and property under his jurisdiction.

Morgan pulled up his horse at the edge of town, to consider his situation. He had left Stilwell's in such haste, and in the midst of such domestic anguish, that he had neglected to bring one of the rancher's rifles with him. His only weapon was his revolver, and the ammunition at his belt was scant, due to the foolish security of the days when he believed Seth Craddock never would return. He must pick up a gun somewhere, and ammunition.

There was some scattered shooting going on in the direction of the square, but whether the citizens were gathering to the defense of the town, or the raiders were firing admonitory shots to keep them indoors, Morgan could not at that distance tell. He rode on, considering his most urgent necessity of more arms, concluding to ride straight for Judge Thayer's house and borrow his buffalo rifle.

He swung into the road that led past Judge Thayer's house, which thoroughfare entered the square at the bank corner, still about a quarter of a mile away. As he came round the turn of the road he saw, a few hundred yards ahead of him, a man hurrying toward the square with a gun in his hand. A spurt of speed and Morgan was beside him, leaning over, demanding the gun.

It was the old man who had jumped out of his reverie on the morning of Morgan's first return to Ascalon, and menaced him with the crook of his hickory stick. The veteran was going now without the comfort of his stick, making pretty good time, eager in the rousing of fires long stilled in his cooling heart. He began trotting on when he recognized Morgan, shouting for him to hurry.

"Lend me your gun, Uncle John--I left mine in the hotel," Morgan said.

"Hell, what'll I do then?" said Uncle John, unwilling to give it up.

Morgan was insistent. He commandeered the weapon in the name of the law. That being the case, Uncle John handed it up to him, with a word of affection for it, and a little swearing over his bad luck.

It was a double-barreled buffalo rifle, a cap-and-ball gun of very old pattern, belonging back in the days of Parkman and the California Trail, and the two charges which it bore were all that Morgan could hope to expend, for Uncle John carried neither pouch nor horn. But Morgan was thankful for even that much, and rode on.

A little way ahead a man, hatless, wild-haired, came running out from his dooryard, having witnessed Morgan's levying on Uncle John's gun and read his reason for it. This citizen rushed into the road and offered a large revolver, which Morgan leaned and snatched from his hand as he galloped by. But it hadn't a cartridge in its chambers, and its caliber was not of Morgan's ammunition. Still, he rode on with it in his hand, hoping that it might serve its turn.

Morgan galloped on toward the square, where a great volume of smoke hid the courthouse and all of the town that lay before the wind. He hoped to meet somebody there with a gun worth while, although he had no immediate plan for pitching into the fight and using it. That must be fixed for him by circumstances when he confronted them.

Women and children stood in the dooryards watching the fire that was cutting through the thin-walled buildings on that side of the square--the hotel side--as if they were strawboard boxes. They were silent in the great climax of fear; they stood as people stand, straining and waiting, watching the approach of a tornado, no safety in flight, no refuge at hand. There was but one man in sight, and he was running like a jack rabbit across the staked ground behind Judge Thayer's office, heading for the prairie. It was Earl Gray, the druggist. He was covering sixteen feet at a jump. When he saw Morgan galloping into the town, Gray stopped, darted off at an angle as if he were going on some brave and legitimate excursion, and disappeared.

The Elkhorn hotel was well under way of destruction, its roof already fallen, its thin walls bending inward, perforated in a score of places by flames. The head of the street was unguarded; Morgan rode on and halted at the edge of the square.

Smoke blotted out everything in the square, except for a little shifting by the rising wind which revealed the courthouse, the pigeons in wild flight around the tower. There was not a man in sight, neither raider nor defender. Across on the other side of the square, as if they defended that part from being set on fire, the citizens were doing some shooting with rifles, even shotguns, as Morgan could define by the sound. The raiders were there, for they were answering with shot and yell.

Morgan caught the flutter of a dress at the farther corner of the bank--a little squat brick building this was--where some woman stood and watched. He rode around, and at the sound of his approach a gun-barrel was trained on him, and a familiar fair head appeared, cheek laid against the rifle stock in a most determined and competent way.

"Dora! don't shoot!" Morgan shouted. In a moment he was on the ground beside her, and Dora Conboy was handing him his own rifle, pride and relief in her blue eyes.

"I knew you'd come, I told them you'd come!" she said.

"How did you save it--what are you doing here, Dora?" he asked in amazement.

"I was layin' for Craddock! If he'd 'a' come around that corner--but it was you!"--with a sigh of relief.

"Have you got any shells, Dora?"

"No, I didn't have time to grab anything but your gun--I run to your room when they set the hotel afire and drove us out."

"You're the bravest man in town!" he praised her, patting her shoulder as if she were a very little girl, indeed. "Where are they all?"

"They've locked Riley, and Judge Thayer, and all the men that's got a fight in 'em up in jail with the sheriff. Pa got away--he's over there where you hear that shootin'--but he can't hit nothin'!" Dora said, in hopeless disgust.

Morgan saw with relief that the magazine of his rifle was full, and a shot in the barrel. He took Dora by the hand, turning away from his haste to mount as if it came to him as an after-thought to thank her for this great help.

"There's going to be a fight, Dora," he said. "You'd better get behind the bank, and keep any of the women and children there that happen along. You're a brave, good little soul, I'll never forget you for what you've done for me today. Please take care of this gun--it belongs to Uncle John."

He was up in the saddle with the last word, and gone, galloping into the pitchy black smoke that swirled like a turgid flood from burning Ascalon across the square.

Morgan's thought was to locate the raiders' horses and cut them off, if it should be that some of the rascals were still on foot setting fires, as it seemed likely from the smell of kerosene, that they were. It would increase his doubtful chances to meet as many of them on foot as possible. This was his thought.

He made out one mounted man dimly through the blowing smoke, watching in front of the Santa Fé café, but recently set on fire. This fellow doubtless was stationed there on the watch for him, Morgan believed, from the close attention he was giving the front door of the place, out of which a volume of grease-tainted smoke rolled. He wondered, with a little gleam of his saving humor, what there was in his record since coming to Ascalon that gave them ground for the belief that it was necessary to burn a house to bring him out of it to face a fight.

Morgan rode on a little way across the square, not twenty yards behind this raider, the sound of his horse silenced in the roar of fire and growing wind. The heat of the place was terrific; burning shingles swirled on the wind, coals and burning brands fell in a rain all over the square. At the corner of the broad street that came into the square at Peden's hall, another raider was stationed.

The citizens who were making a weak defense were being driven back, the sound of firing was behind the stores, and falling off as if the raiders pressed them hard. Morgan quickly concluded that Craddock and the rest of the outfit were over there silencing this resistance, probably in the belief that he was concerned in it.

This seemed to be his moment for action, yet arresting any of them was out of the question, and he did not want to be the aggressor in the bloodshed that must finish this fiendish morning's work. Hopeless as his situation appeared, justified as he would have been in law and reason for opening fire without challenge, he waited the further justification of his own conscience. They had come looking for him; let them find him here

TRAIL'S END

in their midst.

Fire was rising high among the stripped timbers of Peden's hall, purging it of its debauchery and blood. On the rising wind the flames were licking up Gray's drug-store, the barber shop beside it, the newspaper office, the Santa Fé café and the incidental small shops between them and Peden's like a windrow of burning straw. A little while would suffice to see their obliteration, a little longer to witness the destruction of the town if the wind should carry the coals and blazing shingles to other roofs, dry as the sered grasses of the plain.

The sound of this fire set by Seth Craddock in celebration of his return to Ascalon was in Morgan's ears like the roar of the sea; the heat of it drew the tough skin of his face as he rode fifty yards from it into the center of the square. There he stopped, his rifle across his breast, waiting for the discovery.

The man in the street near Peden's was the first to see and recognize him as he waited there on his horse in the pose of challenge, in the expectant, determined attitude of defense. This fellow yelled the alarm and charged, breakneck through the smoke, shooting as he came.

Morgan fired one shot, offhand. The charging horse reared, stood so a moment as rigidly as if fixed by bronze in that pose, its rider leaning forward over its neck. Then, in whatever terrible pang that such sudden stroke of death visits, it flung itself backward, the girths snapping from its distended belly. The rider was flung aside, where Morgan saw him lying, head on one extended arm, like a dog asleep in the sun.

The others came whooping their triumphant challenge and closed in on Morgan then, and the battle of his life began.

How many were circling him as he stood in the center of the square, or as close to the center as he could draw, near the courthouse steps, Morgan did not know. Some had come from behind the courthouse, others from the tame fight with the citizens back of the stores not yet on fire.

The dust that rose from their great tumult of charge and galloping attack, mingling with the smoke that trailed the ground, was Morgan's protection and salvation. Nothing else saved him from almost immediate death in the fury of their assault.

Morgan fired at the fleeting figures as they moved in obscurity through this stifling cloud, circling him like Indians of the plains, shouting to each other his location, drawing in upon him a little nearer as they rode. He turned and shifted, yet he was a target all too plain for anything he could do to lessen his peril.

A horse came plunging toward him through the blinding swirl, plain for a flash of wild-flying mane and tossing rein, its saddle empty, fleeing from the scene of fire-swept conflict as if urged on by the ghost of the rider it had lost.

Bullets clipped Morgan's saddle as the raiders circled him in a wild fête of shots and yells. One struck his rifle, running down the barrel to the grip like a lightning bolt, spattering hot lead on his hand; another clicked on the ornament of the Spanish bit, frightening his horse, before that moment as steady as if at work on the range. The shaken creature leaped, bunching its body in a shuddering knot. Blood ran from its mouth in a stream.

A shot ripped through the high cantle of the saddle; one seared Morgan's back as it rent his shirt. The horse leaped, to come down stiff-legged like an outlaw, bleeding head thrust forward, nose close to the ground. Then it reared and plunged, striking wildly with fore feet upon the death-laden air.

In leaping to save himself from entanglement as the creature fell, Morgan dropped his rifle. Before he could recover himself from the spring out of the saddle, the horse, thrashing in the paroxysm of death, struck the gun with its shod fore foot, snapping the stock from the barrel.

Dust was in Morgan's eyes and throat, smoke burned in his scorched lungs. The smell of blood mingling with dust was in his nostrils. The heat of the increasing fire was so great that Morgan flung himself to the ground beside his horse, with more thought of shielding himself from that torture than from the inpouring rain of lead.

How many were down among the raiders he did not know; whether the people had heard the noise of this fight and were coming to his assistance, he could not tell. Dust and smoke flew so thick around him that the courthouse not three rods away, was visible only by dim glimpses; the houses around the square he could not see at all.

The raiders flashed through the smoke and dust, here seen in a rift for one brief glance, there lost in the swathing pall that swallowed all but their high-pitched yells and shots. Morgan was certain of only one thing in that hot, panting, brain-cracking moment--that he was still alive.

Whether whole or hurt, he did not know, scarcely considered. The marvel of it was that he still lived, like a wolf at the end of the chase ringed round by hounds. Lived, lead hissing by his face, lead lifting his hair, lead knocking dirt into his eyes as he lay along the carcass of his horse, his body to the ground like a snake.

Morgan felt that it would be his last fight. In the turmoil of smoke and dust, his poor strivings, his upward gropings out of the dark; his glad inspirations, his thrilling hopes, must come to an obscure end. It was a miserable way to die, nothing to come out of it, no ennobling sacrifice demanding it to lift a man's name beyond his day. In the history of this violent place, this death-struggle against overwhelming numbers would be only an incident. Men would say, in speaking of it, that his luck failed him at last.

Morgan discovered with great concern that he had no cartridges left but those in the chambers of his revolver. He considered making a dash for the side of the square not yet on fire, where he might find support, at least make a further stand with the arms and ammunition every storekeeper had at hand.

As these thoughts swept him in the few seconds of their passing, Morgan lay reserving his precious cartridges. The momentary suspension of his defense, the silence of his rifle's defiant roar, which had held them from closing in, perhaps led his assailants to believe him either dead or disabled. They also stopped shooting, and the capricious wind, now rising to a gale as it rushed into the fiery vacuum, bent down and wheeled away the dust and smoke like a curtain suddenly drawn aside.

Craddock and such of his men as were left out of that half-minute battle were scattered about the square in a more or less definite circle around the spot where Morgan lay behind his horse, the nearest to him being perhaps thirty yards away. The citizens of the town who had been resisting the raiders, had come rushing to the square at the diversion of the fight to that center. These began firing now on the raiders from windows and doors and the corners of buildings. Craddock sent three of his men charging against this force, now become more courageous and dangerous, and with two at his side, one of whom was the Dutchman, he came riding over to investigate Morgan's situation.

Morgan could see the Dutchman's face as he spurred on ahead of the others. Pale, with a pallor inborn that sun and wind could not shade, a wide grin splitting his face, the Dutchman came on eagerly, no doubt in the hope that he would find a spark of conscious life in Morgan that he could stamp out in some predesigned cruelty.

The Dutchman was leaning forward as he rode, revolver lifted to throw down for a quick shot. When he had approached within two lengths of his horse, Morgan lifted himself from the ground and fired. The Dutchman sagged over the horn of his saddle like a man asleep, his horse galloping on in panic. As it passed Morgan the Dutchman pitched from the saddle, drug a little way by one encumbered foot, the frantic horse plunging on. Fred Stilwell, closely followed by his father, came riding into the square.

Morgan leaped to his feet, new hope in him at sight of this friendly force. Craddock's companion turned to meet Fred with the fire of two revolvers. One of the three sent a moment before to dislodge the citizens, turned back to join this new battle.

Morgan had marked this man as Drumm from the beginning. He was a florid, heavy man, his long mustache strangely white against the inflamed redness of his face. He carried a large roll covered with black oilcloth behind his saddle.

Morgan wasted one precious cartridge in a shot at this man as he passed. The raider did not reply. He was riding straight to meet Stilwell and Fred, to whom Craddock also turned his attention when he saw Morgan's rifle broken on the ground. It was as if Craddock felt him out of the fight, to be finished at leisure.

Morgan left his dubious shelter of the fallen horse and ran to meet his friends, hoping to reach one of them and replenish his ammunition. Fred Stilwell was coming up with the wind, his dust blowing ahead of him on the sweeping gale. At his first shot the man who had left Craddock's side to attack him pitched from his saddle, hands thrown out before him as if he dived into eternity. The next breath Fred reeled in his saddle and fell.

The man with the oilcloth roll at his saddle yelled in exultation, lifting his gun high in challenge to Stilwell, who rode to meet him. A moment Stilwell halted where Fred lay, as if to dismount, then galloped furiously forward to avenge his fall. The two raiders who had gone against the townsmen, evidently believing that the battle was going against them, spurred for the open country.

Craddock was bearing down on Morgan, the fight being apportioned now man to man. Morgan heard Stilwell's big gun roaring when he turned to face Craddock, vindictive, grim, who came riding upon him with no word of challenge, no shout of triumph in what seemed his moment of victory.

Morgan was steady and unmoved. The ground was under his feet, his arm was not disturbed by the rock of a galloping horse. He lifted his weapon and fired. Craddock's horse went down to its knees as if it had struck a gopher hole, and Craddock, horseman that he was, pitched out of the saddle and fell not two yards from Morgan's feet.

In falling, Craddock dropped his gun. He was scrambling for it when Morgan, no thought in him of mercy, threw his weapon down for the finishing shot. The hammer clicked on an empty shell. And Craddock, on hands and knees, agile as a bear, was reaching one long hairy arm to clutch his lost gun.

Morgan threw himself headlong upon the desperado, crushing him flat to the ground. With a sprawling kick he sent Craddock's gun far out of reach, and they closed, with the weapons nature had given them, for the last struggle in the drama of their lives.

The stage was empty for them of anything that moved, save only Craddock's horse, which Morgan's last shot, confident as he was when he aimed it, had no more than maimed with a broken leg. To the right of them Fred Stilwell lay, his face in the dust, his arms outspread, his hat close by; on the other hand the Dutchman's body sprawled, his legs, flung out as if he had died running. And near this unsightly wreckage of a worthless wretch Morgan's horse stretched, in the lazy posture of an animal asleep in a sunny pasture.

Behind them the fire that was eating one side of the square away rose and bent, roared and crackled, sighed and hissed, flinging up long flames which broke as they stabbed into the smoke. Morgan felt the fire hot on his neck as he bent over Craddock, throwing the strain of every tendon to hold the old villain to the ground.

Craddock writhed, jointless as a snake, it seemed, under the grip of Morgan's hand at his spiney throat, squirmed and turned and fought to his knees. They struggled and battled breast to breast, until they stood on their feet, locked in a clinch out of which but one of them, Morgan was determined, should come a living man.

Morgan had dropped his empty revolver when he flung himself on Craddock. There was no inequality between them except such as nature had given in the strength of arm and back. They swayed in silent, terrible determination each to have the other's life, and Morgan had a glimpse, as he turned, of women and children watching them from the corner near the bank, huddled groups out of which he knew many a hope went out for his victorious issue.

Craddock was a man of sinews as hard as bow strings; his muscles were like dried beef. Strong as Morgan was, he felt that he was losing ground. Then, by some trick learned perhaps in savage camps, Craddock lifted him, and flung him with stunning force against the hard ground.

There they rolled, clawing, striking, grappling at each other's throats. As if surf made sport of them on the shelving sands they rolled, one uppermost now, the other then. And they fought and rolled until Morgan felt something hard under his oppressed back, and groped for it in the star-shot agony of sinewy fingers choking out his life. His empty gun. It seemed that he grasped it in delirium, and struck with it in the blindness of hovering death.

When Morgan staggered to his feet there was blood in his mouth; the sound of the fiery turmoil around him was hushed in the roar of blood in his ears. He stood weakly a moment, looking at the pistol in his hand. The blow he had laid along Craddock's head had broken the cylinder pin. Meditatively Morgan looked at it again, then threw it down as an abandoned and useless thing. It fell close by where Craddock lay, blood running from a wound on his temple.

CHAPTER XXVII

ABSOLUTION

Morgan stood looking down on the man whom he had overcome in the climax of that desperate hour, wondering if he were dead. He did not stoop to investigate; from where he stood no sign of life disturbed Craddock's limp body. Morgan was thinking now that they would say of him in Ascalon that luck had been with him to the last.

Not prowess, at any rate; he did not claim to that. Perhaps luck was as good a name as any for it, but it was something that upheld his hand and stimulated his wit in crises such as he had passed in Ascalon that eventful fortnight.

A band of men came around the corner past Peden's hall, now only a vanishing skeleton of beams, bringing with them the two raiders who had attempted to escape by that avenue to the open prairie. The two were still mounted, the crowd that surrounded them was silent and ominous. Morgan waited until they came up, when, with a sign toward Craddock, which relinquished all interest in and responsibility for him to the posse comitatus, he turned away to hasten to Fred Stilwell's side.

Tom Conboy had reached the fallen youth--he was little more than a boy--and was kneeling beside him, lifting his head.

"God! they killed a woman over there--and a man!" Conboy said.

"Is he dead?" Morgan inquired, his voice hoarse and strange.

"He's shot through the lung, he's breathin' through his back," Conboy replied, shaking his head sadly. "But I've seen men live shot up worse than Fred is," he added. "It takes a big lot of lead to kill a man sometimes."

"We must carry him out of this heat," Morgan said.

They carried him across the square to that part of the business front the fire had not yet leaped over to and taken, and laid him in a little strip of shade in front of the harness store. Conboy hurried off to see if he could find the doctor.

Morgan wadded a handkerchief against the wound in Fred's back, whence the blood bubbled in frothy stream at every weak inspiration, and let him down gently upon that insufficient pad to wait the doctor, not having it in his power to do more. He believed the poor fellow would die with the next breath, and looked about to see if Stilwell were in sight. Stilwell was nowhere to be seen, his pursuit of Drumm having led him far. But approaching Morgan were five or six men carrying guns, their faces clouded with what seemed an unfriendly severity.

"We want to have a word or two with you over in the square," one of them said.

Morgan recognized all of them as townsmen. He looked at them in undisguised surprise, completely lost for the meaning of the blunt request.

"All right," he said.

"The doctor will be here in a minute, he's gone for his case," one of them volunteered.

Relieved by the word, Morgan thanked him, and returned with them to the place where a growing crowd of men stood about Seth Craddock and the two prisoners who had been taken in their attempt to escape. Craddock was sitting on the ground, head drooping forward, a man's knee at his back. And Earl Gray, a revolver in his hand, no hat on, his hair flying forty ways, was talking.

"If he'd 'a' been here tendin' to duty under his oath, in place of skulkin' out and leavin' the town wide open to anybody that wanted to set a match to it, this thing wouldn't 'a' happened, I tell you, gentlemen. Look at it! look at my store, look at the ho-tel, look at everything on that side of the square! Gone to hell, every stick of it! And that's the man to blame!"

Gray indicated Morgan with a thrust of his gun, waving one hand dramatically toward the ruin. A sound, more a growl than a groan, ran through the crowd, which now numbered not fewer than thirty or forty men.

The sight of the destruction was enough, indeed, to make them growl, or even groan. Everything on that side of the square was leveled but a few upstanding beams, the fire was rioting among the fallen rafters, eating up the floors that had borne the trod of so many adventurous feet. The hotel was a ruin, Gray's store only a recollection, the little shops between it and Peden's long, hollow skeleton of a barn already coals.

Men, women, and children were on the roofs of buildings across the street from Peden's, pouring precious water over the fires which sprang from falling brands. It seemed that this shower of fire must overwhelm them very soon, and engulf the rest of the business houses, making a clean sweep of everything but the courthouse and the bank. The calaboose, in its isolation, was still safe.

"Where was you last night?" Gray demanded, insolence in his narrow face as he turned again to Morgan, poking out with his gun as if to vex the answer from him as one prods a growl from a dog.

"None of your ---- business!" Morgan replied, rising into a rage as sudden as it was unwise, the unworthiness of the object considered. He made a quick movement toward Gray as he spoke, which brought upon him the instant restraint of many hands.

"You don't grab no gun from nobody here!" one said.

"Why wasn't you here attendin' to business when that gang rode in this mornin'?" one at Morgan's side demanded. It was the barber; his shop was gone, his razors were fused among the ashes.

Morgan ignored him, regretting at once the flash of passion that had betrayed him into their hands. For they were madmen--mad with the torture of hot winds and straining hopes that withered and fell; mad with their losses of that day, mad with the glare of sun of many days, and the stricken earth under their bound and sodden feet; mad with the very bareness of their inconsequential lives.

Seth Craddock heaved up to his knees, struggled to his feet with quick, frantic lumbering, like a horse clambering out of the mire. He stood weaving, his red eyes watching those around him, perhaps reading something of the crowd's threat in the growl that ran through it, beginning in the center as it died on the edge, quieting not at all. His hat was off, dust was in his hair, a great welted wound was black on his temple, the blood of it caked with dust on his face.

The two prisoners on horseback, one of them wounded so badly his life did not seem worth a minute's reprieve, were pulled down; all were bunched with Morgan in the middle of the mob. Gray began again with his denunciation, Morgan hearing him only as the wind, for his attention was fixed on the activities of Dell Hutton, working with insidious swiftness and apparent success among the mob.

Hutton did not look at Morgan as he passed with low word from man to man, sowing the poison of his vindictive hate against this man who had compelled him to be honest once against his bent. A moment Hutton paused in conference with the blacksmith, and that man came forward now, silenced Gray with a word and pushed him aside.

The blacksmith was a knotty short man of Slavic features, a cropped mustache under his stubby nose. His shop was burning in the ruin of that tragic morning; the blame of it was Morgan's. Others whose business places had been erased in the fire were recognized by Morgan in the crowd. The proprietor of the Santa Fé café, the cobbler, the Mexican who sold tamales and chili--none of them of any consequence ordinarily, but potent of the extreme of evil now, merged as they were into that unreasoning thing, the mob.

There were murmured suggestions, rejections; talk of the cross-arms on the telegraph poles, which at once became determined, decisive. Men pushed through the press with ropes. Seth Craddock looked across at Morgan, and cursed him. One of the prisoners, the unwounded man, a youth no older than Fred Stilwell, began to beg and cry.

Morgan had not been alarmed up to the moment of his seeing Hutton inflaming the crowd against him, for the mob was composed of men whose faces were for the greater part familiar, mild men in their way, whom the violence in which they had lived had passed and left untouched. But they held him with strong hands; they were making ready a noose to throw over his head and strangle his life out in the shame that belongs to murderers and thieves.

This had become a matter beyond his calculation; this should not be. There were guns in men's hands all about him where guns did not belong. Morgan threw his determination and strength into a fling that cleared his right arm, and began a battle that marked for life some of them who clung to him and tried to drag him down.

They were crushing him, they were overwhelming him. Only a sudden jerk of the head, a dozen determined, silent men hanging to him, saved Morgan's neck from the flung rope. The man who cast it cursed; was drawing it back with eager haste to throw again, when Rhetta Thayer came.

She came pushing through the mad throng about Morgan, he heard her command to clear the way; she was beside him, the mystery of her swift passage through the mob made plain. Seth Craddock's guns, given her as a trophy of that day when Morgan lassoed the meat hunter, were in her hands, and in her eyes there was a death warrant for any wretch that stood in her way. She gave the weapons to Morgan, her breathing audible over the hush that fell in the failing of their cowed hearts.

"Drop your guns!" Morgan commanded.

There was a panic to comply. Steel and nickel, ivory handle, old navy and new Colt's, flashed in the sun as they were dropped in the little open space at Morgan's feet.

"Clear out of here!"

Morgan's sharp order was almost unnecessary. Those on the edge of the crowd were beginning already to sneak off; a little way, looking back over shoulders, and they began to run. They dispersed like dust on the wind, leaving behind them their weapons which would identify them for the revenge this terrible, invincible, miraculously lucky man might come to their doors and exact.

The thought was terrifying. They did not stop at the margin of the square to look back to see if he pressed his vengeance at their heels. Only the shelter of cyclone cellar, sequestered patches of corn, the willows along the distant river, would give them the respite from the terror of this outreaching hand necessary to a full, free breath.

The sheriff had released himself from jail, with Judge Thayer and the valorous Riley Caldwell, and twenty or more others who had been locked up with them. The sheriff, humiliated, resentful, red with the anger that choked him--for it was safe now to be as angry as he could lash himself--came stalking up to where Morgan held Craddock and the unwounded raider off from the tempting heap of weapons thrown down by the mob.

The sheriff began to abuse Craddock, laying to him all the villainy of ancestry and life that his well-schooled tongue could shape. Morgan cut him off with a sharp word.

"Take these men and lock them up!"

"Yes, sir, Mr. Morgan, you bet your life I'll lock 'em up!" the sheriff agreed.

"Hold them for a charge of arson and murder," Judge Thayer commanded sternly. "And see that you do hold them!"

Judge Thayer came on to where Morgan stood, the surrendered weapons at his feet, Rhetta beside him, pride higher than the heavens in her eyes.

"I can't apologize for them, I can't even try," said the judge, with a humility in his word and manner quite new and strange, indicating the members of the fast-scattering mob. He made himself as small as he felt by his way of approaching this man who had pitched his life like a coin of little value into the gamble of that tragic day.

"Never mind trying--it's only an incident," Morgan told him, full of another thought.

"I'll see that he locks Craddock and the other two up safe, then I'll have these guns picked up for evidence. I'm going to lay an information against every man of them in that mob with the prosecuting attorney!"

"Let them go, Judge Thayer--I'd never appear against them," Morgan said.

Judge Thayer appeared to be dazed by the events of that day, crowded to their fearful climax of destruction of property and life. He was lacking in his ready words, older, it seemed, by many years, crushed under the weight of this terrible calamity that had fallen on his town. He went away after the sheriff, leaving Morgan and Rhetta, the last actors on the stage in the drama of Ascalon's downfall, alone.

Beyond them the fire raged in the completion of the havoc that was far beyond any human labor to stay. The heat of it was scorching even where they stood; coals, blazing fragments, were blown about their feet on the turbulent wind. The black-green smoke still rose in great volume, through which the sun was red. On the flank of the fire those who labored to confine its spread shouted in the voice of dismay. It was an hour of desolation; it was the day of doom.

"Thank you for my life," said Morgan. "I've put a new valuation on it since you've gone to so much trouble to save it."

"Don't speak cynically about it, Mr. Morgan!" she said, hurt by his tone.

"I'm not cynical," he gravely assured her. "My life wasn't worth much to me this morning when I left Stilwell's. It has acquired a new value now."

TRAIL'S END

All this time Morgan had stood holding Seth Craddock's big revolvers in his hands, as if he distrusted the desolation of the fire-sown square. Now he sheathed one of them in his holster, and thrust the other under his belt. His right hand was bleeding, from wounds of the bullet that had struck his rifle-barrel and sprayed hot lead into his flesh, and from the blows he had dealt in his fury amongst the mob.

Rhetta put out her hand and took his, bleeding and torn and battle-maimed as it was, and lifted it tenderly, and nestled it against her cheek.

"Dear, brave hand!" she said.

"You're not afraid of it now!" he wondered, putting out his free hand as if he offered it also for the absolution of her touch.

"It was only the madness of the wind," she told him, the sorrow of her penance in her simple words.

CHAPTER XXVIII

SUNSET

Evening saw the fires of Ascalon subdued and confined. With the falling of the wind the danger of the disaster spreading to embrace the entire town decreased almost to safety, although the wary, scorched townsmen stood watch over the smoldering coals which lay deep where the principal part of Ascalon lately stood.

Fred Stilwell had been taken to Judge Thayer's house, where his mother and Violet attended him. The doctor said youth and a clean body would carry him through. As for Drumm, whose bullet had brought the young man down, his horse with the black saddle-roll had stood hitched to Judge Thayer's fence until evening, when the sheriff came with a writ of attachment in Stilwell's favor and took it away. Drumm's body was lying on a board in the calaboose, diverted for that dark day in Ascalon's history into a morgue.

The sheriff reported that the Texas cattleman had carried more than fifty thousand dollars in currency behind his saddle. That was according to the custom of the times, and usage of the range, where many a man's word was as good as his bond, but no man's check was as good as money.

Tom Conboy was already hiring carpenters to rebuild the hotel, his eye full of the business that would come to his doors when the railroad shops were running, and the trainmen of the division point were there to be housed and fed. Dora and Riley had been wandering around town all afternoon, very much like two pigeons looking for a place to nest.

And so evening found peace in Ascalon, after all its tragedy and pain.

Calvin Morgan and Rhetta Thayer stood at the bank corner at sunset, looking down the square where the great gap in its front made the scene unfamiliar. Morgan's disabled hand was bandaged; there was a cross of surgical tape on his chin, closing a deep cut where some citizen had tapped him with a revolver in the last fight of that tumultuous day.

Little groups of desolate, disheartened people stood along the line of hitching racks; dead coals, which the wind had sown as living fire over the square, littered the white dust. Morgan had taken off his badge of office, having made a formal resignation to Judge Thayer, mayor of the town. Nobody had been sworn in to take his place, for, as Judge Thayer had said, it did not appear as if any further calamity could be left in store among the misfortunes for that town, except it might be an earthquake or a cyclone, and a city marshal, even Morgan, could not fend against them if they were to come.

"You have trampled your place among the thorns," said Rhetta.

"It looks like I've pulled a good deal down with me," he returned, viewing the seat of fire with a softening of pity in his grave face.

"All that deserves to rise will rise again," she said in confidence. "It's a good thing it burned--it's purged of its old shame and old monuments of corruption. I'm glad it's gone."

There was a quiet over the place, as if the heart of turbulence had been broken and its spirit had taken flight. In the southwest, in the faces of the two watchers at the margin of this ruin, a vast dark cloud stood like a landfall rising in the mariner's eye out of the sea. It had been visible since four o'clock, seeming to hesitate as if nature intended again to deny this parched and suffering land the consolation of rain. Now it was rising, already it had overspread the sunset glow, casting a cool shadow full of promise over the thirsting prairie wastes.

"It will rain this time," Rhetta prophesied. "It always comes up slowly that way when it rains a long time."

"A rain will work wonders in this country," he said, his face lifted to the promise of the cloud.

"And wisdom and faith will do more," she told him, her voice tender and low.

"And love," said he, voice solemn as a prophet's, yet gentle as a dove's.

"And love," she whispered, the wind, springing like an inspiration before the rain, lifting her shadowy hair.

Joe Lynch came driving into the stricken square down the road beside

TRAIL'S END

them, bringing a load of bones.

"Had to burn the town to fetch a rain, huh?" said Joe, his ghostly dry old face tilted to catch the savor of the wind. So saying, he drove on, and paused not in his labor of off-bearing the waste of failure that must be cleared for the new labor of wisdom, faith, and love.

* * * * *

Thirty years will do for a cottonwood what two centuries will do for an oak. Thirty years had built the cottonwoods of great girth, and lifted them in dignity high above the roof of Calvin Morgan's white farmhouse, his great barns and granaries. Elm trees, bringing their blessings of wide-spreading branch more slowly, led down a broad avenue to the white manse with its Ionian portico. Over the acres of smooth, luxuriant green lawn, the long shadows of closing day reached like the yearning of men's unfinished dreams.

Before the house a broad roadway, smooth as a city boulevard, ran straight to the bright, clean, populous city where Ascalon, with its forgotten shame and tragedies, once stood. And far and away, over the swell of gentle ridge, into the dip of gracious valley, spread the benediction of growing wheat. Wisdom and faith and love had worked their miracle. This land had become the nation's granary; it was a land redeemed.

* * * * *

Under the giant cottonwoods, gray-green of leaf as the desert grasses were gray-green in the old cattle days, the brown walls, the low roof, of a sod house stood, the lawn clipped smooth around its humble door, lilac clumps green beside its walls, sweet honeysuckle clambering over its little porch. And there came, in the tender last beams of the setting sun, a man and woman to its door.

Not old, not bent, not gnarled by the rack of blind-groping, undirected toil, for such of the chosen out of nature's nobility are never old. Hair once dark as woodland shadows was shot with the sunlight of many years; hair once bright as the mica tossed by joyous waves upon a sunny beach was whitened now by the unmelting snows of winters numbered swiftly in the brief calendar of man. But shoulders were unbent by the burdens which they had borne joyously, and their feet went quickly as lovers' to a tryst.

This little sod house stood with all its old-time furnishings, like a shrine, and on this day, which seemed to be an anniversary, it had been brightened with vases of flowers. This man and this woman, not old, indeed, entered and stood within its door, where the light was dimming through the little window high in the thick wall. The man crossed the room, and stood where a belt with holsters hung upon the wall. She drew near him, and lifted his great hand, and nestled it against her cheek.

GEORGE W. OGDEN

"Old Seth Craddock's guns," he said, musing as on a recurring memory.

"His guns!" she murmured, drawing closer into the shadow of his strength.

CPSIA information can be obtained
at www.ICGtesting.com
Printed in the USA
LVOW13s1105270218
567908LV00029B/141/P

9 781985 382275